Deborah Sheldon, a professional writer from Melbourne, Australia, writes across the darker spectrum of crime, noir, and horror. Deb's short stories have appeared in many well-regarded literary magazines and anthologies. Her published fiction includes short story collections, novellas, and novels. Other writing credits include television scripts, feature articles, radio plays, award-winning medical writing, and non-fiction books for Reed Books and Random House.

Visit her website: http://deborahsheldon.wordpress.com

Deborah Sheldon's titles published by IFWG Publishing Australia

Dark Waters / Ronnie and Rita (novellas, 2016)

Perfect Little Stitches and Other Stories (collection, 2017)

Perfect Little Stitches and other Stories

By Deborah Sheldon

This is a work of fiction. The events and characters portrayed herein are imaginary and are not intended to refer to specific places, events or living persons. The opinions expressed in this manuscript are solely the opinions of the author and do not necessarily represent the opinions of the publisher.

Perfect Little Stitches and Other Stories

ISBN-13: 978-1-925496-38-3

V1.0

Stories first publishing history at the end of this book.

Printed in Palatino Linotype and Signo.

IFWG Publishing Australia
Melbourne

www.ifwgaustralia.com

For Allen and Harry.

…the bright day is done,
And we are for the dark.

Iras

William Shakespeare, *Antony and Cleopatra*

Table of Contents

Perfect Little Stitches

Angelo De Luca took up the scalpel and opened the cadaver's thigh, from hip to knee, with a single stroke. There was very little subcutaneous fat. Using firm, continuous passes of the scalpel, Angelo pared through the muscle within seconds and exposed the femur without scratching it.

"Very nice, as usual," Gary Mathews said. "Ah shit, you know what? I just went and notched mine at the hip-end."

"At the lesser trochanter?"

"I think so, yeah, the top bit that sticks out a little."

Angelo De Luca glared across the stainless-steel table at his new assistant, Gary Mathews, who was harvesting from the cadaver's other leg. Gary had started his working life as a butcher and still acted like one, even though the meat now was human, and therefore precious.

"If you would put your mind to the study of anatomy," Angelo said, "and learn about the attachments of soft tissue, you wouldn't keep making these basic errors. Haven't you read the books I loaned you?"

"Relax. Most of the bones we get are in shit condition anyway."

"That's no reason to damage them further."

Gary sneered. "Even with this bloke? He's almost ninety. How good are his bones going to be? Swiss cheese. The poor bastard who gets these femurs will bust them in half on his first step from the hospital bed."

Angelo could not trust himself to speak.

Whistling, Gary returned his attention to the cadaver's thigh, slicing briskly towards the kneecap. Angelo heard the muted snicking sound as the scalpel contacted the femur, over and over. Oh, how Angelo despised Gary Mathews with his uncouth footy-beer-and-barbecue personality, his ginger hair sprouting thick as fur over pale forearms, his skin freckled and wrinkled as if he had been pressed out of dough and left in the sun to crack; Gary Mathews, the jovial, under-educated idiot, the very antithesis of everything that a funeral director ought to be.

Angelo felt the familiar stab of regret.

This funeral parlour, *De Luca and Son,* had been named after his father, Giovanni, and himself. It was supposed to be Angelo's legacy but his own sons had not wished to continue the family trade. Once Papa Giovanni had died, money became tight. Staff members—those who are not relatives—expect and must receive full pay and entitlements. Then there was the outstanding balance of Sofia's stupendous medical bills. Bankruptcy had loomed.

Until the arrival three months ago of Angelo's saviour: Heather.

Once Angelo had agreed to her unusual business offer, Gary Mathews was made the sole member of Angelo's staff, without consultation, by Heather the Body Wrangler. That was what she actually called herself, Heather the Body Wrangler. Angelo did not know anything about her apart from a mobile number.

Unlike organs such as the heart, certain tissues including bones and skin are still viable for transplant after death. Heather would pay up to four thousand dollars in cash for a complete set of usable parts, removed surreptitiously, from a young and healthy corpse. Age and medical conditions lessened the remuneration on a fixed scale. At the very least, a diseased and elderly corpse meant a few hundred dollars.

The money had staved off the bank manager.

Yes, Angelo would go to jail if the police found out, but morally, it made irrefutable sense. Living patients either died or suffered permanent disability without these transplants. Voluntary donors were scarce. When cadavers would be wasted anyway, burned to ashes or buried to make worm shit, what was the harm in first recycling their viable parts? No harm at all.

As long as the relatives never found out.

Because realising that your loved one's remains had been pillaged, defiled and dismantled would have to be the worst kind of unimaginable horror. Dear God, if such a fate had befallen Sofia…he could hardly bring himself to think of it. And so, occasionally, when Angelo could not sleep, he feared that he had made a pact with the Devil. A widower for nearly a year, he would turn to the empty side of his bed and weep to Sofia for forgiveness.

Now, Gary Mathews gazed at Angelo across the naked and muscle-splayed cadaver on the stainless-steel table, waggled the scalpel and said, "Mate, you couldn't cut butter with this bloody thing. Just let me go get my boning knife."

"No." Angelo's moustache quivered as he fought to maintain a neutral expression. "Our deceased clients are offering the living a wonderful gift. We will not desecrate them with implements intended for the carving up of animals."

Gary dropped the scalpel to the stainless-steel table and put his fists on his hips. "You know what's going on? What we're doing?"

Angelo flushed. "Yes, of course."

"Nobody has signed any release forms. Every document is forged. What we're doing, right here, is some seriously criminal shit."

"Please continue with the harvesting," Angelo said. "Once we've gathered the long bones, we'll move onto the saphenous veins, ligaments and tendons. I'd like your help to sew the PVC pipes inside the limbs, and to remove the skin and heart valves, if you wouldn't mind. After that, I'll take the corneas myself, thank you. Please take your break at that point. Embalming will begin promptly at three o'clock."

Gary stared back, nostrils flared. Angelo decided to continue with the removal of the femur. For a time, the only sounds were the flit of his scalpel, the steady drip-drip-drip of the tap into the scrub-sink.

"Nobody is giving anybody a gift," Gary finally said. "We're stealing these body parts. We're stealing them for money. I'm a grave-robber and so are you."

Gary unfastened his bloodstained apron, flung it across a bench, and peeled away his latex gloves. He headed to the exit of the preparation room.

"Where are you going?" Angelo said, hoping that the *bastardo* had quit.

"To the boot of my car," Gary said, "for my knives."

Oh, she was beautiful.

She was the first cadaver of the day, this warm spring day that had followed a long, torturous night of rain and shrieking wind. Angelo slowly unzipped the body bag the rest of the way.

A child: such a beautiful young child.

Her jet-black hair lay in a halo of ringlets about her pale face. Angelo wanted to weep. The forensic pathologist must have been similarly affected. Following autopsy at the Coroner's Court, the typical cadaver arrived at Angelo's funeral parlour in disarray, tacked together as roughly as a hessian sack, but not this child. The forensic pathologist had taken great care. The single incision from throat to pubis had been closed using small, neat sutures, as precise as any of Sofia's hand-sewn embroideries. Had there been an examination of the brain? Angelo couldn't see any sign. He smoothed back the ringlets framing the child's forehead. And yes, hidden away within the hairline lay the tidy stitches circumnavigating the scalp.

According to the paperwork, the cause of death was inconclusive. Teresa-Kate, eleven years of age, had died in hospital three days ago from an unidentified infection that had first paralysed her, and then triggered multiple and catastrophic organ failure. More than likely, she had acquired the infection from the bite of an unknown animal, probably a dog. The included body diagram showed a large 'X' on the upper back. Angelo put down the paperwork.

Gently, he turned the child onto her side. Just above her right scapula, into the tissue of her trapezoid muscle, lay the bite mark.

Could the paralysis have been symptomatic of some new strain of rabies? But Angelo was no microbiologist. If the experts at the Coroner's Court were unable to establish an exact cause of death, it was not for him to speculate. He zipped the bag closed and placed Teresa-Kate in the refrigerator unit. Then he washed his hands and retired to the lunchroom, where he washed his hands again.

As he ate his sandwich, Angelo perused his work diary. He had spoken to Teresa-Kate's parents that morning. Anglicans, they wished to hold a home viewing before the funeral and burial, which necessitated an open casket. Teresa-Kate was already so perfectly preserved that Angelo's embalming and cosmetology skills would render her almost life-like. After lunch, he would ring the family's priest to discuss and confirm details of the service. Satisfied, he had just started on an apple when Gary Mathews shouldered through the lunchroom door.

Dropping the pizza box onto the table and sitting down, Gary said, "We'll get the whole four-grand out of that kid."

A chunk of apple nearly stuck in Angelo's windpipe.

Gary folded a slice of pizza in half, and crammed most of it into his mouth. A Hawaiian pizza, of course: a disgusting abomination that turned Angelo's stomach.

"She's perfect in every way," Gary said, talking as he chewed, "young and in good nick. This time, mate, we've hit the jackpot."

"No," Angelo said. "No, we haven't. You're wrong."

Gary stopped chewing, raised an eyebrow.

Angelo said, "Haven't you read the report? Seen the biohazard tape on the body bag? She died of a disease that sounds very similar to rabies. Her soft tissues could infect every single transplant recipient."

"I've already called the Body Wrangler," Gary said. "We're doing the kid."

Angelo felt blood mottle his cheeks. "If it has to be done, fine, I'll do it myself. You'll not go anywhere near her. You and your boning knives can burn in hell first."

Gary shrugged, kept eating his pizza.

Teresa-Kate lay naked on the stainless-steel table. Her arms and legs were thin, hairless and unblemished, pre-pubescent. What might she have done with her four-score and ten? That would be the question to torment her parents until the release of their own deaths. And in a lesser way, that same question would also haunt Angelo. Since going into business with Heather, Angelo dreamed about many of his harvested clients, each one berating him and wailing for their missing body parts.

Enough.

He was a professional.

And according to protocol, he had to first take the leg bones.

He picked up the scalpel. The multiple bulbs of the overhead light beamed bright and white. The tap over the scrub-sink dripped in a steady beat. It was almost 9 p.m. Gary had been sent home hours ago. Angelo had arranged to meet Teresa-Kate's family priest tomorrow morning to discuss details of the funeral and burial.

The harvesting would be now or never.

As softly as the kiss of a downy feather, he touched the tip of the scalpel to Teresa-Kate's hip without breaking the skin. A moment passed. He held the blade over her anterior superior iliac spine—the outer crest of the pelvis—where, beneath the epidermis, dermis and layer of subcutaneous fat, the attachments lay for the inguinal ligament and the sartorius muscle. One deep and decisive cut, following along the length of the femur, was the starting point.

Angelo could not do it.

Sofia came to mind, back when she first became seriously ill, confused, trying to cut rolled pastry on the kitchen bench with her hands as if her fingers had become knives. Leading her away, Angelo had shown her some of the framed embroidery she had made over the years. Placated, Sofia allowed him to administer her medication. *Look at my nails,* she had said. *Tesorio mio, watch me as I rend the world.*

These had been the last complete sentences she had ever spoken to him.

After forty-two years together, God, how he missed her.

Now, Angelo sniffed, scrubbed at his tears with the heels of both latex gloves. Then he pressed the scalpel into Teresa-Kate's left hip and dug in deep, slicing down towards the kneecap. He worked quickly, efficiently. After next stripping the tibia and fibula, he moved to the other leg, repeated the procedure. Then he deboned her right arm, her left arm. The meat of Teresa-Kate's flayed limbs lay shockingly red against the pallor of her torso. From the box of PVC pipes, he found the lengths that would fit. He spent the next hour neatly reconstructing Teresa-Kate's body, using suture as translucent as fishing wire, making stitches so discreet that they brought Sofia's best handiwork to mind.

At close to 10.30 p.m., Angelo packed up his harvesting equipment. No matter what Heather the Body Wrangler demanded, he would not take this child's soft tissue. She had died from a rabies-like disease. How could Angelo claim to be helping the living if he deliberately offered up corneas and tendons that might carry infection?

It was time for the embalming procedure. He measured and mixed the chemicals. An incision near her collarbone exposed both the carotid artery and the jugular vein. One small incision in each, and he would insert the tubes: one to drain any remaining blood, the other to fill the circulatory system with embalming fluid. He pressed the tip of the scalpel into the carotid artery.

Teresa-Kate opened her eyes.

Angelo staggered back, dropped the scalpel.

The girl sat up, gazing at him, blinking dopily as if coming awake from a deep sleep. The sclera of both her eyes was black, as black as a fathomless pit.

"*Dio mio,*" he said, and tried to cross himself.

Teresa-Kate looked at the stitched wounds along her arms and legs, gaped at the line of sutures down the midline of her body, and gave a silent scream. The stretching of her mouth peeled back her lips, splitting the skin across her teeth. Her incisors, pre-molars and molars were long, fanged: no longer human.

Teresa-Kate leapt from the table.

As she came at him, Angelo grabbed a stainless-steel instrument tray and struck her across the face. It slowed her momentarily.

He hit her again, and again. When she staggered, dropped, he picked up the bone-dust vacuum and brought it down onto the crown of her head, cracking her skull. She sprawled across the floor.

Angelo watched her for a long, long time.

When she still hadn't moved, his senses began to return. He put down the vacuum. The first thing he realised was that he had wet himself. The second thing was that, somehow, Teresa-Kate had been alive and now she was dead.

Angelo groped for a chair and sat down.

The dead coming back to life, he had read of such things occurring from time to time in faraway places like Zimbabwe, the Philippines, and Venezuela, where the deceased wakes up during their funeral. But no, this was not a misdiagnosis, a case of some poorly-trained doctor confusing coma with death. At the Coroner's Court, Teresa-Kate's internal organs had been removed, inspected, weighed, sliced, and then tumbled together into a plastic bag, which was then sewn up inside her abdominal cavity. Good God, her brain had received the same treatment.

She still hadn't moved.

Incrementally, Angelo slid from the chair, approached. He used the tip of his shoe to turn her over. This time, she was definitely dead. One side of her face was smashed into a pulp of ruined skin and splintered bone.

Teresa-Kate had been alive.

And he had murdered her.

He vomited a little, wept. After a time, he regained control.

The child had already been issued a death certificate. Angelo would tell no one what had happened. Instead, he would spend the night using all his skills to repair and mask the damage he had inflicted upon her. Tomorrow morning, he would give Teresa-Kate to her family so they could hold, in the lounge-room of their home, the girl's open-casket viewing.

Gary Mathews drove the hearse. Angelo's nerves weren't steady enough.

They delivered Teresa-Kate, dressed and perfect, in her casket. While shaking hands with her father, Angelo began to cry. Moved to tears herself, Teresa-Kate's mother attempted to embrace Angelo, for the love of everything holy, as if to *console* him after the evil he had done to their daughter.

It was true; he had indeed made a pact with the Devil.

During the drive back to the funeral parlour, Gary harangued him about failing to strip the girl's corpse for the entire four thousand dollars. Angelo did not have the strength to reply. Staring sightlessly at the passing scenery, he kept seeing Teresa-Kate's face, repaired to the absolute best of his abilities, yet, on expert inspection, still carrying the marks of violence inflicted by his own hands.

He assigned Gary to meet with Teresa-Kate's priest.

Angelo got through the rest of the day on automatic pilot. In the evening, once Gary had left the funeral parlour, Angelo took from the locked drawer of his desk the business card of Heather the Body Wrangler, and called the number.

"You beat me to it," she said. "I was just about to ring. Gary reckons you took the girl's bones and nothing else. Frankly, that's a wasted financial opportunity."

It struck Angelo that Heather did not care about the living patients who needed transplants. This epiphany took his breath. It meant that he was, irredeemably, a sinner. Clearly now, he saw that his financial strife and the grief over Sofia's passing had muddied his judgement, allowed him to be led astray, led straight into the pits of hell.

"I'm sorry," Angelo whispered to the ether, to God Himself.

"I understand," Heather said. "A little girl; hey, things can get sentimental."

"No, I mean I'm sorry, but I can't do this anymore."

"Can't do what?"

Angelo squeezed the handset. "I'm terminating our arrangement."

"Terminating our…? Okay, calm down. The arrangement stays."

"No. Things have happened. Thank you and I wish you all the best."

Finally, she said, "I hope, for your sake, that you haven't snitched."

"Snitched? To the police?" Angelo gave a crazed laugh. "I haven't told anybody. Why would I? I'm as guilty as you. I don't want to go to jail either."

"Listen, hang tight, I'll be in touch. Don't do anything stupid."

Heather ended the call. Angelo stared at the handset. When he returned it to the cradle, he thought of Sofia, of Teresa-Kate, and then of Sofia again, until he wanted nothing more than to lose himself in alcohol.

At home, drunk, Angelo lolled across the couch. Later, his mobile rang. It was on the coffee table. Stirring from his stupor, groggy, Angelo reached to the table and took a gulp of warm sherry before grabbing the phone. He said, "*Pronto.*"

"Excuse me?"

Angelo consulted his watch, swiped a hand over his numb face. Night lay heavy around the curtains. "Yes, this is De Luca and Son Funeral Directors."

"Mr De Luca? Oh, thank the baby Lord Jesus."

Prescience needled Angelo fully awake. He said, "How may I help you?"

"I'm the mother of Teresa-Kate. You delivered her body this morning for the viewing. Something terrible has happened. She's gone."

Angelo sat up. "Gone?"

"I couldn't sleep. I went to check on her. The casket is empty."

"Empty? You mean your daughter's body has been stolen?" The shock rendered Angelo sober. "Did you call the police?"

"I've called everybody," the mother said. "Help me. Please, help me."

"I'll try my very best." Shaking in fear and anger, he hung

up and called Heather the Body Wrangler. As soon as Heather answered, Angelo yelled, "Why did you do it? To blackmail me, is that it? A single X-ray will reveal the PVC pipes. Is that what you're planning? To hold that X-ray over my head?"

"Angelo?" Heather sighed. "You sound drunk. It's late. Let's talk tomorrow."

"Tell me what you did with Teresa-Kate."

"Who?"

"The little child: the girl with the raven hair."

"That kid you didn't complete?"

"Tell me where she is."

"I don't know what you're talking about." Heather paused. "Are you high? Having some kind of stroke? Look, I think maybe you should call an ambulance."

Unnerved, Angelo disconnected the call. Heather had not stolen the child's body. So where was it? He thought of the child leaping from the table, coming for him, and he shuddered. Perhaps Heather was right. Perhaps there was something wrong with him, like a mental breakdown. The strain of stealing from the dead must be unravelling his mind. Surely, he had hallucinated Teresa-Kate's resurrection. And those inhumanly long teeth? Why, gums always shrink after death.

Oh, deliver me. He put his face into his hands. *Deliver me, even though I don't deserve it.* The house shifted and creaked in the wind. Frightened, Angelo stared at the doorways leading to the kitchen and entrance hall. Nothing happened. Over the next few hours, he drank the sherry bottle dry. At around 4 a.m., he lurched towards bed. The mattress swam up and hit him. For the longest time, he didn't dream.

And then he dreamed of Teresa-Kate. He woke up.

Or, at least, he thought he did.

Teresa-Kate wrapped her fish-cold arms about his neck and sunk her bite into the meat of his shoulder. The pain, the wet and sloppy sound of her fangs chewing into his flesh, made him shriek over and over.

As he drowsed awake, the sound came to him slowly, a soft and familiar sound, regular as a pulse, making him feel comforted. Angelo tried but was unable to open his eyes. Confused, he attempted to sit up, failed. Cold steel lay beneath his naked body. And now he knew where he was: on the preparation table in his funeral parlour. That sound, that regular sound, was the dripping of the tap into the scrub-sink.

Panic lurched through him.

Had he been drugged? Kidnapped by Heather and her body snatchers? The last thing Angelo remembered…drinking, passing out, the nightmare, that terrible nightmare about Teresa-Kate. How much time had passed since then?

What in God's name was going on?

More sensation returned to his body. He became aware of a strange emptiness within his chest, an abnormally heavy weight within his belly. Gradually, he understood what it meant. He had undergone autopsy. His internal organs, including heart and lungs, were in a plastic bag sewn inside his abdomen. His death certificate would echo Teresa-Kate's: Angelo De Luca, fifty-nine, succumbed to an unidentified infection, administered by the bite of an unknown animal, probably a dog.

He wanted to scream. Was he dead? Undead? Had Teresa-Kate been conscious like this when he had harvested her bones?

The door of the preparation room opened. Footsteps approached. Whistling started—it was Gary Mathews. Angelo strained to give a signal, but could not wiggle his fingers, his toes; in fact, could not even take a breath.

"Sorry, old mate," Gary said. "But you know how it is. Business is business."

The rip of velcro, the one-two unfolding of heavy fabric. Angelo recognised those noises. Gary had opened the roll-bag of his butcher's knives. The subsequent *whisk-whisk-whisk* must be Gary honing a blade against the sharpening steel.

And that blade would be the boning knife.

When This You See, Think of Me

The beach house turned out to be a cruddy little shack. Zane cut the engine.

"Be careful of the mud," he said, grabbing their suitcases from the backseat.

Connie got out of the SUV. The wind held needling rain, salty from the ocean. Zane ran ahead and opened the front door. Connie ducked inside.

"I'll get your esky," Zane said, dropping the cases. "Take a look around."

At what? It's a shithole.

But their relationship was only a few months old, too fragile for honesty.

No oven. She tried the gas on the stovetop: nothing. *What about lunch?*

Shockingly, the detritus of Zane's wife littered the bathroom: comb, mousse, bobby pins. The wife had had long hair. It must have wound about her like seaweed as she had drowned herself. Perhaps she had cradled her pregnant belly as she died.

Zane came back with the esky.

"Your wife's things are still in the bathroom," Connie said.

He blanched. "I thought my sister cleaned out the place."

Zane's sister had rung Connie once. *Stay away*. But Connie had not been at fault. If anyone was to blame, it was Zane for straying.

"There's no gas," Connie said. "How can I cook the turkey?"

"You brought turkey?"

"And vegetables, stuffing, gravy, the lot."

"Don't worry," Zane said, putting down the esky. "We'll have takeaway."

"No. What about my groceries?"

"There's a charcoal chicken shop," he continued. "I won't be long."

He left.

Goddamn it.

Zane doesn't want his family to meet me, she thought. That's why he pushed for us to have this Christmas-in-July bullshit, to keep me away from the December barbecue. On the bedside table lay a paperback with a hand-stitched bookmark. Sewn by the wife? Connie threw the paperback into a drawer.

The wind carried a sudden, chilling wail.

At first, it reminded her of a seagull, a lonely howl that rose and fell. After a while, it began to sound human. Christ, was it a child?

Oh yes, oh God: a crying, screaming child.

Galvanised, Connie ran outside. The rain gusted in sheets. She sprinted to the sea. Wet sand bogged beneath her shoes. The grey surf slopped and surged. The wailing sounded on and on. She scanned the waves. There, in the shallows, a toddler, desperately waving her chubby arms.

"I'm coming to get you," Connie shrieked into the wind.

She waded through the icy water. The toddler kept waving, just out of reach. The sand disappeared underfoot. Connie began to swim. Glancing over her shoulder, the lights from the shack seemed far away. The bookmark came to mind: *when this you see, think of me*. A crawling dread moved through her.

The toddler disappeared.

In its stead materialised a woman with long hair: impassive, staring, motionless as if untouched by the tide. Panicked, Connie turned back towards land, retching and gasping. Zane stood on the beach. Help me, she tried to call.

Then, something—was it seaweed?—curled around Connie's ankle and pulled her under.

In The Company of Women

Philantha saw the horses first. Their corral was built under the boughs of a giant plane tree. Immediately, Philantha left the dirt road and walked across the meadow of wild grasses towards them. The horses nickered at her approach, shifting on nervous hooves. There was not a house or hut in the area, no signs of domesticity at all apart from the corral, which seemed to consist of fallen branches elaborately interwoven, reminding her of a nest. Then Philantha noticed the man. Naked apart from a filthy rag of cloth around his loins, the man sat under the tree and watched her get nearer. He did not stand up or wave. Perhaps he was an injured Trojan. But even if he were a Greek attempting an ambush, it would not matter; she would take one of his horses anyway. Philantha adjusted her grip on both the spear and shield.

Early yesterday morning, after killing the soldiers who had captured her, she had headed northeast, where Thermodon and her home city of Thermiskyra lay on the horizon. On foot, the journey would take at least two weeks. Philantha had no intention of walking the whole way. During that last, desperate fight to save Troy, a stinking Greek had managed to nick her forearm with his sword before she ran him clean through with her spear. Her injury, though trifling, had become infected. Without medical care, she risked sepsis. And since the Marmara region was now overrun with enemies, her only safety lay in reaching Thermiskyra, fast, and on horseback.

The low-lying valley baked under the midday summer sun. A pheasant cock called somewhere behind her in the woods. Dry grasses scratched at her bare legs. The man still had not moved. Perhaps he was dead. Philantha turned her attention to the plane tree, which appeared to be diseased. Instead of deep green, the foliage was a haphazard patchwork of grey, white and black. Despite this, the tree had reached a vast old age, judging by its great height and rounded canopy. There were no other plane trees in the meadow.

Philantha went right up to the man and stopped. He sat cross-legged, taking his weight on one arm extended behind him, gazing at her with interest. A chain around his ankle tethered him to the tree trunk. Covered in mire, his hair matted into muddy knots, she could not discern his race. The air stank of shit and putrescence. A fluttering motion caught her eye, and she turned, spotted the ravens nearby. The birds pecked and worried at a scattering of raw, wet bones: the remains of a recently butchered horse. There was no evidence of a cooking fire.

The man sat up straight. "You're an Amazon," he said. "I can tell by your tit."

His accent revealed him to be a Turk. Philantha looked about. The man appeared to be alone. The chain that bound him to the tree was about three metres long, while the butchered horse and attendant ravens were much further away.

"When does your master come back?" she said.

"Mistresses. I don't know. You'd better run before they get here." He clicked his fingers as if remembering something. "Hey, I thought Amazons carried a bow and arrow."

The soldiers had taken these from Philantha, along with her armour. Of her uniform, only the short tunic and girdle remained. What those bastards had done with her warhorse, only Ares knew. She scanned the corral. Ignoring the ponies—too small and weak for long-distance travel—she quickly assessed each horse by its coat, musculature, and posture. Two of them were Andravida, the Greek cavalry breed. The bay stood with its head hanging and its mouth open. The other one, the palomino, looked in reasonable condition.

"I'll take the palomino," she said.

"The horses aren't for sale."

"I'll take a bit and bridle too, if you have them."

"You're not leaving here with a horse," he said. "You're not leaving here at all."

Philantha went over to the palomino. The other horses and ponies bunched anxiously. The palomino stood its ground and stared. Putting down her shield, Philantha ran her hand along the horse's broad nose, up to the rough coarse hair of its mane.

As much as she despised the Greeks, she had to admit that their Andravida was a fine breed. With its stocky legs, deep chest and legendary stamina, this palomino would carry her speedily back to Thermiskyra, perhaps within five days if she rode the animal without mercy. Did she have five days? Philantha studied the wound on her forearm. An obscene mouth, the lips of it gaped and puckered. She pressed a finger experimentally against the inflamed skin. Thick beads of pus welled up. Already, she could feel an unnatural heat rising within her blood, a headache clenching the base of her skull.

Walking into the shade of the tree, she said to the man, "Have you any water?"

He shook his head.

"Food?"

With a smirk, he waved a hand at the bones and ravens. "Be my guest."

"Have your mistresses gone to collect water and food?"

"Uh-huh. You should get out of here while you still can."

Philantha laid her shield and spear next to her in the grass, and sat down to wait. Once the women returned, she would take their provisions, and leave on the palomino.

The man sighed. "Don't say I didn't warn you."

Philantha wondered what had happened to her regiment. She had not seen any of her fellow warriors since escaping the Greeks yesterday. Perhaps a force of retreating Amazons was already ahead of her on the road to Thermodon. She wondered how many had survived. Once inside the city walls, the Greeks had fought strongly and well, perpetrating a brutal massacre. Then again, most of the Trojan army was drunk, prematurely celebrating victory after ten long years of war, and plenty of

Amazons were drunk too. Philantha tightened her jaw. Those lousy Greeks, those cowards; hiding inside a goddamned peace offering. Where is the honour in that? At least Philantha had killed her share of those yellow dogs for the everlasting glory of Queen Penthesilea of Thermodon. The allied armies would regroup. Troy may be lost for now, but surely the battle wasn't over yet.

"Don't you want to know why I'm chained to this tree?" the man said.

Philantha glanced at him and looked away towards the distant road. The man's mistresses would most likely be travelling by horse-drawn trap. A deer trotted out of the woods on the other side of the dirt road, lifted its nose to sniff the air, and then bolted back into the cover of trees. If only Philantha still had her bow and arrow. Her mouth watered at the thought of venison steaks. Since escaping her captors, she had eaten just a handful of wild and bitter olives.

"Aren't you curious?" the man said at last. He lifted his foot and shook it, rattling the chain. "It's an interesting story."

She turned to him. Over his shoulder, she noticed the tree trunk. It was not disease that had turned it white, black and grey, but excrement; litres and litres of what seemed to be bird shit. In fact, more bird shit than she'd ever seen in her life. From the ravens, perhaps? She looked up through the befouled branches, searching for the rest of the flock, for birds that must number in the hundreds, but the tree was empty. The only ravens were the three still pecking at the carcass. She looked about for a stone or rock. Instead, she found a bloodied rib bone next to her in the grass. She threw the bone at the ravens. They startled, flapped their dark glossy wings, and settled back down again.

"Some time ago," the man said, "I worked as a day labourer on a farm."

Philantha cut her eyes at him. "In a time of war, farming is the job of the very young and the very old. You don't appear to be either."

He huffed out an impatient breath. "Anyway, one particular day, my mistresses came along and removed me from the farm.

We've been together ever since. One of them likes to have sexual relations with me. It's a singularly bizarre kind of coupling. Shall I tell you about that? Considering you don't seem interested in my chain."

"I'll break your chain with my spear. Then you can return to the farm."

The man snickered. Lifting his leg, he slipped off the chain, waggled his free foot, and put the chain back on again. Philantha did not know what to make of that. Puzzled, she stared at him.

"So? I don't like farming." As if discomfited, the man started to pout. "You've got no right to judge me," he continued. "I've lived a difficult life until now."

The more Philantha learned about the ways of men, the less she liked them. Unexpectedly, her heart gave a savage twist for Thermiskyra, for the mountains of the Thermodon nation, the sight of the Black Sea at dusk shining like a rippling skin of molten silver. By Ares, she longed to be home again in the company of women. The wound throbbed. The gods alone would decide whether she made it back in time. She concentrated on watching the road for the horse and trap. In the distant sky, two large birds were flying in from the south. The slow and ponderous action of their wings and frequent gliding identified them as vultures. They carried objects in their claws: parts of dead soldiers from Troy, no doubt.

The man began to chuckle and tut-tut. Philantha ignored him. The dirt road stayed empty. Her brow sweated with fever. How much longer before the trap appeared? She felt weary and ill, in need of rest. The ravens abandoned their meal and took off. The horses jostled and whinnied. The man laughed out loud. Wary, but not sure why, Philantha stood. She scrutinised the road, the woods, all directions: nothing.

"You've only yourself to blame," the man said, stretching out on his back and lacing his fingers behind his head. "I told you to leave. More than once, actually."

The horses began to crowd each other, stamping, bumping against the walls of the corral in a sudden panic. The vultures were close. How had they crossed such a great distance so quickly? The horror of it became clear. They were not vultures but harpies.

Harpies.

She would rather face a squad of Greeks.

The hairs rose on the back of Philantha's neck, and her breath quickened. She grabbed the spear and shield. Harpies were evil creatures, half-hag and half-bird, voracious carnivores and killers of lone travellers. At certain times of the year, flocks of them infested the shores of the Black Sea. Naturally, they knew better than to harass Thermodon, but every Amazon had at least a basic knowledge of the dangers that harpies posed. By Ares, how had Philantha not recognised the diarrhoetic dung slathering the tree? The nest-like construction of the corral? Because of sickness and fatigue, of course, but it was too late, far too late now, to worry about anything else but survival.

The thick, cloying stink typical of the harpy choked the air. Philantha dug her toes into the ground and lifted her spear. As the creatures came in to land, they dropped their cargo: bloated goatskins containing either wine or water. Philantha felt the dizzying strength of her thirst.

"They'll eat you alive," the man said, "and take your soft parts first: tongue, guts; the flesh between your legs. The pain will make you scream in a hundred new ways. Don't be ashamed. They don't give anybody, not even a soldier such as you, an honourable death."

The harpies landed awkwardly in the manner of bats, overbalancing, bracing themselves on the knuckles of their huge leathery wings and tottering forward a few steps on clawed feet. Philantha had never seen a harpy this close before. They were about a metre high, hunched, and bony. Their small eyes glittered. While breasts and arms were reminiscent of a human woman, their faces shone like flayed skulls, the lipless mouths sporadically flexing open and shut, sphincter-like, revealing yellowed fangs.

One harpy poured a stream of shit onto the ground. A second later, the other one followed suit. The stench momentarily closed Philantha's throat. She focused. There were differences between the harpies. One was smaller, thinner; lame in one leg with missing toes. Philantha would attack this harpy first.

Walking to the end of his chain, the man approached the lame harpy and put his arm about her filthy neck. Her wing on that side fluttered, stretched to enclose him.

"This is Elae, my lover," the man said. "Like a bird, she has but one hole down there for everything, so in effect, I screw her in the arse. What do you think of that?"

He laughed. Philantha didn't reply. Elae raised her yellowed teeth at the man. In response, he ran his tongue over them in a long, single lick.

"And this is Odarg," he added, gesturing towards the bigger harpy, "Elae's sister."

"Which one is in charge?" Philantha said.

"I am." Odarg's voice sounded raspy and dry as if seldom used.

Philantha struck her shield with the spear, once, and said, "Give me a goatskin of water and the palomino. Comply, and I will go on my way without incident."

The man giggled. Odarg approached on the knuckles of her wings, her scaly legs following behind in a slithering waddle. Philantha took a step back and lifted her shield, putting her weight into her front foot.

"Stranger, you look like *Antianeirai*," Odarg said, using the insult that translates as *those who fight like men*. "You need to make peace with your gods."

"My advice to you is the same," Philantha said.

The harpies exchanged glances.

The man snickered into his hand. "Oh, she's very bold."

"Bold for no reason," Odarg said. "Amazon, your queen's blind deference to Priam was the death of you all. The Greeks wiped out your regiment in Troy."

Philantha tightened her grip on the spear. "There is still Aeneas."

"Not for long. A force of our harpy sisters is attacking the once-mighty Aeneas and his troops as they flee the city of Troy, tails between their buttocks. This is the truth. You see, there is no hope. Drop your spear."

"Come and take it from me."

Odarg angled her head from side to side, gazing at Philantha with one eye and then the other, in the manner of a bird. "My talons are poisoned," she said. "One scratch and you will die within days."

"My aim is true. I will kill you outright with my spear."

"Hah. There are two of us."

"But I am a warrior, not an old man or a child, you cowards."

Odarg leaned back on her dirty wings and curled her body, aiming her wet and winking cloaca at Philantha. "I'll shit on you directly," Odarg said. "While you vomit, I'll gouge your face to shreds."

Philantha smiled. "I have disembowelled countless Greeks, felt the spray of their shit and blood across my face in every battle. Rotting bodies offended my nose every day. Come on, you devil. Give it a try. I'll spear you through your arse."

Sighing, Odarg at last sat down, tucking her legs beneath her like a broody hen. Finally, she said, "I'm curious. Where is your armour?"

"After the battle of Troy, a dozen Greeks captured me, and removed it."

"I see," Odarg said. "Then they took turns on you, no doubt."

"They tried."

The harpy skewed a piggish eye. "Meaning what? That you killed them?"

"To the last man."

With a nod, Odarg said, "Stand down, Amazon. Leave us in peace."

"Agreed." Philantha lowered the spear and shield. "I want the palomino."

"It's yours."

"And a goatskin of water."

"Go ahead. That's yours too."

Philantha picked up one of the sewn goatskins, walked to the corral, draped the goatskin over the palomino's back and began to dismantle one side of the corral. The palomino waited patiently, watching her with its calm, apple-sized eye.

"You're letting her go?" The man ducked out from under the wing of the lame harpy. "Wait a minute. She deserves to be punished. Listen, she tried to screw me."

"Amazons screw to reproduce," Odarg said. "She wouldn't reproduce with the pitiful likes of you if her remaining tit depended on it."

"No, I'm telling you, she grabbed my sack, told me to get it up or else."

Sniffing, Odarg rose slightly on one leg to dribble a puddle of shit.

The man added, "She also tried to break my chain and steal me away."

The man's lover, Elae, showed her fangs. "Bitch, I'll kill you."

"Now that's more like it," the man said, and laughed into his fists.

Elae awkwardly approached on wing and foot. Philantha put down the corral branch and grasped her spear, holding it loosely in one hand. Elae stopped and looked behind at her sister, who had not moved.

Odarg shrugged. "If you fight the Amazon, you'll fight her alone."

Philantha said, "Odarg, call off your sister before I slaughter her."

Odarg shrugged again. "She has her own mind."

"Will you keep out of it?"

"You have my word."

Sick as she was, Philantha knew she could manage a single, crippled harpy. Two harpies, however, would be a different story. In tandem, they would attack her from the air, moving as fast as lightning streaks, one assailing her front and the other her back, talons slashing and threshing down to the bone. Philantha swiped the perspiration from her forehead. She hefted the spear into her dominant hand, lifted the shield.

Elae was already upon her with claws outstretched.

Philantha struck blindly. It was a lucky blow, and she knew it.

The spear found Elae's breast. The impetus of the harpy's attack drove the spear all the way through the creature's body. There was little resistance, the bones light and brittle, the meat stringy. Elae gave a startled gasp. Then she went limp, and fell to the ground. Philantha put her foot against the harpy and wrenched out the spear in a fountain of guts and blood.

With an agonised howl, the man fell upon Elae, crying and clutching at her corpse. The intensity of his grief turned Philantha's stomach.

"I should kill you," she said to Odarg, "and your pet human, too."

"But you're injured."

"No. The harpy cripple never touched me."

Odarg offered a sly grin. "I mean the injury on your forearm, the one that speaks of infection. The Greeks must have given it to you as their parting gift."

Philantha removed the last tree branch from the corral and led the palomino free. Then she reconstructed the corral to keep the other animals inside. The palomino stood tall, snorting gently through its nostrils, shaking its head. Philantha arranged her spear and shield in one arm. Grasping the mane, she tried to mount the horse and somehow failed, a swoon of vertigo tilting the earth beneath her feet.

"Tell me," Odarg said, "can you feel the exhalation of Thanatos on your neck?"

Philantha managed to climb onto the horse. "Our business here is done."

"Is it? You killed my sister."

Philantha considered. Evidently, Odarg planned to attack at a later point. There was only one road to Thermodon. Unless Philantha wasted precious time slogging through woodland—time which she could not afford—Odarg would find her simply by flying over the road. And harpies travelled as quietly as owls, as quickly as sound. Odarg would close in when Philantha, exhausted, might be dozing on horseback.

"Don't come after me," Philantha said. "I'll kill you like I killed your sister."

Odarg stood up from her squat, tottered side to side on scaly feet, and fanned her wings. The ghoulish skull-mask of her face stretching into a rictus, she said, "You think I'd attack you alone? Unlike Elae, I'm not insane. No, I'll ask the flock currently spiting Aeneas if they can spare a few sisters."

"Understood. I'll be waiting for you."

Odarg gave a screeching laugh. "Let's be honest. You won't make Thermodon."

The harpy released a stream of shit and trod into it, joyfully, as if in celebration. The weeping of the man over the fallen Elae went on and on. With a cluck of Philantha's tongue, the palomino began to trot through the meadow.

Odarg called, "Amazon, last of the *Antianeirai* fighters of Troy, you are already dead, one way or another, by a Greek's hand or my own."

Philantha kept the shield on her lap, the spear in her fist. Once at the dirt road, she used the gentle pressure of her knees to urge the palomino into a steady, three-beat canter. The meadow soon fell behind. After a while, she broke a stitch on the goatskin, sucked at the flesh, and tasted wine instead of water. The gods had again abandoned her.

No matter, she would continue to journey without them.

The afternoon sun bore down, hot as fire stones. Spangles affected her vision. To keep focus, Philantha recalled the Black Sea and its rolling waves, its spume foaming across the beach, its water that had cooled her feet ever since she was old enough to walk, the boats working their fishing nets on its horizon.

Across The White Desert

Both of them were going to die. John knew this to be true. Every time he tried to mentally prepare, however, the goddamned soldier next to him on the dogsled kept arguing the impossible.

"Circle back," the soldier said again. "Seven downed men: that equals seven field-packs with food, weapons and ammo. We need those supplies."

John said, "Circle back? How? This is Antarctica, dickhead. No cover."

The dogs sprinted over the snow, kicking up powder. John felt the muscular strength of each Siberian husky through the reins. His two other dog teams, their sleds now empty, kept pace alongside. Run, he thought; for the love of Christ, *run*. Those *things* still tracked close behind. Circle back? My arse. Didn't the soldier understand? Hadn't the dumb bastard witnessed that ambush out of nowhere? Seen the massacre himself?

John yelled, "Hike!"

His lead dog, Nikita, picked up the pace. The four dogs in her chain followed suit. The dogs were gasping, their breaths freezing overhead and raining plumes of ice crystals along their backs. The sled flew over the wasteland. Ice sheared up in dual waves. John ducked his head into the wind. The blue sky sat over them like a glass dome. We're trapped, John realised, a few insignificant figures in a snow globe.

"I can't protect you," the soldier said, "without weapons and ammo."

John sneered. "Protect me?"

"Hey, I'm your only means of defence."

What arrogance, what stupidity. On the plane ride here, the machismo of the eight army soldiers had made John uneasy. Their boundless enthusiasm suggested greenness. John was a Vietnam vet. When approaching a drop zone, experienced soldiers tend to be quiet, focused, usually a little frightened. In hindsight, the stupendous amount of cash the Defence Force had offered should have warned him away, but mortgage payments, bills, the hope for one last hurrah backpacking through Asia before his arthritis got too bad…

John glanced back. The *things* had dropped away. Thank God for the speed of his dogs. For the first time since John and the soldiers had approached the craft, the clutch of panic around his throat loosened off. Maybe we'll make it, he thought. Maybe we'll get to one of the research stations.

The wind felt cold enough to strip the skin from his face, despite his layers of balaclava. It had been many years since he'd run a dogsled in Antarctica; not since 1994, when politicians had introduced the ban for fear of dogs passing distemper to the fucking seals, for Christ's sake. Ever since, stranded back home in Australia, he had offered a tourist show in the Victorian Alps for five hundred bucks per dogsled ride; wasting his life whisking red-cheeked and excitable families through meagre snow, growing old at an exponential rate, sixty-seven yet feeling infinitely more decrepit with boredom, restlessness, depression…

Until the knock on his door yesterday.

The man and woman were military. John could tell from their posture, their attitude, the way they wore their suits.

"John Lansky?" the woman said. "Can we talk, sir?"

They walked inside. Before he shut the door, John noted three black sedans parked out front, windows tinted. Why would the military give a rat's arse about him? There was a sofa and a couple of kitchen chairs in his cabin, but the visitors chose to stand. John sat down and lit a cigarette.

Without any preliminaries, the woman said, "We're from the Australian Defence Force, here under direct orders from the

Minister of Defence. We want you and your dogs to take eight soldiers into Antarctica."

Surprised, John smiled. "The Antarctic Treaty bans military manoeuvres."

"We have to leave tonight," the man said.

John laughed. "Tonight? I can't get ready that fast."

"You'll have all the help you need. Let's begin."

John felt a sudden apprehension. "Hey, take it easy. What's the rush?" He looked from one blank face to the other. "What's going on?"

The man said, "An unidentified craft landed on Australian territory."

Oh, Christ. Now John knew why the Defence Force had come to his door: because of that one experience he'd had in Nam; one insane, inexplicable mind-fuck of an experience that had landed him and the survivors of his scout party a psych evaluation each and one week's leave. A crawling sensation moved through his body. Jesus, he could even feel the shrivelling of his ball sack.

"Why not use vehicles?" he said. "The weather this time of year is okay for choppers or Hagglunds."

The man said, "There's a constant EMP surrounding the area of the craft."

"Like a force field? I didn't think an EMP could work like that." When they did not answer, John added, "Do you realise how old I am? Besides, I haven't done any soldiering for a long time."

"We need your dog skills," the woman said. "But according to your war records, an incident happened to you in Vietnam that would also make you handy as a consultant."

So after all this time, he thought, the Defence Force believes me. Arseholes.

"A consultant?" John mashed out his cigarette. "Forget it. I've seen that particular sci-fi movie, and I know how it turns out."

The woman said, "Twenty thousand dollars for the weekend. Cash."

Twenty *thousand*? More than he made in a whole year? Even though his balls had been trying to crawl back into his body,

John had shaken hands on the deal.

Idiot, he thought. Now he and this soldier were going to die somewhere in this vast, white Antarctic desert, and die horribly. He should have listened to his balls.

"Where are we headed?" the soldier said.

"I think we're closest to the French claim," John said. "We're too far away to reach Davis, Casey or Morgan."

"Who are they?"

Oh Jesus, was the bloke kidding? John said, "Australia's three permanent research stations, you fucktard. Don't you bastards prep for missions anymore?"

But John was underprepared too. The Defence Force had packed him and the dogs last night and flown them to Antarctica. While the commanders and soldiers discussed the mission, John was out shooting a couple of seals, gutting and skinning them, making the weekend's dog food. By the time he returned, the soldiers were kitting up, so he never got properly briefed. He hadn't had time to read up on anything, had not stepped foot on this continent for over twenty years, could not get his bearings from the landscape. Right now, John was trying to navigate by the sun, for Christ's sake. Dumont d'Urville Station wasn't very big. In all likelihood, his estimations were a few kilometres out and they would miss it. Even if he found the station, it might be shut. Due to katabatic winds and ice, the French kept the station closed for months at a time. Which months? John couldn't remember.

The dogs were tiring. He could feel it through the reins.

Dear God, he thought, I don't want to die here.

The soldier, hindered by his armour and snow gear, twisted to look behind. The sled momentarily lost its centre of balance. John leaned over to compensate as a fountain of ice flew up from a blade.

"Watch it," he said. "If you tip us over, I'll leave you behind."

"I can't see them." The soldier faced front, wiped ice crystals from his goggles. "You think they've frozen to death?"

"Who can tell?"

"It's common sense," the soldier said. "Fucken giant cockroaches or whatever. They didn't have equipment, no gear, no protection. They've frozen to death for sure."

John glanced back. Only a flat sheet of ice as far as the eye could see, a mountainous range shimmering like a mirage on the horizon, everything tinted a cool blue from the sky and, just visible, a glint of sunlight reflecting off the alien craft. Yes, of course it was alien. The suits had said on the plane ride over that it might be North Koreans. Bullshit. John had taken one look at that smooth, organic, luminescent UFO and known it was nothing from this earth.

He checked his watch. He and the soldier had been sledding for about an hour. So they had travelled about fifteen kilometres from the craft. If he slowed the dogs, let them trot, he would conserve their strength. The dogs were not endurance runners. They were used to carrying families on short jaunts, not slogging through snow for 140 kilometres at a stretch. Maybe he could stop after another hour. They could all rest, eat something. He would swap out Nikita's team with either Buck's or Samson's.

"What's your name?" John said to the soldier.

"Papadopoulos. The team calls me Pup. I mean, they used to call me Pup."

"If we can't make it to the extraction point," John said, "what's the contingency plan?"

"Did you see what those fuckers did to Corporal O'Rourke? Burrowed into his guts and turned him inside out. I never would have believed it possible."

"Yeah, I saw it." The *things* had been hiding, had ambushed the soldiers. The attack had lasted mere seconds. John said, "What's Plan B?"

"And Dobson. Shit, it was like he walked into a couple of rotor blades."

"Tell me about Plan B."

Pup looked around at him, swivelling his head on top of his neck. The goggles didn't show the boy's eyes, but John recognised shock in the body language.

"We go back to where we landed," Pup said. "Pick up is nine hours after drop-off. Three hours on the sleds, three hours of recce, three hours to get the fuck out of there." He put his gloved hand on John's arm as if to take the reins. "So you see? We've got to turn around."

John shook him off. "No way."

"But the extraction team won't be able to find us."

"Once we get out of the EMP force field, we can make contact via radio. You've got a radio, haven't you?"

"No sir. The radio's in Tobin's gear. Tobin is the radioman. I mean, he used to be the radioman. Did you see what happened to him back there?"

"I don't know one of you bastards from the other."

"A fucken giant cockroach dug into his throat and punched out his guts. Wham, fast as a bolt of lightning."

"Have you got any other way of contacting the commanders?"

Pup whistled as if in admiration. "Like a fucken bolt of lightning."

John looked back. The horizon was empty.

"Easy!" he yelled to Nikita.

She slowed. The other dogs followed suit, dropping their heads, exhausted already. But so was John. Despite his warm and waterproof clothing, his arthritic joints were hurting, stiffening, his fingers hardening into claws on the reins.

Stop bitching, he thought, and concentrate.

From memory, Dumont d'Urville Station was a scattered collection of red buildings arranged as if at random across the rocky outcrop of the archipelago. The young John Lansky had thought the station resembled carriages of a derailed red-rattler. Very hard to miss. Now there was nothing but ice.

"You got a compass?" he said.

Pup began to pat at his pockets, as if searching absentmindedly for lost cigarettes. God, John could do with a smoke. Depending on how the compass reacted, he might be able to figure their position in relation to the geographic and magnetic South Poles. He peered at the sun. It should be low and moving in a counter-clockwise position at this time of day and year. Shouldn't it?

Okay, they could be lost.

The idea of it chilled him to the marrow, colder than any

Antarctic wind. Before them lay ice, ice and more ice. Where was Dumont d'Urville? He looked behind them again. No sign of those *things*.

"Tell me," he said. "Can we contact the extraction team ourselves?"

Pup did not answer. It sounded like he was humming a tune.

"We'll keep going for another hour or so," John said. "Then we ought to stop for a break, drink some water, eat something, and rest the dogs. Okay, Pup?"

The boy kept humming.

The dogs huddled together, dozing, bellies full of seal meat. With the portable cooker, Pup had rehydrated two ration packs: beef curry with rice. Now, they drank coffee.

"Lance Corporal Lee reckoned you fought these cockroaches before," Pup said, "back when you served in Nam."

John sighed. "I saw them but I didn't fight them."

"What happened?"

"No one believed me. That's what happened."

Pup waited.

John sipped at his coffee. Finally, he said, "Me and some other blokes were the scouts. We heard screaming from behind. I figured the Viet Cong had done their usual trick: skip the scouts to catch the main party unawares. So we all ran back to help." John's throat closed, made a faint choking sound.

"And what did you find?" Pup said.

John flung the coffee dregs into the snow, where they hissed and pitted into holes of their own making. "Those *things*."

"Doing what?"

"What they did to your blokes: running through everyone like buzz saws, like each man had somehow swallowed a grenade and triggered it."

Jesus Christ, each *thing* as big as a rat, with about twelve legs, an articulated exoskeleton, numerous sets of mandibles swirling and chopping. But the *speed* of those creatures was the heart-stopper. As if the laws of physics didn't apply. Living things of that size and bulk could not move that fast, John knew, could not fly without wings, could not change course in mid-air like that, could not smash through armour and helmets and bodies like a mortar shell and not incur any damage themselves.

Pup nodded. "Back there at the spaceship; did you see those other pricks?"

John held his breath. So he had not been dreaming. Yes, at an opening in the craft's skin had stood tall, impossibly skinny, bone-white figures. He said, "It's like they're the ones in command, and these…cockroaches…are their guard dogs, chasing off any intruders."

"Dirty shitsacks," Pup said. "Okay, what's the plan?"

"We exit the EMP range, find the French station, use their radio to contact the extraction team, and get the fuck out of here."

"And if we can't find the French station?"

John got up from his seat on the sled. "Let's go. We've been here twenty minutes already."

John and Pup were travelling with Samson's team. They would make better time if Pup drove his own sled, but John did not trust the boy's state of mind. Nikita and Buck trotted their teams alongside. The pace was brisk but sustainable. John figured they would exit the EMP range any minute now. But where was Dumont d'Urville station?

As if the same thought had occurred, Pup said, "Fuck. We're lost."

John hesitated. "Against this landscape, we stand out like proverbial dog's balls. The chopper pilot will find us, easy." Unless the suits had decided to let them die, and burn all paperwork. Clearly, this was in no way a legal reconnaissance.

Pup flung out his arm and pointed.

Dead ahead, 12 o'clock, a line of *things* was coming at them.

Goddamn, John thought, a classic pincer move. They circled ahead of us. How far must they have ranged to the left and right on this endlessly flat landscape to keep out of sight? How fast could those *things* actually travel?

"Whoa," he yelled to Samson. The lead dog pulled up. Nikita's and Buck's teams pulled up too. Alarmed, the dogs flattened their ears and began whimpering.

"We've got to turn back," Pup said, trying to take the reins.

But John knew better. This was a trap. The oncoming *things* were hoping to direct the dogsleds 180 degrees where the ambush waited. Lions hunted in the exact same way. Oh God, John thought, his legs beginning to shake.

These *things* are hunting us.

"Gee!" he cried. Samson aimed the dog team to the right.

"Don't run at a fucken right-angle," Pup said. "They'll catch us. Turn back."

"No, it's a pincer move."

The dogs dragged the sled at top speed over the snow. As if anticipating this reaction, a scattering of *things* lay ahead in wait. Shit, they had created a giant loose circle; the majority at the front and back, some on either side.

"Ready your weapon," John said.

Pup fumbled next to him. John had his .22 but it was unloaded. The magazines were in his pack.

Fuck.

Samson wailed. John wouldn't give the command to change course. Samson, God bless him, would not disobey. Pup kept fumbling with his weapon. The *things*, about a dozen of them, gained ground at astonishing speed. They were on a collision course. John felt his bowels start to involuntarily loosen.

Buck, heading an empty sled, balked, howled and peeled off to the left.

"On by!" John yelled, ordering Buck to ignore the distraction. "Buck, on by!"

No good. Buck and the chained four dogs ran higgledy-piggledy across the snow and away. The approaching *things* seemed to hesitate. Some peeled off to chase Buck's team. The remainder, about half a dozen, came straight at John and Pup.

Crack.

The tremendous noise punched John's eardrums. Flinching, disorientated, he almost lost footing on the sled.

Crack.

Shit, it was Pup, his F88 Austeyr rifle on single-shot mode, picking off the *things* one by one.

Crack.

John saw a *thing* arc up into the air and flip into the snow. He chanced a look to the left. Buck's team was down, blood spraying in giant red Catherine wheels. Buck, Panda, Fritz, Sugar, Rufus… John's heart squeezed down into a fist at the loss.

Crack.

The remaining *things* were almost upon them. Pup killed them in a flurry of shots, and then shouldered his F88 as if he thought nothing of it. They were sledding across clear snow, the carnage behind them dwindling into the distance. The *things* attacking Buck's team were not following.

"Holy shit, boy," John said. "Did you miss a single shot?"

"Not one."

John clapped him on the shoulder. "That's the best shooting I've ever seen."

"Oh, fucken hell," Pup moaned. "Fuck me dead."

John looked at Nikita, running her team alongside. She gave him a wounded glance. John scanned the landscape: ice, ice and more ice. The sun looked in the same spot as before. If they were not lost before, they were definitely lost now. At least they were alive. In a little while, he'd steer the dogs back to their original course in hopes of finding Dumont d'Urville. At least they must be clear of the craft's EMP by now.

Pup said, "I'm gonna spew."

"Whoa," John said, and the team stopped.

Pup shifted the layers of his balaclava and emptied a stomach's worth of curry into the snow. John caught sight of a meagre beard. The poor kid, John thought, he's too young. Every soldier is too damn young.

"Hike!" John yelled, and Samson began to sprint. The other dogs followed suit. The slushy sound of the blades cleaving snow began again.

"Sorry about that," Pup said. "Look, I'm not a pussy."

"There's no shame in losing your lunch. Not in a situation like this. Better drink something before you dehydrate."

They had come to a stop. No choice.

The dogs snarled, whimpered and barked, tails down, ears flattened. Working quickly, John swapped the gear back to Nikita's sled. Meanwhile, Pup turned on the spot in a tight circle, F88 at his shoulder, trying to cover every point. When John began to unchain Samson and his team, Pup said, "What are you doing?"

"Giving them a fighting chance. If we survive, we'll head out on Nikita's sled. Do your best to protect Nikita's team if you can, okay?"

"Okay."

"How much ammo have you got?" John said.

"Not enough."

"How many *things* do you count?"

"Hard to tell," Pup said, flat and lifeless. "Maybe thirty or forty."

Fuck. John's rifle held five bullets in a magazine, and the damn thing was bolt action too. Scrambling, the sweat pouring from his armpits despite the cold, his knees trembling, he dug from his pack the handful of magazines. As he slid one into the .22, the rest into his pocket, he said, "What are they doing now?"

"Just watching, I guess."

John looked around. The *things* had them fenced on all sides. The distance between us and them, he figured, about fifty metres. "See how they're hesitating?" he said, unable to mask the quaver in his voice. "That's good. They're unsure of us."

"But creeping in closer and closer," Pup said. "How near do you want them to get before we start shooting?"

"I don't know. They'll probably attack as soon as we shoot."

Samson and his unchained team raised their hackles and bared fangs. As if aware of their own helplessness, Nikita and her chained dogs crowded together and whined. The wind gusted hard, full of gritty snow.

"You got any tactical suggestions?" John said. "We could stand back to back."

A deafening stutter of bullets erupted from Pup's F88. For about two seconds, he swung it from left to right. A dozen or more *things* jumped and split apart in a line of bloodless grey guts. Then Pup was out of ammo and fitting another box magazine.

A suspended moment, then everything occurred at once.

Chaos, John thought, utter chaos.

The *things* flew over the snow at them, the free dogs ran out to meet them, and John fired, reloaded, fired. One of his dogs, Simba, turned inside out in an explosive aerated spray, followed by Raven. Dear God. Pup let loose another devastating round of automatic fire.

His own rifle empty, John swung with his machete. The *thing* felt dense and heavy against his blade, like a lump of clay. His arthritic joints burned. Then the *things* retreated. John leaned on his knees, shaking, trying to catch his breath. The air was so cold, it felt as if he were breathing needles.

"What the fuck are they doing?" Pup said.

"Having second thoughts. How many do you reckon are left?"

"About a dozen."

We can win this, John thought. A wave of strength surged into his limbs. Hurriedly, he reloaded his .22. "Let's finish off the bastards," he said.

"Look," Pup said and pointed.

About five kilometres away was a dark line in the snow. John squinted. Even as he watched, the dark line came perceptibly closer. With a sickening lurch in his stomach, he realised what it was: reinforcements. No wonder these *things* had withdrawn. They were waiting for back-up.

"Get on the sled," John said.

"What for? Your dogs are knackered, and this place is bigger than the whole of fucken Australia."

"We'll find the French station."

Pup laughed. "No we won't."

"Then what's your plan? Stay here and die? Get on the sled."

"Aw, fuck this for a joke."

Pup started off at a shambling trot toward the nearby *things*, shooting on automatic. He killed most of them. One was all it took. The boy's tiered armour made no difference. The *thing* ploughed into him and came out the other side. Pup dropped and began staining the snow red.

Barking, the free dogs charged.

John found his feet and leapt onto the sled, yelling, "Hike! Hike!"

Nikita and her team sprinted. John gave out a sob. Oh God, Pup, that poor boy…John glanced behind. Samson, Willow and Voodoo were fighting the remaining *things*. Meanwhile, the dark line of reinforcements edged closer.

Pup was right, John thought, I can't outrun them. Holding onto the sled with one hand, he opened Pup's kit and dug through it. Surely, there must be more firearms, a semi-automatic pistol, anything. He found a holster with a gun, thank Christ. But no, it was a flare gun, goddamn it, useless as a weapon.

You idiot, he thought a split-second later.

I have a flare gun.

It was a single-shooter, the holster with thirteen flares. He loaded, aimed overhead, and squeezed the trigger. The loud report hurt his ears. If he lived, he would need bloody hearing aids. A glowing orb streaked into the sky. As it reached the top of its arc, it smoked, leaving a long red trail.

The extraction team would see that, unless they were blind or turning a blind eye. They'd see it, by God.

Behind him, the dark line was close enough to show detail: scores and scores of *things*. Why wouldn't they quit? One old man and five dogs, so what, why the hell wouldn't those *things* ever quit? Awkwardly, scared of falling off the sled as it jounced and jostled over the ice, John put another magazine into the .22 and hung the machete from his belt.

The dogs were slowing down.

"Hike," he shouted.

Nikita tried. She and her team did not have the strength.

He shot another flare.

The *things* were closing in. Turning to face them, he lashed himself to the sled with the reins. He cocked his rifle and peered down the scope. For a time, all he could hear was his heart. Then he heard another sound, like a droning bee. He scanned the blue dome of the sky. And there, far away, small as an insect, was a helicopter.

He put his eye back to the scope: the *things*, a kilometre away, were closing.

Here it is, the moment of truth, John thought with a surreal kind of surprise. What'll come first: the chopper or those *things*? A strange calm descended like it often had back in Vietnam, the world dwindling down to a pinpoint, as if viewed through the wrong-end of binoculars.

"Hike!" he shouted, again and again.

The chopper sounded louder, but he could not look up from his scope.

He pulled the trigger, cocked the rifle, and fired again. Three more shots remained.

Sarah Jane Runs Away With the Circus

At ten years of age, Sarah Jane leaves the orphanage to come and live with these people. This is your family now, a nun says at the gate. When Sarah Jane turns eleven, her new parents give her a colouring book. She hates colouring. She does not want to stay within the lines. Her teacher makes her stay within the lines.

Mum raises both eyebrows. "Well, what do you say?"

"Thank you," Sarah Jane replies. "Thank you very much for my present."

"You're welcome," Dad says.

Her parents attend to breakfast. Her four brothers are slouched at the kitchen table. They are much older, in high school. All the members of Sarah Jane's new family have red hair, blue eyes, and freckles. She has dark hair, brown eyes, and olive skin. She is the colour of shit, so her brothers tell her. Why did these people take her from the orphanage? She asked one time, and made her new parents furious. Sarah Jane wishes to find her real family. Once, the nuns took the children on a trip to the circus. As Sarah Jane watched the trapeze artists, a beautiful woman and a handsome man, she knew they were her real parents. That's not true, the nuns said.

Sarah Jane slips into a chair at the kitchen table and waits. Mum puts toast in front of her. Dad pours her a cup of milk. Late last night in bed, she heard them arguing in the next room, a familiar argument.

"What can we do?" Dad said. "She's not a dog we can take to the pound."

Sarah Jane eats her toast, drinks her milk, and recalls the shivering dachshund in a pink tutu skirt, trundling on a miniature tricycle, doing laps of the circus ring under hot lights while the audience pointed and laughed. The dog could do nothing but pedal, pedal, look this way and that with its wet, brown eyes, and keep pedalling.

Today is Sarah Jane's birthday, but it is also Sunday. Aunty, Uncle and the cousins will visit after lunch, as they do every weekend, so the men can play cards, the women can gossip, and the children can tease Sarah Jane. They tease her in the rumpus room if the weather is foul, in the backyard if the weather is fine. *You're not one of us*. Clenched, Sarah Jane does not reply. Her silence inflames them. They shove or hit her. She falls down and gets up again. Eventually, her stoicism makes the younger children cry in fright. The older children get angry. *What's wrong with you?*

After lunch, Aunty, Uncle and the cousins arrive. Everyone takes a seat in the open-plan kitchen and lounge room. Sarah Jane has nowhere to sit. As usual, she is stranded on the rug by the radiator. The visitors find out it is her birthday.

"Oh?" Aunty says, and winks. "You know, I think I've got a present for you."

Aunty glances about. Sarah Jane knows it must be a trick, but hope flutters in her chest anyway. Finally, Aunty takes a heavy-gauge wire coathanger from the clotheshorse set up next to the radiator. A titter of laughter rolls around the room.

"Here you go," Aunty says. "Happy birthday."

Sarah Jane takes the coathanger. The brothers and cousins nudge at each other. Everyone is looking at her, their eyes gleaming. They lean forward, waiting. The coathanger is old and buckled. She touches the hook with her thumb. The hook is sharp. She turns the coathanger over and over in her hands. What would be the correct response to a gift like this? The blood is pounding in her head. She feels faint.

"Well?" Mum says, prompting her.

The brothers and cousins smother their giggles.

"Thank you," she replies. "Thank you very much for my present."

Laughter breaks out. Mum sniggers and snorts.

"Hey, that's not nice," Dad says, yet he is smiling too.

Sarah Jane can do nothing but pedal, pedal, keep pedalling. The room is suddenly hot, as if under spotlights. She looks at the jeering crowd. What is expected of her? Should she laugh too? She tries to join in, but no, the crowd laughs harder. Tears rise. She blinks them back.

A lion wakes up inside its cage, inside her ribcage, and roars.

The roar is so loud that it beats at her eardrums.

Sarah Jane listens, and stops pedalling.

The nearest child, one of her cousins, has a fat, round face. The hook of the coathanger splits his cheek from ear to lip. The exposed molars shine white. Everyone recoils, gasps, and freezes. The butchered flesh shivers, glossy and moist, before the blood gushes and the child shrieks. His ruined mouth gapes oh so very wide. Sarah Jane laughs at the spectacle. People scream, jump, dash from one side of the room to the other, a pack of frightened monkeys hooting and whooping inside an enclosure.

They are too slow. Nobody can catch her. Nobody can flee.

Sarah Jane gashes a scalp, ruptures a nose, and tears out teeth, punctures an eyeball. Swooping and diving on the end of the hook, she is a trapeze artist like her real parents, agile and strong, unerring, her grip sure.

The lion roars. The monkeys holler. The blood flows.

Sarah Jane decides to fly through this crowd until she is good and done, for as long as it takes; until the nuns, repentant, show up at the door and hold out their arms.

What the Sea Wants

The gale passes with the dawn. The *Mary Jane* barely lifts on the swell; her mainsail fortified with the bonnet and drabbler to better catch the breeze, her square-sail full on the mast. The North Sea lies as green and calm as an English meadow. Joseph puts on his cap but the cold still bites at his ears. The wintry air, like a ghost, moves through anything it pleases, stinging his fingers and toes, slicing without resistance into his belly, his marrow. It's a familiar discomfort.

Joseph leans on the gunwale to better enjoy this rare moment of rest.

The sky shines pale and clear, a sign of good fishing. Once thrown, the nets will be full of cod and herring within a few hours. Joseph longs for something to eat other than fish. Mostly, he craves bacon and potato pie. His wife, Amelia, is a good cook. He sighs. The *Mary Jane* has been at sea for weeks. It's best not to think about one's wife and the various pleasures that she can offer.

Out of the corner of his eye, he sees Young Thomas approach. The boy tugs the elbow of Joseph's woollen gansey to get his attention. He turns. Young Thomas looks haggard and ill; his first full storm at sea left him puking all night. Joseph, a grown man of nineteen years who has worked on doggers since he was ten, claps a reassuring hand on the shoulder of poor Young Thomas.

"Rough storm," he says. "Don't worry, lad. You'll find your sea legs."

"Does the weather get much worse?"

Joseph considers. Yesterday, after a red sky, the shifting wind began to whip the North Sea into chop and foam. The heavens disappeared behind a veil of mist. Each breath drew salt into the lungs. Without waiting for orders from Skipper, the experienced hands abandoned the gutting of the catch and started to batten down, telling the deckie-learners—including Young Thomas—to do the same.

Soon after, the wind swung around, and blew from ahead.

Skipper ordered the crew to shorten sail. The men scrambled to obey. Water flung aboard the vessel in sheets. Skipper tacked as close to the wind as he could. The ever-increasing swell drove the boat leeward, back towards England and away from the Dogger Bank, despite the dropping of every anchor.

How many storms at sea had Joseph endured? Five hundred? One thousand? He felt keyed up, but not afraid. The dogger is a sturdy craft, fifteen feet at the beam with a draught of five feet; rugged and high-sided, substantial enough to resist the vagaries of the North Sea. Heart pounding, his frozen and wet hands wrestling to knot the weather-cloth over the hatches, he risked a glance behind him.

The sea heaved and pulsed, the foam a series of broken and jagged streaks lacing the rollers. Then a surge loomed. Climbing, it rose more than twenty-five feet, a wall of dirty green water. Its white cap tipped in a long unbroken line over the crest, and barrelled at the dogger as solid as a felled log. Joseph knew that when it hit the side of the boat, this giant wave might capsize the *Mary Jane*.

"Brace yourselves," he yelled, his voice thrown away by the wind.

Whether they heard him or not, it didn't matter; the old hands instinctively knew what was coming by the pitch of the dogger, and immediately clutched at grab rails, ropes, and anything else pinned down. The deckie-learners, terrified, were already holding on fast. The wave crashed into the ship with the power of God's fist, sending a flood of water over the gunwale. The soapy foam snatched Richard, a deckie-learner. Joseph saw the lad wash over the side as the *Mary Jane* almost flipped to starboard. One moment, the lad was there; the next moment, no more. Joseph's heart squeezed down into a tight clutch. Almost immediately, he determined to forget about it. Plenty of men had perished during the years of Joseph's tenure. What the sea wants, the sea will have. Nevertheless, he hoped that Young Thomas was all right.

The waves dumped on the *Mary Jane* one after another, slopping and frothing across the deck, freezing Joseph and smothering his breath. As fast as the sea gushed out through the scuppers, a fresh deluge would come on board. When the *Mary Jane* ascended each crest, Joseph became weightless and lifted from the deck, his feet scarcely touching the planks. When the dogger ploughed her bow into a trough, his body transformed into a ton of bone-cracking weight, crushing down through his spine.

The storm intensified as night fell. The watery blue mist of the sky became black. Joseph did not pray. As a fisherman for some ten years, he understood the futility of the exercise. On and on went the storm. The ferocity left it during the false dawn. Minutes later, the true dawn heralded a change in weather. The storm died. The waves dropped at once, as if God Himself had lost interest.

Now, Joseph and Young Thomas are leaning on the gunwale together, surveying the North Sea, which lies as harmless as a drawn bath.

"Does the weather get much worse?" Young Thomas says again.

"We've had the lowest of it," Joseph says, which is a lie. Actually, the gale was nothing unusual. The North Sea is a contrary and capricious bitch, yet it would not help to inform the lad of this fact. Joseph adds, "Now hurry up and eat breakfast."

The wind is behind. Skipper asks for full sails. The crew complies. The *Mary Jane* skips over the North Sea towards Dogger Bank where the fishing is best. Half the crew finishes gutting, decapitating and salting yesterday's catch, and packing the fish with extra salt into the hold. The rest of the men, including Joseph and Young Thomas, check and repair the trawling nets. No one mentions the lad, Richard, washed overboard during the storm; to do so would be bad luck.

The nets are voluminous, wet and heavy. The salt water stings the various cuts and welts that crisscross Joseph's leathery hands. He notices that Young Thomas' palms are bleeding. To his credit, the lad does not complain. They dole out the nets to starboard. The sea takes the clotted mess of twine and effortlessly plumps it out into the narrow-necked shape of a sack, pluming it in the wake of the *Mary Jane*. Crew members on the port-side do the same. Sweating, Joseph takes off his woollen cap, wrings the sweat and brine from it, and tucks it into the back of his trousers. Solemnly, Young Thomas imitates him.

It is time to adjust the trim of the boat. Most of the hands either move or jettison the boulders and sand in the hull to counterbalance the salted fish in the hold. The work done, the *Mary Jane* bobs higher, jaunty; the North Sea once again kisses at her painted waterline. The crew has a brief rest, each man climbing into his individual berth in the cuddy. Joseph falls asleep at once. He dreams of his wife, Amelia, of her plump arms and warm lips, the moist and welcoming softness between her thighs.

Skipper rings the bell.

The crew turns out. On deck, however, Joseph notices that the sun is too low in the sky. It is not yet noon. The trawling nets will be half-empty. Confused, troubled by the break in routine, he decides to question the Skipper, and turns to find him. The old man, however, is already at Joseph's side. They have fished many times together over the years, and have grown to trust each other's judgement.

"What's the matter?" Joseph says. "The nets aren't ready."

Skipper is a stoic man, never prone to joking around, yet his rheumy eyes are wide and haunted. Uneasy, Joseph crosses his arms. Young Thomas is suddenly by Joseph's elbow, clutching the gansey that Amelia had painstakingly knitted, pulling at the sleeve hard enough to finally rip and unravel the wool. Angered, Joseph raises a hand. Young Thomas cowers. Skipper does not react at all, as if blinded, and this—and nothing else—is what stays Joseph, stops him from slapping the lad.

Joseph says, "Skipper. What is it?"

"Christ almighty," Skipper whispers. "Can't you hear that?"

No.

Not at first.

And then Joseph hears it, lying way out on the edge of his perception.

But it is not a sound to be discerned by the ears; rather, it is a long, high and tremulous note that sings instead through the soft tissues. He experiences the lusciousness of the tune as it runs up his muscles and warms his blood, surging into his cock, stiffening him. The sound flows through his brain and flushes it out.

The catch can go to hell.

Where is the music coming from? He spins around. The crew is doing the same; even Skipper, who is now smiling. The melody forms part of the air itself, coming from nowhere in particular but from everywhere at once. It is the sweetest sound that Joseph has heard in his life, a sound that brings to mind the surfeit of all physical comforts a man could have if he could have them all at once.

He is overwhelmed, dazzled, glutted.

When he returns to his senses and looks about, he notices that some of the men are gathered at the sides of the *Mary Jane*, looking down at the sea. At once, Joseph is compelled to do the same. Running across deck to the gunwale, he gazes into the water, and sees his wife.

Amelia!

She must be lying submerged on her back, as just her face peeps above the surface. Her skin reflects the green tint of the North Sea. Amelia stares up at him with her large, heavily-lashed eyes. As soon as Joseph thinks to call out to her, he realises that he is hallucinating. Amelia could not be floating in the North Sea. No, she would be at home, looking after their baby, tending to the fowls and the vegetable garden. This woman is a stranger.

He gathers together his fractured thoughts.

Without immediate help, the woman will drown. It's a

miracle that she is alive at all. The temperature of the water is a few degrees above freezing. He turns, tries to shout, but the crew is distracted, every man contemplating the sea below. Clearly, there must be other people in the water. Another fishing vessel must have capsized during last night's storm. The captain of that doomed boat is to blame. Joseph feels a flash of temper. What kind of fool tempts fate by allowing a woman on board?

Nevertheless, Joseph must save her.

Like everyone else on the *Mary Jane,* he cannot swim. He would have to throw down a line, and hope that the woman has enough strength to hold on while he drags her aboard. Loops of rope lie amidships. However, his feet will not move. The music somehow pins his boots to the deck.

The woman smiles up at him.

Arching her back, she lifts her naked breasts clear of the water. Never before has a woman so brazenly exposed herself to Joseph. Her nipples are very large and very dark. Despite himself, despite his love for Amelia and their daughter, despite his solemn vow of fidelity, Joseph imagines taking those nipples into his mouth, one at a time and back again, to warm them with his tongue, over and over.

A caudal fin breaks the water.

The music falters.

Joseph knows every fish that swims the North Sea, but he doesn't recognise that fin. A tremor of fear runs through him. The woman allows the whole length of her body to breach. Instead of legs, she has the lower half of a silver-scaled fish.

He grips the gunwale to keep from staggering.

Every sailor knows the folklore of mermaids. Unlucky omens, they foretell maritime disaster. But had not the *Mary Jane* already survived the storm? The sea is flat, the sky is blue. The music intensifies. Now the melody has a form to it; voices, lovely angelic voices, gentle, beguiling, otherworldly. Some of the crew members are climbing the gunwale and dropping out of sight. The occasional splash sounds as each man hits the water. Joseph should ring the bell; call the remaining crew to order.

The mermaid runs both hands over her breasts, along her

stomach, across the scales, finally stopping at a little slit that she holds open. She dips a finger, two fingers, inside herself. Joseph's cock is the hardest it has ever been; swollen enough, surely, to tear its own skin. The mermaid raises her arms to him.

He clambers over the side.

The icy water encloses and shocks him. He remembers that he cannot swim. A flood of panic makes him thrash. The mermaid rises up beneath him like an island. Now, lying face down upon her, he is safe.

She feels as cold as the sea. The choir of countless female voices reverberates throughout Joseph's body and smooths away every trace of concern. His mermaid's hair floats in coils as thick as kelp. She is not green from the reflection of the water; in fact, her flesh itself is green, a light tint, reminding him of the first flush of grass in spring. The mermaid is beautiful.

Her hand reaches between their bodies to unbutton his trousers. Quickly, she guides him inside her. He gasps. Unlike Amelia, the mermaid is ice-cold. The surprise of it frightens him. This moment of clarity—what in God's name is he doing?—shrivels his cock, but the mermaid has muscles that clamp down and ripple in powerful undulations, so that he soon becomes hard again.

He clutches the mermaid's breasts. They are dense, frigid. She lifts her caudal fin between his legs and presses against his buttocks. The realisation that she must want him deeper inside her body speeds Joseph's need to come. He tries to kiss her.

She has no teeth.

The mermaid's upper lip protrudes over her lower lip, which has a barbule. Her eyes are perfectly round and unblinking, the eyes of a fish. Where her ears should be are gills, opening and closing, sucking and expelling. A creeping horror races along Joseph's spine, but it is too late to stop, the muscular actions of the mermaid's innards have brought him to the brink of climax. She wraps her icy arms about him, presses her caudal fin harder against his buttocks, and takes him under.

The music stops.

Water closes over his head. He can't breathe. Traitorously,

his cock ejaculates anyway. He struggles but the mermaid is too strong. He opens his eyes. Through the olive green of the water, he sees the sturdy hull of the *Mary Jane* overhead, and all around, the crew members, each man cinched in the arms of a mermaid, sinking, like Joseph, towards the shallow bottom of the Dogger Bank. There is Skipper, motionless, as if already dead. Nearby is Young Thomas. Joseph feels a pang of terrible guilt. The lad is not yet thirteen. As an apprentice, Young Thomas relied on Joseph for protection and guidance.

The need to breathe is overwhelming. Joseph fights wildly against the mermaid. Her grip intensifies. Beneath the *Mary Jane,* other mermaids armed with knives are sawing at the trawl nets, freeing the captured fish. Joseph thinks of Amelia, and then the baby, not yet one year old. He tries again to free himself for their sakes.

The mermaid's grasp tightens.

As his vision fades, he realises that the *Mary Jane* will drift without a single crew member on board. She will be found at last, perhaps weeks or even months later, derelict, a ghost ship with no signs of battle or theft; food and drink still on the tables, rotting fish in the hold. The manifest will be inspected, to no avail. The fate of the *Mary Jane* will be a mystery that no one alive can ever solve.

Joseph's lungs won't be denied. He takes in a breath of water. It feels cold, heavy. With a cough, he draws in again. The mermaid gapes sightlessly at him as he pulls the North Sea in and out of his lungs. Her lidless eyes are open and staring, her gills fluttering. She won't let go. Locked together, Joseph and the mermaid continue to sink. The soft, sandy bed of the Dogger Bank lies a few feet below them.

Far above, the *Mary Jane* starts to move away on the current.

The Sundowners

"We have a new admission," Dr Chandler said, and indicated the old woman sitting next to him. "Staff, please say hello to Daisy."

The male and female nurses smiled and said, in unison, "Hello, Daisy."

The old woman looked around the table at the dozen or so unfamiliar faces and didn't reply. Dr Chandler started his lecture on Daisy's medical history, but Jill, a senior nurse at the Aged Care Facility, could not concentrate. Here it comes again, she thought, as she dabbed at her sweat moustache. Was this a hot flush or not? No one else seemed to be perspiring. If only Dr Chandler would conduct his meetings in the library, with its garden bed of conifers throwing shade over the windows, instead of here in the staff lunchroom. There weren't any curtains or blinds you could shut. She felt as if she were boiling alive.

"Jill," Dr Chandler said. "You have a farming background. Is that correct?"

"Yes sir," Jill said. "Born and raised a farm girl."

"Any experience with animals?"

"Plenty, but my family had beef cattle in particular."

"Excellent." Dr Chandler rubbed his hands together. "Then I'd like to put Daisy under your direct care and supervision."

"Sundowning makes her fret for a homestead?"

In this secure hospital facility, Jill specialised in helping dementia patients cope with sundowning, the increased confusion and agitation that struck the patients around dusk.

Although scientists hadn't yet found a cause, Jill had her own theory—habits die hard.

One patient, a retired businessman, got angry that he couldn't find the bus stop and would miss the last ride home. Jill's solution: push a bench against a wall, tape above it a handwritten sign that read BUS STOP, and direct him to sit and wait. And whenever he checked his non-existent watch and asked why the fucking bus was running late, Jill would say, "It's coming very soon. Just relax." Jill calmed another patient by letting her set and reset plastic spoons, paper plates and serviettes on one of the card tables. "If I don't get dinner ready on time, there'll be hell to pay," the elderly woman said every evening. "Mike has to leave for the factory at eight. Now where are those kids?" And Jill would say, "Don't worry. They'll soon be home from soccer practice."

And once the daylight slipped away and night stole through the windows, the sundowning episodes passed like magic. The affected patients woke up from their various dreams, but Jill believed that it was always the same dream they shared—their own life, treasured yet long gone, replaced by locked doors and medications by the hour.

Oh yes, Jill thought grimly, habits die hard.

"Daisy is an unusual case," Dr Chandler said, and leaned forward in his chair. "Personally, it's the first case I've encountered. According to her referral letter, Daisy has clinical lycanthropy."

One of the male nurses, Xavier, started to laugh. "Lycanthropy? You mean she's a werewolf?"

Giggles rippled around the table. Jill glanced at the old woman, who sat with her hands folded in her lap, watching intently with her large, brown eyes.

Dr Chandler smiled, shook his head. "The psychiatric term 'clinical lycanthropy' refers to the delusion that one turns into an animal, not specifically a wolf. In Daisy's case, she has a particular type of lycanthropy known as boanthropy. During an episode, she believes herself to be a cow."

"A cow?" Xavier raised his eyebrows and grinned. "And her name is Daisy?"

Some of the other nurses laughed, but not Jill. There but for the Grace of God go I, she thought, and wondered if Xavier realised that he would likely develop some kind of dementia if he lived long enough. Meanwhile, Daisy looked from one face to the other, as if committing each to memory. Jill noticed the woman's careful gaze. She didn't much like it.

"Stop playing the fool, Xavier," Dr Chandler said. "Everyone pay close attention. This isn't a straightforward case of sundowning. Her dementia is complicated by psychotic breaks of boanthropy, which are a rare manifestation of her schizophrenia. Daisy behaves like a cow only during a full moon."

"Like a werewolf," Xavier said with mock innocence. "Or is the correct term 'were-cow'?"

A few nurses tittered. Jill wanted to slap them. The room felt too hot.

"Sundowning is provoked by disturbances in circadian rhythms," Dr Chandler said, "and moon phases can be a trigger for some patients. So if it's easier for you to understand, Xavier, then yes, Daisy is a were-cow."

The room fell quiet. Jill could hear the urn simmering, the hissing of the fridge compressor. The young nurses gazed at Daisy as if she might transform in front of their very eyes. Jill's temper rose.

"That's fine, Dr Chandler," she said. "I'll take good care of her."

"Thank you, Jill. You have my greatest confidence."

Xavier flipped through his work diary and tapped his finger on a page. "Look out," he said. "The next full moon is in ten days. Better hope she doesn't grow horns."

The first time Daisy turned into a cow, Jill felt uneasy. After lunch, in the middle of the recreation room, Daisy calmly took off her clothes, got down on all fours and made lowing sounds. Most of the residents panicked. A couple leaned down to get a better look, whooping and wailing. With the help of Xavier and another male nurse, Jill manhandled Daisy into one of the storerooms. There was nowhere else to put her. The dorms and private rooms didn't have door locks.

The room was tiny, with a single window set high on a wall. The men put Daisy on the floor. Daisy bellowed frantically, kicked, and hobbled on her hands and knees around the room, bouncing off filing cabinets.

"What the fuck?" Xavier said. "What the actual fuck?"

"Keep your voice down," Jill said.

"It's not even night-time."

"Good Lord, she's a psychiatric patient, not a werewolf in a comic book."

Daylight shone through the window. A full moon hung faintly in the blue sky. How did Daisy know? You couldn't see the moon from the recreation room. On tiptoes, Jill dragged shut the stiff grey curtains, raining a cascade of dust over her upturned face. She would not switch on the electric light. Keeping a sundowning patient in the dark sometimes tricked them into thinking that night had already fallen. Perhaps this would work on Daisy.

"You right?" Xavier said, white-faced, already out the door with the other boy.

"Fine, be off with you," Jill said. "Look after the others. Play some Vera Lynn or some bush ballads, for goodness sakes."

The door slammed.

Jill turned, regarded Daisy with some trepidation.

Panting, the old woman swung her head from side to side. Exactly like a fearful cow, Jill thought in amazement. Since a cow's eyes are on either side of its head, it can't judge distance with only one eye. Jill moved to stand directly in front of the old woman. The head swinging stopped.

"Can you recognise me?" Jill said. "We do jigsaw puzzles. Remember?"

Daisy shuffled uneasily on her hands and knees, and threw her head around, dropping it a couple of times as if preparing to charge. The behaviour was spot-on. Uncanny, Jill thought. The hairs lifted on the nape of her neck. In the faint light, the old woman's boxy, stout body and wide back looked almost bovine.

Jill clenched her jaw. She knew cattle and she knew sick people. And if this poor sick old lady believed herself to be a cow, then Jill was the absolute best remedy.

"Hush now," Jill whispered. "Everything is all right. You're safe." And then she began to murmur nursery rhymes, one after the other, like she used to as a girl back on the farm. She could have recited her times-tables and got the same result. Any frightened cow is soothed by the sound of a quiet, calm voice.

Daisy stopped her shuffling and head-throwing. Only panting and drooling remained. She looked exhausted. Her large, brown eyes glittered wetly.

"Can I give you a pat?" Jill said and approached with her hand out, palm down. "It's all right, Daisy. You're a good girl, aren't you? Yes, you're my good girl."

Daisy tensed a little, watched the progress of the hand. Finally, Jill touched the old woman's head and began to stroke and pat, making shushing noises all the while. Daisy's panting slowed down. Was the old woman cold? She was buck naked, after all. Jill decided to stock blankets in preparation for the next full moon. Daisy lowered her face and made slobbering noises. She's looking for pasture, Jill thought. As well as blankets, Jill would have to cache this room with some feed.

Jill reported to Dr Chandler later that day. His large, sunny office had mahogany furniture and framed pictures of his family ranging across the desk.

"I don't think Daisy's behaviour is linked to the moon," Jill said. "A full moon lasts two or three nights but her delusion stopped after an hour or so."

Dr Chandler looked smug. "By strict definition, the moon is full—that is, illuminated one hundred per cent—for only about one minute. Today's full moon occurred at 2.53 pm precisely. Daisy might be exhibiting pre- and post-lunar responses."

"Yes sir." Jill consulted her notes. "When Daisy came out of her delusional state, she repeated the words 'hath or', a quote from Old English, I guess, or maybe a fragment of a poem. Otherwise, it could be gibberish."

"Hathor? Are you positive?"

Jill nodded.

"Fascinating," he continued. "Hathor is the Egyptian goddess of fertility, protector of women and children, helper of the deceased on their journey to the Underworld. Hathor is always depicted as a cow." Dr Chandler stared off into the mid-distance for a moment with a rapt expression. "This could be the link we're looking for. Various institutions are interested in Daisy's case, but she's *our* patient. Perhaps Daisy had a prior enthusiasm for Egyptian mythology, which influenced her psychosis. I'll check with her family. Well done, Jill. Keep reporting back. A peer-reviewed paper might be in the offing."

Dr Chandler bent his head to his laptop and started typing furiously with his two forefingers: peck, peck, peck. Dismissed, Jill left the room. Closing the door behind her, she decided to Google Hathor, goddess of fertility, just as soon as she got home.

Her husband, Graeme, turned the steaks. Fat sizzled. Jill exited the back door with two beers, and gave a can to Graeme. The moon hung low in the night sky, a brilliant white orb. It looks full to the naked eye, Jill thought, but it's not. Daisy knows this somehow. She *knows*.

"Is that barbecue too hot?" Jill said.

"Don't worry," Graeme said. "I'm sealing the steaks on the flat plate, and then I'll finish them on the grill for medium-rare. They'll be juicy as hell, you wait."

"Okay," Jill said. "After tonight, I'm thinking we shouldn't eat beef anymore."

"Yeah, right." He laughed. "Just as soon as I stop breathing."

She sat on one of the wrought-iron chairs and contemplated her husband, her sweetheart since high school. On their wedding day, she'd imagined a future for them that had never come true. On impulse, she said, "Let's try again for a baby."

Graeme jolted, looked at her sideways. "You told me you'd

had all the miscarriages you could stand."

She shrugged.

"Come on now," he said. "We're too old."

"Old? We're both only forty-eight."

"And you're going through the change."

"I get a hot flush here and there, so what? I still have my monthlies."

"Well, shit, isn't this a turnaround." Graeme sighed, fussed with the steaks, dabbing at them with the tongs. "Sometimes I don't know what gets into you."

"Hope," she said. "Is that so bad? Tell me, is that so bad?"

In the days leading up to the next full moon, Daisy caused havoc at the Aged Care Facility. Patients shied away from her, some of them hysterical, even though Daisy did nothing but quietly complete jigsaws in a corner of the recreation room.

Xavier went up to Jill and said, "I'm getting the willies. They're acting like dogs before a thunderstorm."

"Watch your mouth," Jill said. "Show some respect."

But Xavier was right. The patients knew something was about to happen to Daisy. How? It gave Jill the willies too. Every patient's medications had been increased. The retired businessman with his make-believe bus stop had begun punching at the keypad locks on the exterior doors as if desperate to get out.

None of the patients would sit with Daisy, so Jill spent as much time with her as possible. The day before Daisy's metamorphosis, they were completing a jigsaw together when Daisy stopped and regarded Jill, not with the blank, anaesthetised gape as usual but with a look that could only be described as sentient. Jill held her breath.

"Where are your children?" Daisy said. Her voice was low, monotonous, a kind of hum. This was the first complete sentence Daisy had uttered in this place.

"I never had any," Jill said, heart thudding. "My hubby and I weren't blessed."

Daisy grabbed Jill's hand and squeezed it, hard. "Where are your children?"

Perturbed, Jill moved away. Besides, it was time to placate the few men in the facility that thought every evening was Happy Hour. Jill played the role of bartender, serving them cordial which they took to be whiskey. Every time she glanced over at Daisy, she found the old woman staring back, nodding her large head.

When Daisy turned into a cow, Jill was prepared. She had lined the storeroom floor with blankets and hidden a bag of spinach in a cabinet. Two male nurses carried Daisy into the storeroom and put her down. Jill closed the curtains. Tossing her head, Daisy stared around nervously, the whites of her eyes showing all the way around, wet nostrils flaring, false teeth spat out and gums bare. The nurses couldn't leave fast enough. Jill locked the door, got a handful of spinach and dropped to her haunches.

"Come on, girl," she said, holding out her hand. "Are you hungry? It's all right. Hush now, you can relax."

Head lowered, Daisy approached on all fours, sniffed at the leaves. Finally, she took up the spinach with her slavering lips, jaws moving sideways. Jill dragged a blanket over Daisy's broad back.

"There you go," Jill said. "Is that better, Daisy? Or would you prefer I call you Hathor? I can do that if you like."

Daisy continued to eat from Jill's hand. The rough tongue against Jill's palm brought back memories of the farm. She could almost hear the lowing from the pasture, smell the sweetness of hay, feel again her youth, energy and optimism, the trust she'd had that life would be fair and turn out just fine. Tears came to her eyes.

The cow finished eating.

Impetuously, Jill knelt and pressed her face against the warm, blanketed belly. "Give me a child, Hathor," she whispered. "A child is the only thing I've ever wanted."

Jill wriggled across the bed and nudged Graeme. He half-turned his head in the dark.

"What's wrong? You got another muscle cramp?"

"No," she said, and pressed herself close. "It's not that."

She squirmed against him until he rolled over and pushed her onto her back. When he came, she felt the miracle, a sensation of white light piercing her womb.

Jill counted the days. After she missed her period, she typed her symptoms into a medical search engine—fatigue, bloating, weight gain, appetite loss, constipation, heartburn, pelvic pain, frequent urination—and the answer came back as various ghastly diseases, mainly types of cancer. But what did search engines know? Jill rubbed her burgeoning belly.

One Sunday morning while Graeme made coffee, she lifted her pyjama top to show off her little bump.

"Better lay off the desserts," he said, chuckling. "You're getting middle-age spread."

But that wasn't true, could not be true.

After breakfast, she went into the den and again Googled Hathor. Searching compulsively, scanning page after page, she at last found something that caught her interest—the English translation of an ancient Egyptian poem dedicated to the goddess. The proper recitation of the poem required, as far as Jill could fathom, a tambourine. Monday morning, from the local music shop, Jill bought a medium-sized calfskin tambourine with six pairs of jingles. To be honest, calfskin seemed a sacrilegious choice for the drum, but it was calfskin or nothing, and what did Jill really know about praying to a cow goddess?

The next full moon, she locked the storeroom door and rapped the tambourine. The skin sounded dull. The jingles jangled. Daisy looked up with her wet snout and long, luscious eyelashes.

"I don't know the tune," Jill said, "but I hope you'll like this poem anyway."

Daisy lowered her head to the bowl of spinach and ate.

Jill intoned, "We play the tambourine for Your ka. We dance for Your Majesty. We exalt You to the height of heaven. You are the mistress of Sekhem, the Menat and the Sistrum, the mistress of music for whose ka one plays…"

Nothing happened. Daisy kept eating the spinach, oblivious.

Jill faltered, unsure of what she had expected.

"Please, Hathor," she whispered, "let this baby hold. Don't let it slough away in a river of blood like the others."

Jill turned over and over in bed.

Graeme sighed. "For Christ's sake, what's the matter?"

"Sorry. Go back to sleep."

"Are you still hurting? You ought to see the doctor."

"No," she said. "There's no need." She preferred to live in hope. What if the pain was just kidney stones again? She had to be pregnant. She just had to be.

The agony kept zigzagging through her abdomen like the riffle of a knife. It took her breath. Nothing but growing pains, she thought. My womb has been the size of a pear my whole life, and now it is stretching and growing.

The silence went on and on until she figured Graeme must have fallen asleep.

Then he muttered, "You can't be pregnant."

Jill bit her lips.

When the cramps lanced her again, she decided to hold still and bear it. For her child, she could bear anything. Their baby would have green eyes with hazel flecks like Graeme, olive skin and stubby toes like herself, and share their combined love of the outdoors. As soon as their child was old enough, they would go on camping holidays all around Australia—the Grampians, Wilsons Promontory, Kakadu, Bribie Island. Jill gritted her teeth, willing herself to rise above the cramps.

Eventually, Graeme began to snore again.

Jill needed to buy bigger trousers. The pregnancy took her strength, made her slow at work, testy with Xavier and the other youngsters who constantly fooled around.

And pain made her mean. One night, when the patient needed to lay the table for the non-existent Mike and the soccer-playing children, Jill withheld the plastic cutlery and paper plates until the woman became frantic. When Jill at last threw the items across the card table, the woman scrabbled after them, sobbing.

"What the fuck is wrong with you?" Xavier said.

I don't know, Jill thought desperately, but said nothing. How could she confide in Xavier? From across the recreation room, Daisy stared and nodded.

Jill kept track of the lunar calendar with increasing dread.

In time, the patients became distressed and Daisy took off her clothes and went on all fours. Hefted into the storeroom with its closed curtains, Daisy munched spinach and wore a blanket. Jill tapped half-heartedly at the tambourine and recited the poem. The cow lay on the floor, tucked in its legs, and twitched both ears.

"Something's wrong," Jill whispered. "Please, is my baby okay?"

In response, the pain flared worse than ever before, much worse, tearing at Jill's guts. Rather than the elbows and knees of a restless foetus, it felt more like the sharp and flailing hooves of a spooked animal. Collapsing, Jill doubled up into a tight clutch. Her teeth began to chatter and her limbs trembled.

These cramps will pass, she reassured herself.

They didn't.

At first, she thought she'd lost control of her bladder. The hot rush of liquid turned out to be blood. It quickly soaked through her clothes. The realisation came, too late, that Hathor was not just the goddess of fertility but also of the dead. I'm miscarrying, Jill thought. Or is it me getting carried into the Underworld? She crawled to the door. No, she couldn't reach the handle. Blood pumped steadily across the tiles. In the dim light, the blood seemed shiny and black.

"Help me," she whispered.

The cow chewed its cud.

After a while, blood began to seep under the door. The sight triggered shrieking, running footsteps, and soon the hammering of fists as Xavier kept shouting, "Open up." but Jill was too exhausted to answer.

The cow approached. Jill listened to its slow, easy steps. One cloven foot stepped on the tambourine and broke the skin with a loud pop and a final, plaintive shiver of jingles.

"Get the key," Xavier yelled to someone, who sprinted along the corridor.

Bang, bang, bang. It sounded like Xavier was repeatedly slamming his shoulder against the door. The lock held.

Jill tried to remain awake, hopeful. The staff might reach her in time.

Humid breath snorted over her face.

She opened her eyes. Hathor's calm and empty gaze, as flat as a mill pond, told Jill in an instant that everything was lost.

Flight Path

Jack held out his hand and his wife, Margaret, took it. As she alighted from the wreckage, she smiled and said, "Goodness me, would you just look at this mess."

Jack turned. The plane, or what was left of it, was smashed to pieces. The pieces were strewn along, in a more or less straight line, as far as the eye could see which was very far indeed. He and his wife stood on an expanse of white ground that stretched from one horizon to the other and shimmered under a sun that blazed out of a cloudless sky. It was like they had crashed on the moon. Jack couldn't see a single tree or blade of grass anywhere, and his eyesight was still good, despite his age.

Margaret said, "What is this place?"

"I'm not sure. Looks like a salt flat."

"Salt flat? I don't know," she said, and took a few steps. "The ground's soft and wet."

"So?"

"So, if it was a salt flat, then it'd be hard and crunchy. Well, wouldn't it?"

He shook his head. "It's soft and wet because of the water. This right here, what we're standing on, used to be a lake. Where do you think the salt came from?"

Margaret slapped a foot against the ground, splashing at the thin sheet of water. Jack noticed that she was wearing her sandals but he recalled that she had removed them right before take-off and kicked them underneath the seat in front.

Margaret said, "Does this mean we're in Utah?"

"You mean Utah as in Utah America?"

"Isn't that where the salt flats are? They have all those attempts at land speed records in Utah, don't they?"

"Yeah, but Australia has salt flats too, like in South Australia. Haven't you heard of Lake Eyre? Correct me if I'm wrong, but I think that's one of the biggest salt flats in the world."

"So we're in South Australia?"

Jack set his teeth. She was winding him up, playing dumb. When they had first met, this coquettish routine had had a physiological effect—he used to imagine he could feel the extra blood pumping into the muscles of his chest, back and arms—but now, after thirty-odd years of marriage, her eyelash-batting could really annoy him.

"Margaret, stop it. We're not in South Australia and you know it. We were flying straight down the coast from Brisbane to Melbourne, so Lake Eyre would have to be at least eleven hundred kilometres to the west or even more, I don't know, depending on the flight path."

"Maybe the pilot got lost."

Jack threw up his hands. "Now you're being stupid."

"Oh yeah? Well maybe the pilot put the plane on automatic and forgot to update the address."

"Jesus, Margaret, it's not like the bloody GPS in the car."

"And how would you know? Stop talking down to me, why don't you, you've never even flown a plane."

Jack harrumphed, propped his fists on his hips and turned away from her. Now he was facing the plane. Actually, it didn't look much like a 737, more like a giant-sized collection of rubbish, like a kicked-over bin. Through the mush of buckled metal right in front of him he could see a tangle of blue, red, yellow and green wires, tied together into a bundle as thick as his thigh. Amazing. He touched a section of the plane's ruined skin, expecting it to give under his fingertips like aluminium foil, and was surprised to find that it was as hard as concrete. He whistled. It must have been one hell of a crash to pulp such a solid aircraft.

One helluva crash…

Then Margaret came up behind him and slipped a hand into

the back pocket of his shorts.

"Let's get our cabin luggage," she said. "It's too bright out here. I need my sunglasses."

"Where would we even start looking?"

"We were near the wings, weren't we? Let's find the wings and then we'll find our bags."

Jack sighed. "All right, fine, let's find the wings," and he started walking. Margaret fell in beside him.

His runners sank and slurped at the ground with each step, which irritated him. The crush of plane parts was incomprehensible. Jack figured that the wreckage stretched a couple of kilometres or more, as if the plane had pin-wheeled over and over for a long time, throwing off bits with every impact until there was nothing left to throw off. Then it occurred to Jack, as he trudged alongside the wreckage with his wife in tow, that nothing about this situation made sense.

He stopped. Margaret stopped too and gazed at him expectantly.

Jack said, "Where's everybody else?"

Margaret hesitated, grinned and said, "What do you mean?"

"I mean the other passengers. There must have been at least a hundred and fifty people on board with us."

"That many? Really?"

"Oh, come on, Margaret, it's summer, peak tourist season for Queensland, the plane was packed, don't you remember? You wanted to pinch the window seat but I told you it'd be taken and it was, wasn't it?"

Margaret blinked at him, her dumb blonde routine again.

Jack jammed his fists onto his hips. "The bloke who took the window seat, remember?" he continued. "The bloke with the acne scars and the sideburns?"

Margaret looked off into the distance and bit at her bottom lip.

He said at last, "You know what I'm talking about, don't you?"

She looked at him and smiled. "Of course I do. And the stewardesses were so nice, weren't they? I liked the one with the bun. She had such a happy face."

A faint curl of adrenaline tightened around Jack's insides. He said, "Are you all right, Margaret? Are you feeling okay?"

"I feel wonderful." She pirouetted, fanning out her sundress. "See that? I'm in fine form. My hip doesn't hurt a bit."

"Now, wait a minute, you were barefoot on the plane, I know you were, so at what point did you put those sandals back on?"

She giggled. "You're asking the strangest questions. Are you sure you're okay? Maybe you bumped your head." She took his hand. "Let's keep going, sweetie. Let's find those wings."

They started walking again.

After a while, Jack said, "There's absolutely no one here but us. How do you explain that?"

"I don't know. They're gone, I suppose."

"Gone? Gone where?"

"Rescued."

"Rescued how?"

Margaret stopped and crossed her arms at him. Then she tipped her head to one side, considering, and Jack thought of the first time he had ever seen that gesture of hers, the night they had met. He had been at this particular pub with his mates, celebrating their ten-pin bowling victory, and Margaret, wearing a blue wraparound dress that cinched her waist, had been at the bar with a girlfriend. She had tipped her lovely blonde head as the singer of the crappy pub band had leaned over to say something to her, and Jack, sipping at his beer, had decided *I want that woman.* He could still feel that initial longing for her, all these years later, and the clarity of the memory frightened him more than the wreckage.

He grabbed her shoulders.

She shook him off and pushed her fringe back from her face. "Jack, what the hell is the matter with you?"

"Everything. For God's sake, doesn't any of this seem weird to you?"

"Look, you panic merchant, the other people on the plane must have been rescued by helicopter while we were unconscious."

Jack laughed. "That's it? That's your theory?"

She started walking again. He put his hands on his knees and laughed and laughed. Then he ran up to her and said, "So nobody stays behind to clear up the mess? Air crash investigators don't come out here to measure things with instruments? No media?"

Margaret had her lips pursed and was frowning. She would not look at him.

"You're always so condescending, Jack. Did you know that? Everything I say, you've got to ridicule. I'm getting mighty sick of it."

"Please, Margaret, wait."

She kept stomping alongside the wreckage. Jack staggered and sat down. A film of warm water seeped through his shorts and he found the sensation reassuring. He scanned the scene. He thought of their daughters, Vicky and Julia; Vicki married with a baby on the way and Julia doing her final year at nursing school. Both of them still needed him. Both of them still needed their mother. Unexpectedly, his eyes misted over.

Then Margaret turned on her heel and stormed back to him. She said, "Do you want me to get snow blindness?"

"This is salt, not snow."

"You know what I mean. Are you going to help me find my sunglasses or are you going to sit here like a baby and sulk?"

Jack said, "Tell me what you remember about the crash."

"What?"

"The plane crash."

Margaret regarded him very carefully. Something about the stillness of her face made his heart jitter. He put his hands into the warm, wet dirt and dug into it with his fingers, kneading at the earth, feeling himself still on the planet.

Margaret shrugged. "All right, let's see. I flipped the dial on the armrest, looking for the comedy channel. You were doing a crossword, a cryptic crossword. The clue was something about a chef and a tree branch, or whatever."

"Go on."

She smiled. "Well, that's it. That's the last thing I can think of."

"I don't remember the crash either."

Jack lowered his head.

After a moment, Margaret walked over and sat down next to him. She put one arm along his shoulders and tucked her cheek against his face. She said, "It's just the trauma, sweetie. A person's mind can block out horrible things."

"I don't know if that's it."

"Then what? Is this a dream, is that what you think?" She tittered and kissed Jack with a loud smacking sound. "Maybe you're right. Maybe the plane is flying its merry way back to Melbourne and I'm asleep with the headphones on and I'm dreaming whatever the comedian is saying and you're part of my dream but in reality, you're sitting next to me on the plane doing your dumb crossword." She laughed again, rocking back and forward. "I should've conjured up a beach and a butler instead. So pinch me, why don't you? Wake me up."

Jack flung himself away and stood over her, chest heaving. She flicked back her fringe and waited. Jack could hear the pulse thrumming in his ears. He looked over his fifty-eight-year-old life, mentally weighing it, trying to work out if it was enough or whether fate had ripped him off, and he could not decide.

He said, "We're not injured, not even a scratch. Nothing."

"Jack, it's okay, really. The rescue helicopter's going to come back for us too. It really will. Just be patient."

"How can you talk like this, like everything's normal? You're not yourself."

"Aren't I? Then you must be asleep on the plane with the crossword book in your lap and I'm next to you eating peanuts." She laughed and reached out her hand, the hand that had run through his hair or cupped his face or caressed his body thousands of times, a hand that he had always trusted, and now was too afraid to touch.

Then Margaret's eyes left his face and gazed over his shoulder. Her expression made him spin around. High in the sky, next to the blaring ball of the sun, was a single white-hot spangle.

"What in blazes is that?" he said.

"It's the chopper, you dummy, the rescue chopper. It's come back for us."

Jack looked at the glint of bright white and started to shake.

Margaret stood up and put her arms about him. "It's okay, sweetie," she said. "We've been through a lot."

"It's not a chopper."

"Of course it is. It just looks like a star because the metal's reflecting the sunlight, that's all. Why are you always such the cynic? Be happy, Jack, we're getting out of Utah."

"We're not in Utah."

"Say goodbye to the salt flats. We'll be home before you know it."

Jack shrank before the expanding ball of light and whispered, "Whatever happens, Margaret, I love you. I've always loved you. I always will."

"Oh, don't be so melodramatic." She stepped away from him and began waving her arms at the light, as if guiding it to ground. "Look," she said, as the light grew bigger, "they know we're here. It's coming right at us."

A Faithful Companion

The man in the hospital bed next to her made a noise on every exhalation: sometimes a moan, but most often an *argh* sound, breathed with great effort like a fat man easing into a chair. Elsie couldn't concentrate on the paperback her sister had brought for her. Be quiet, she wanted to shout. Instead, she stared at the ceiling with her arms held tightly against the sheets. The television bolted overhead wore a sticker: THIS IS A RENTAL TV – HIRE CHARGES APPLY. She read it over and over and over.

Argh...argh...argh...

If only he would stop. Even for a minute.

The curtain between them was now closed, but she had caught a glimpse as the porters had wheeled him in some half an hour ago. He appeared to be aged in his seventies, like Elsie. Maybe that explained the pairing. Still, putting a man in a woman's room was highly inappropriate. And they were expected to share a bathroom too. She had never in her life shared a bathroom with a man and did not intend to start now. A nurse came in, the one with the red hair and glasses, the one Elsie disliked.

"Good morning, Elsie," the nurse said. "Good morning, Don, and welcome to Ward Two South. It's nearly brekkie time. You both hungry?"

The curtains formed a T-shape that divided the room in half and allowed space for a little hallway from the door to the bathroom. The nurse opened all of the curtains, including the one that separated Elsie from the old man, Don. He was lying on his back, his mouth gaping in either sleep or stupor.

Argh…argh…argh…

Elsie said, "Why does he keep making that awful sound?"

"Let's have a bit of sunshine," the nurse replied, opening the window blind.

"I haven't had my heart medicine," Elsie said. "No one has given me the injection in my tummy. And why is there a man in here?"

The nurse offered a brittle smile and swept from the room.

Elsie fussed with her sheet. She glanced out the window. There was a small car park and, beyond that, a three-storey brick building. More wards, she supposed. As usual, most of the windows had their blinds drawn. Those that didn't remained dim, as if sunlight could not penetrate the glass. Elsie opened her book and frowned at a page while the *argh…argh…argh…* continued, regular as the beat of a pulse.

And then it stopped.

Elsie dropped the book.

He had rolled towards the window. Since she could see only the back of his head, she could not tell if his eyes were open or not. He began to make tutting noises.

"You miscreant," he shouted, making her jump, for he had a voice for the stage, deep and stupendously loud so the people in the cheap seats could hear him all the way at the back of an enormous theatre. "Get away with you, lad. Be off with you."

Elsie looked outside for the cause of his consternation. Nothing and nobody; at this time of the morning the visitors' car park was empty. She pursed her lips.

A handful of cockatoos flew through the blanched wedge of sky and disappeared behind the building. On the top floor through one of the shadowed windows a shape moved, round and pale, bobbing as if on a string. Elsie decided that it must be a balloon. Yes, a child's balloon tied to the end of a bed, jouncing in the breeze from the air conditioning. A family must be visiting a loved one. Elsie imagined kisses, smiles, light conversation. Yet it was only a few minutes past seven o'clock. Visiting hours began strictly at eight. An arm materialised near to the window, unmistakably the arm of a child. The hand cupped the balloon in its palm and brought it closer to the glass.

With a jolt, Elsie realised that it was not a balloon after all.

It was some kind of head, a monstrous, round, bald head, as white as bone. The only features were two large black patches where the eyes should be. And the fingers that held that monstrous head were not those of a child; they were unnaturally long and spindly with big knuckles. The fingers of a skeleton.

Elsie's heart broke into a jittery gallop.

The balloon-head sat in the palm and moved about quite naturally, as the head of any real person might if they should look out a window, chin in hand. Then those black patches instead of eyes gazed across the distance between them and saw her. The arm dropped away and the balloon-head rose, as if the body beneath it had stood to its full height. Elsie felt caught by those hollowed sockets. With effort, she turned away. Don't look back. She mustn't dare look back.

But what if the balloon-head still stared at her?

When she peeked with just the tail of her eye, the balloon-head was gone, the window again a dingy, empty rectangle like the others. Elsie let out the breath she did not know she had been holding. At her age, she should not be so impressionable. It was just a balloon with a face printed on it. Or a mask. Yes, a child wearing a mask to delight the relatives. And it was October. Wasn't Halloween in late October? All Hallows Eve, when the veil between this world and the next is at its thinnest, when the ghosts of the dead come back to haunt the living.

"You saw him, didn't you?" Don said. "That miscreant is always nearby."

"What miscreant?" she said, as the skin on her arms crawled and crept into gooseflesh. "Who are you talking about?"

Don closed his eyes and bawled at the top of his lungs, "I want to go toilet!"

She flinched. "Oh, for goodness' sake, use the buzzer if you need a nurse."

"I want to go toilet! I want to go toilet!"

Elsie put her fingers in her ears. Two nurses rushed in. With considerable exertion, they helped Don out of bed and to the bathroom. No one thought to close the door. Elsie could see him sitting there, hunched over, his face screwed up and bright red, grunting as if he were trying to pass a rock. Elsie ran a trembling hand over her face. For the love of God, why on earth did she have a share a room with this disgusting man? At last, the nurses escorted Don back to bed and tucked him in.

"Please shut the curtain," Elsie said, but the nurses were gone.

Their breakfast trays arrived soon after.

"Would you mind shutting the curtain?" she said, but the food staff was gone.

Elsie drew her overbed table close and began determinedly buttering her toast. Don sat up with a huffing and puffing and struggling of limbs. Elsie refused to look. Finally, he was still. She could hear him clumsily fingering the items on his breakfast tray. Elsie kept her eyes on her own food: plain toast and black tea. As usual, the toast was soft and almost wet, as if steamed. After three weeks on this ward, Elsie had come to appreciate its unusual texture. Her sister, Meredith, would scoff at that, if only she knew.

Thinking of Meredith reminded Elsie of home. Two months ago, she and Meredith had sold their home of fifty years and moved to a unit. The unfamiliar environment had been Elsie's undoing. While negotiating the stairs that led to the back patio, she had taken three habitual steps instead of the required five. The fall broke her hip. Following surgery, she caught pneumonia. For a time, she was in intensive care with an oxygen mask. Once she could breathe without the mask, they moved her to this general ward. She did not like it here. The walls were a sickly, jaundiced yellow and the fluorescent bulbs shone a meagre light so that everyone, including the young nurses, looked sallow. Meredith chose not to visit. The ward gave Meredith the heebie-jeebies. Instead, Meredith phoned her every day at precisely 3 p.m.

"Hah, that's the ticket!" Don shouted. "Good idea. She's perfect."

Elsie glanced at him. He was facing her, sitting on the edge of his bed with legs spread wide and his blue hospital gown bunched in his lap. Shocked, she looked away but too late. In that split second she had already seen, drooping beneath a scattering of grey pubic hair, his withered penis.

Oh God, a *pervert*.

Frightened and angry, she turned back and glared at him. In return, he smiled and nodded with vacant eyes, his gesture of greeting as automatic and meaningless as a tic. Elsie hesitated. Some type of dementia, perhaps? He had the reddened cauliflower nose of a heavy drinker. Alcohol abuse must have pickled his brains. She offered a brief smile before looking down at her breakfast tray. Now her mind was made up. She would definitely ask the nurses to move him. She did not want to share a room with a man not in charge of his faculties. What if he attacked her?

"The miscreant likes you," Don murmured, and when she looked around, he was smiling and intently focused, as if he'd picked her out from a crowd. "Let me be frank," Don continued. "I happen to be dying. My last request needs accommodation. Madam, are you ever lonely?"

Pervert. Elsie ignored the comment. If she could reach the curtain, she would close it. She attended to her breakfast. After a while, Don followed suit, as if he had forgotten all about her. He made sloppy noises as he ate. The noises roiled her stomach.

Then he retched.

It was as if the two halves of Don's face were unaware of one another. While his mouth spewed a thin gruel, his eyes roamed the breakfast tray with a joyful and curious interest; gazing upon the single-serve box of cereal, the orange juice, milk jug, cup of coffee, paper napkin, plastic bag of chilled cutlery. Elsie watched him heave semi-solid cornflakes into the bowl, and then spoon them happily into his mouth again.

She pushed away her overbed table, gasping, and buzzed for a nurse.

Don ate and vomited, drank and vomited. Every now and then, he made sounds of appreciative enjoyment. Oh God, where were the nurses? Don kept pausing to wipe regurgitate from his chin. Sometimes he used his gown; other times, his sheet or blanket.

"Hurry up," Elsie called at last. "You must hurry."

Two nurses rushed in. They removed Don's polluted breakfast tray, changed his gown, and remade his bed with fresh linen. Elsie saw everything. Finally, the nurses put Don back to bed, then left. One of them partially shut the dividing curtain on her way out.

"Please, where is my heart medicine?" Elsie said.

No answer. With tears pricking at her eyes, Elsie tried to calm herself, and took a sip of lukewarm tea. Then she noticed the curtain, moving in and out, in and out, as if alive and breathing. Filling and emptying, filling and emptying. It must be the current from the overhead air-conditioning vent, blowing intermittently, that transformed the curtain into a mockery of a living thing, the mimicry of a lung. Yet it had never happened before. Not once in her three weeks of residence on this ward. God, it was so stuffy in here. For a moment, Elsie felt the overwhelming, choking panic of claustrophobia. She interlaced her fingers and squeezed them, hard. It had to be the drugs. The doctors gave her so many, many drugs; there must be side effects, interactions.

Argh…argh…argh…

The curtain just happened to billow in time with Don's exhalations. The coincidence unnerved her. No, she ought to forget this nonsense and read the paperback. The book sat on her bed. She reached for it. When something moved at the window, Elsie bit her lip. Don't look. It was just a bird; a sparrow or pigeon. But in the corner of her eye, the shape seemed so white, so still. Incrementally, she ran her gaze along the length of the bellying, panting curtain, and stopped. Last chance… Instead, with resolve, she looked straight at the window.

Oh God, oh yes, she must be hallucinating.

Or the sunlight on the glass was playing tricks on her.

Those slender fingers clutched tight against the outside sill, as if the being were dangling its feet off the ground, could not be real. And that head, the top of its bulbous skull as thin as tissue paper, as translucent as a balloon… It might actually be a balloon, the string slipped from a child's hand and now caught in a tree, if not for those fingers on the sill, those black sockets that stared at her and corked the breath in her throat.

"Be off with you!" Don bellowed. "Go on, you damned miscreant!"

"What is that thing?" she said. "There, outside the window. Can you see it?"

But Don must have fallen into an instantaneous doze.

Argh…argh…argh…

Thank heavens; the window was fixed and unable to be opened. Elsie turned her back and pressed her fingers to her mouth. If Meredith could see her now, quavering and tremble-chinned, she would sneer, and for good reason. There must be a rational explanation. Yet the only rational explanation was Don's presence.

Argh…argh…argh…

She had to get rid of Don. How? She couldn't leave her bed without assistance.

Like magic, Don provided the answer.

Blowing and gasping, he sat up. From behind the half-closed curtain, she could hear the flapping back of sheets, the squeaking of the rubber mattress, the drag of his hand on the creaking side-rail. The man couldn't stand up unaided. Elsie, in good conscience, should buzz for a nurse. But what if Elsie happened to be asleep? She closed her eyes tightly. She listened to the dry thump of Don's feet hitting the linoleum floor. Even if Elsie thumbed the buzzer, the nurses were always so busy; they would not attend for at least five or ten minutes, perhaps even twenty.

Don sobbed with effort as he got out of bed. He shuffled for three uncertain steps. The metal hooks on the dividing curtain shrieked against the rails as he grabbed at the fabric and toppled. Shrouded within the curtain, he slammed into Elsie's overbed table and bashed it into the frame of her bed. She jumped in fright. His body hit the floor. He began a pitiful mewl. Elsie looked at the window. The balloon-head had vanished.

She thumbed the buzzer, and cried, "Help! Oh, please help!"

Nurses and more nurses filled the room. The dividing curtain was drawn back. Don blinked about, confused and distressed. One of his arms flailed like that of a drowning swimmer. Elsie, to her surprise, didn't feel a jot of guilt.

"I didn't see what happened," she said. "I was fast asleep, and bang, crash, boom."

The nurses hauled Don back onto his bed. He had incurred a nasty gash on his elbow, which Elsie kindly pointed out. Apart from that, he had no other injuries.

"An unwitnessed fall," a meaty-faced man announced, perhaps a doctor. "Let's move him to a room near the nurses' station where we can keep an eye on him."

Porters wheeled his bed from Elsie's room as Don waved at her, grandly, a king in his bulletproof Rolls Royce. A nurse came in, the friendly one with the Spanish accent, who put Elsie on the bedpan, and gave the long-overdue heart pill and tummy injection. Elsie ate lunch with a renewed appetite. The window overlooking the car park and opposite building did not frighten her. Scudding clouds suggested a fresh wind. The air must smell of magnolia and daphne. Elsie settled herself for an afternoon nap. Faintly, coming from somewhere down the hall, she could hear it…

Argh…argh…argh…

A tremor played along her nerves. However, the dividing curtain, pulled back, no longer respired. The window held no monsters. She drifted off.

Something woke her.

Many hours had passed. The room lay in shadow. Meredith had not called. Shivering, Elsie put her arms beneath the covers. In the grey reflection of the overhead TV set, right next to her in the visitor's chair, sat the balloon-head monster.

Thrashing, Elsie sat up and stared at the empty chair.

She rubbed at her eyes.

Yes, the chair was empty. It had been a dream, nothing but a bad dream.

Argh…argh…argh…

She dropped back to the pillows, clutched fretfully at the

sheet, and gazed up at the TV screen. There again was the reflection of the visitor's chair with the balloon-head monster. It sat with its impossibly thin arms resting on its impossibly thin legs, while its hands with their impossibly thin fingers dangled between its knees. Those black pits for eyes contemplated the floor as if the monster, forlorn, was lost in thought. Dumbstruck, Elsie kept looking between the reflection and the empty chair. Fear tightened her throat.

Argh…argh…argh…

If only Don were here. What in God's name was going on?

Argh…argh…

Don stopped breathing.

Elsie waited, her own breath held. A piercing alarm went off. Soon after, she heard running footsteps. Nurses sprinted down the hall, some pushing wheeled equipment. The hairs rose on Elsie's neck. She could feel the approach of doom as surely as her arthritic joints could feel the coming of a storm.

"MET call in Ward Two South, bed five," spoke a bland female voice over the various speakers in the ceiling. "MET call in Ward Two South, bed five."

After all this time in hospital, Elsie knew that the acronym MET stood for 'Medical Emergency Team'. Somehow she knew that Don occupied bed five. Her heart shrivelled into a cold and frightened lump, hard in her chest.

"Elsie, my dear, he's all yours now," boomed Don's theatrical voice, echoing down the hall and sending an electric shock through her system. "Be careful of mirrors. He can reach out of mirrors. You don't ever want the miscreant to touch you."

"No, I won't have him," she cried. "Don, take him back. Oh, please."

The alarm screamed on and on.

"Don?" she shouted, louder this time.

He didn't answer.

Elsie pulled the sheets to her chin, her mind scrabbling over the possible consequences. She would have to cover every mirror in the house. How could she explain that to her sister? Oh God, Elsie would never again see her own face as long as she lived.

Would she glimpse the monster in every reflection? When passing shop windows, would the monster walk at her side? At home, would it gaze out from darkened panes of glass, from every shiny surface, no matter how small: the stainless-steel kettle, the hollow of a spoon, the blade of a butter knife? She would go mad. She would go mad like Don and turn to drink, become a deranged and babbling shell of her former self, and then, in her dying moments, have to give the monster to somebody else, picked out by chance. For all she knew, this monster had been animate for centuries, for millennia, since the beginning of time, haunting one person after another for reasons unknown and it would go on haunting people until the last turn of the world.

Elsie flung the sheet over her head. Perhaps she was going mad already.

The alarm stopped.

Elsie stiffened; her senses alert.

No more footsteps ran along the corridor. Quietness enveloped the ward. Don was lying in bed five with a sheet on his face, just like Elsie, but he was free at last with a doctor signing a death certificate and nurses telephoning family members. With luck, the monster may have even passed with him.

Timidly, Elsie lowered the sheet.

She had to put a palm over her face and peek through her fingers, like a child watching a pantomime. *It's behind you…behind you…* She looked again at the TV screen. The balloon-head was no longer in the visitor's chair. With a spindly hand gripping the side-rail and the other on the headboard, the monster was now leaning over the bed, its hollow-socket skull mere inches from her as if to steal a kiss.

She wrenched away.

Gaping around the room, Elsie couldn't see the monster. She waved her arm through empty air and felt nothing. But when she lay back on the pillows, rigid with fear, panting, eyes screwed shut, she thought she could sense a dank breath fanning her lips, one exhalation after another. Elsie tried to scream. The scream came out strangled and truncated, a weird stuttering noise that sounded like…oh God, sounded like…

...Argh...argh...argh...

...and the terror stripped her mind empty and clean like a hard gust of wind, like a tropical cyclone that shears everything away that isn't nailed down.

Will o' the Wisp

I murdered my child, but not the way you might think.

My child, Adam, was born in early November. Our village had just completed the last ploughing of the year. The crops hadn't suffered any frosts, which meant, for once, we'd harvested more than enough food. Everyone felt in high spirits. The village midwife, Cecily, had divined that our bounteous crop was an omen, especially for me; that this time, I would deliver a live child, and not have my heart broken by yet another stillborn.

On the day of Adam's birth, the men including my husband, Gilbert, repaired fences and tools, and the women did their typical chores. I hauled water and chopped wood. Then, I took two of our buckets and headed into the woodland to collect acorns for the pigs. While Lord Ralf owns the estate and all its beasts, he has no use for acorns, and allows us to gather them freely.

The woodland is broadleaved, growing mainly oak and ash, and spans as far as you can see in both directions. You must approach it by crossing a meadow. At first, the trees are sparse, dotted occasionally in the lush grass. Squirrels dart and skip about. This first sight of the woodland is pleasant, welcoming. As you advance, however, the trees grow closer and thicker. Their branches gnarl, twist and knot, gradually snuffing out the light, so the further you gaze into the woodland, the blacker it becomes. No one in the village knows what lies on the other side. To explore would be too dangerous. Bears and wolves prowl within. Cecily says that at the woodland's dark heart lies a deep, tarry marsh that so resembles solid ground you'd think nothing of taking a step into it and disappearing forever.

I went to the edge of the woodland. As soon as the dappling of sunshine through the canopy began to falter and turn to shadow, I put down the buckets, took off my shoes, and knelt. Acorns lay thick on the ground. Heavy with child, puffed, I waited to catch my breath. Overhead, the autumn clouds spun together into bunches, heralding a rainstorm. I wished I'd worn my sheepskin cloak. Then I contemplated my filthy, callused hands and wished for so many other things.

A glowing object caught my eye.

I looked into the trees. At first, I saw nothing. Then I saw it again: a white ball of light, round as a wheel of cheese and soft as the flower-head of a dandelion, bobbing and swaying in the murky depths of the woodland. The light didn't zigzag like an insect; it wasn't a firefly. The movements didn't follow the up-and-down of a person's gait; it wasn't a villager holding a candle. A shiver seized me.

All at once, dozens of other lights dropped from their hiding places and joined the first one. Their swirl, churn and surge looked so beautiful, so enchanting, that I soon forgot my fear. The lights paused, came closer, slipping through the trees, shining brighter. A sensation of warmth and relaxation ran through me. For a dazzling moment, I could imagine how it might feel to rise, freshly soaped, from a bath. I closed my eyes, intoxicated. When I opened them again, I was on my feet.

The lights were stretched out, side by side in a straight line, like a chain of beacons enticing a ship to shore, waxing and waning, each throb urging me to step forward. I began to walk.

An agonising cramp overwhelmed me.

My waters broke. The hot fluid soaked my woollen stockings.

The baby!

I abandoned the lights, the acorns, the buckets—even my shoes—and stumbled barefoot across the meadow towards the village, clutching my belly with both hands, my waters gushing from me now, the spasms doubling down and threatening to take me out at the knees.

The house I share with Gilbert lies at the edge of the meadow. I could see him at the back wall of our house, chocking the gaps with daub. I tried to call to him. Another labour pain strangled me.

I lost my footing, and cried out, "Gilbert, help."

He turned, somehow spotted me. Shouting to his nearest neighbours, he sprinted across the meadow. Two of our neighbours ran close behind him. Gilbert skidded, dropped to the ground, and gathered me in his arms.

"Beatrice," he said, "is it time?"

I nodded.

With the help of one neighbour, Gilbert picked me up. The other ran to the village to get Cecily, the midwife. As my husband and neighbour carried me across the meadow to home, I looked back at the woodland. The oak and ash trees at its core lay in darkness, as if the beacons had never been.

Cecily attended the birth, as she had for my other doomed babies.

"Remember the harvest," she kept saying, as I strained, wept and screamed.

The storm broke, whipping our thatched roof with rain. Thunder rolled around the heavens. Lightning flashed. I could hear our animals shrieking in alarm. Gilbert would be out there with them, hushing them, stopping them from dashing madly at our fences. Hours passed, as did the storm.

The straw mattress I share with Gilbert jumps with fleas and lice. Onto this seething crawl of life, Adam was delivered in a rush of gore. My heart seemed to stop. Then I heard Adam's cry. But his cry was weak, a spiritless mewling, as if he felt disappointed in his surroundings, in me, at the hard-scrabble life that I had given him.

"What did I tell you?" Cecily said. "The harvest was indeed your good omen."

She scrubbed at Adam's face and body to bring the blood into him, then wrapped him in linen and put him at my breast. He looked like an angel: clear skin, blonde hair, blue eyes; the most perfect thing I had ever seen.

"Be careful," Cecily whispered. "The faeries might want this one." She cut the cord, dealt with the afterbirth. Then she opened the curtain that separated our bedroom from the common room, and announced, "Gilbert, come and meet your son."

My husband approached. He had joy on his face, tears wetting his cheeks. When he gathered the baby and me into his arms, kissing us both, I felt him tremble.

"Beatrice," he said, "our hardships lie behind us. Don't be scared any more. Life will be kind from here on in. I promise."

In the common room, as Cecily washed her hands in a bucket of water, she said, "Hang a pair of open scissors over your son's place on the bed."

Gilbert said, "The Lord will keep this child safe."

"Not until he's baptised. If you won't hang scissors, put pins in his clothes in the shape of a cross."

"Woman, I believe in the mercy and might of our Lord," Gilbert said. "And apart from Him, there is nothing in this world but dirt, sunshine and rain."

"At least tie a red ribbon to the child's blanket."

"It's all right, Cecily," I said. "Gilbert will see the priest tomorrow and arrange for Adam's baptism on Sunday."

"But today is only Tuesday," she said.

"Thank you for delivering my son," Gilbert said. "I'll come to your house shortly with the payment: two pounds of potatoes, as we agreed."

Cecily nodded, went to leave, and then fixed me with a hard stare. "Keep the baby at your side. Don't leave him by himself. Not even for a moment."

Kind neighbours shared their dinner, since I hadn't had time to make any food of our own. When dusk fell, Gilbert and I began to usher our chickens, pigs and goat from our yard into the common room. Most of our animals are comfortable with the routine and trot into the house without complaint. Some make the round-up difficult for us. The brown hen ran me around the yard in circles, as is her habit.

Annoyed, exhausted from giving birth just a few hours before, I put my hands on my hips and said, "If you like, madam, I shall leave you outside to wander off and get taken by wolves."

The hen stopped, regarded me with her glossy eye. And behind her, beyond the meadow, deep in the pitch-black of the woodland, I saw the lights come on. They shimmered and roiled, winking in and out of existence as they moved between the trunks. The eerie sight froze my blood.

Gilbert came out and grabbed our recalcitrant goat by its horns, intending to drag it into the house, as he must do every single night.

"Do you see that?" I said, and pointed.

"See what?"

"Out there, amongst the trees."

He glanced up, went back to wrestling the goat. "Beatrice, get the brown hen. Corner her in the vegetable patch if you have to, but mind the lettuce."

Digging in his heels, grunting, he hauled the protesting goat across our tiny yard and through the doorway. Frightened, I turned back to the woodland.

The lights were gone.

Panic jolted me. Both our windows are without panes, since glass is too expensive. The bedroom window has a view of the woodland. I imagined that those mysterious lights had streamed one by one into our house, buzzing like hornets, and were now alighting on my child. Forsaking the hen, I hurried inside, pushed through the common room full of animals, and wrenched open the bedroom curtain.

There on the mattress lay Adam, undisturbed in sleep.

"The hen," Gilbert said. "I need to block the door before the goat escapes."

"I'll get her straight away."

But as I flapped aside the curtain at our door, the hen ran between my feet and into the house, as if spooked by something in the dark.

"The wolves must be out already," Gilbert said, as he slotted the first of the boards into place across the doorway. "Are you cold? I'll stoke the fire."

I shoved through our menagerie back to the bedroom. Despite the noisy grunting, cackling and farting of our creatures, Adam still slept. I placed a hand on his chest to feel the rhythm of his heart, his body heat, the rise and fall of his ribs with every breath. If only he would suckle.

Tomorrow, I'd seek out Cecily, the oldest and wisest person in the village.

As it happened, Cecily sought me out instead.

With Adam swaddled and tied to my back, I went the following morning to the edge of the woodland to retrieve my shoes and fill my two abandoned buckets with acorns. Meanwhile, I sang lullabies. Adam lay pressed against me, warm as a fresh loaf of bread, a comfort I had thought that I would never experience.

After gathering the acorns, I checked my traps and found one squirrel. Its meat would add to tonight's pottage. Yet I still had to repay my neighbours for feeding us the night before, so I took out my sharpened stick to fossick for hedgehogs. Lord Ralf would cut off both your hands in revenge for killing a single one of his boar, deer or hare, but he has no use for squirrels and hedgehogs, and allows us to take as many as we want to pad out our stews.

I moved through the meadow, listening for the tell-tale snuffling. Someone called my name. I turned. Cecily approached.

"How is Adam?" she said, "Has he taken to the nipple?"

"No. I don't know what I'm doing wrong."

"It's not you who is wrong. Sit with me a while."

Together, we knelt down in the grass.

"Sixteen years ago," Cecily finally said, "before my arthritis took hold, I was midwife to this whole district. I travelled to your village and brought you into this world with my own hands. I had to cut you from the body of your dead mother. You weren't breathing. That first breath, I gave to you myself. I think of you as my own."

My tears rose. I reached out, but Cecily shook me off.

She said, "This summer, you and Gilbert built your new house. It overlooks the woodland, as does mine. Have you seen the lights in the trees?" When I couldn't find my voice, she continued, "You weren't born into this village, you don't know the old tales. It's the faerie folk. Each light is a twist of straw, set on fire like a torch. With these corpse-candles, the faeries try to lure a person into the woodland, to drown them in the bog or make them lose their way and starve to death."

I flushed, remembering how the lights had mesmerised me. "Have no fear. I'll not go into the woodland."

"This is about Adam. I must warn you, since Gilbert won't." She leaned closer, so close that I could see the thready veins in her eyes. "Once every seven years," she said, "the faerie folk owe a tithe to Hell of one faerie child. Instead, they steal a human child for the sacrifice. They replace the human child with a changeling."

"A changeling?"

"A figurine of dirt and twigs, spell-cast to look and act like a baby. Yet the magic isn't perfect. The changeling appears sickly, feeble. That's how you can tell." She gripped my arm. "The lights in the trees are signalling for Adam."

A chill settled over me. "Adam is not the only newborn in the village."

"He is the only male with fair hair, exactly the kind they favour most. Beatrice, make no mistake. The faerie folk want your son."

That night, I couldn't sleep. Instead, I gazed at Adam, lying as boneless on the mattress as a wet rag, until my eyes felt raw. Another baby destined for Hell? I could hardly stand to think of it. My stillborn children were burning in the eternal fires of damnation because they had died before they could be baptised. Although William, Alice and Joan (as I had secretly named them) hadn't committed any sins of their own, they were condemned by

Original Sin. No amount of praying or payments to the Church could ever help them. This is my torment without end.

Dawn came at last.

As Gilbert yawned and stretched awake, I told him of Cecily's warning.

"Don't believe a word of it," Gilbert said. "Never once has the priest spoken of faeries. If the creatures are not in the Bible, they don't exist."

"The Bible doesn't mention squirrels. Nevertheless, we ate squirrel meat last night. I added it to the pot myself."

Gilbert waved a dismissive hand. "You're too easily led. Attend to the baby. Make sure that he feeds."

Then Gilbert got up, unsecured the door, and followed the animals outside. I stayed in bed. I heard his long stream of piss spatter and pound across the garden bed. Today, Gilbert would leave with eight other farmers to visit a distant town. Thanks to this year's bumper harvest, our village could finally afford an ox. It was good news, something to celebrate. But as I watched Gilbert come back inside and shove his spare tunic, sheepskin cloak and mittens into a bag, my lungs began to cramp into airless tangles.

"Don't go," I said.

He turned to me, surprised. "This trip has been long in the planning."

I didn't answer. Sighing, he sat down on the mattress, stroked my hair.

"Beatrice," he said, "there's nothing to fear. I'm your husband. Believe me instead of the old midwife. Now, put her nonsense from your mind."

I nodded, tried to smile. He would be gone until Saturday, the day before Adam's baptism. Gilbert leaned down to kiss me. I clung to him. Eventually, he had to take hold of my wrists in order to free himself.

Gilbert left after breakfast.

I did my chores with Adam strapped to my back. I stopped

every now and then to offer him my breast, which he refused. When it came time to chop firewood, I untied the swaddling and placed Adam on the ground, far enough away to be safe from any flying chips. I brought the axe down on the logs, again and again, stacking the pieces inside the kindling box. Each whack of the axe made a loud noise. Adam didn't startle. Not even once.

Warily, I put down the axe and approached. Clicking my fingers and clapping my hands at his face, I circled him a number of times. No reaction. He stared without interest at the sky. I dropped to my haunches and picked him up. He flopped, soft as a woollen blanket, making me fear that he was dead.

Yet he still breathed.

I raced him to Cecily's house. She was tending to her vegetable patch. When she saw me, she ushered me inside. She invited me to sit, poured me ale. I gulped it.

Pursing her lips, she said, "Let me inspect the child."

With trembling fingers, I kissed Adam before passing him over.

She took him to the mattress and sat down. Arranging him on her lap, she lifted each of his limbs and dropped them, encountering no resistance. Tut-tutting, she massaged his muscles experimentally. Then she put the tip of her little finger into his slack mouth and waited. During this investigation, I felt ill, crazed. Cecily stood up and offered Adam to me. I took him. He sagged in my arms, warm and grizzling.

She said, "You left him alone."

"For a few minutes on the day of his birth; we had to bring in the animals."

"You left Adam? When the faerie folk were lighting their corpse-candles?"

"Yes, I left him." I broke into tears. "I've doomed him to Hell, like the others."

"No, it's not too late." She gripped my shoulder. "This is what you must do: leave the changeling to sleep tonight on the manure pile. This will break the spell."

"But our manure pile is outside. What about the wolves?"

Cecily shrugged. "What kind of wolf eats a figurine made of twigs and dirt?"

"Wait. Let me think. I should discuss this first with Gilbert."

"By the time Gilbert comes back with the ox, your real son will be in Hell."

One of the neighbours helped me to bring the goat inside that night. I chased in the other animals. Fixing the boards across our doorway, I felt torn, undecided. The woodland lay in darkness. Adam still hadn't fed. As the night deepened, I stoked the fire against the chill. Gradually, the noises of the village settled down until nothing stirred. At the very edge of my hearing, I detected the distant howl of a wolf.

I lifted one of the boards from the door, and then picked up Adam—no, I picked up the changeling—and took him outside. Staying close to the house, I crept to the manure pile. From the light cast by the half-moon, I could see the steam rising from the shit. I kissed Adam—no, the changeling—because I couldn't help myself. Then I placed him on the manure.

But I couldn't leave him.

Instead, I sat near to him, keeping in both hands my sharpened stick for hunting hedgehogs, in case of wolves. At some point, I must have fallen asleep. At the first cockerel call, as a false dawn streaked the sky, I jerked awake. Before any neighbours came out, I hurried inside with Adam.

I kissed his little face, over and over.

He was as limp as before. My nipples, dripping with milk, still repulsed him.

Cecily told me to burn a cupful of thorns on a faerie mound. She told me of a faerie mound a few miles north, which turned out to be a hillock about the size of a barn. I burned the thorns. It was a long walk home. In his swaddling, the changeling lay motionless against my back. Perhaps I hadn't gathered enough thorns.

On my return, Cecily told me to brew ale inside an eggshell. The changeling, curious, would ask what I was doing, which would break the spell. I brewed the ale but I must have done it wrong. Gilbert makes the ale, not me.

That night, Friday, I sat within my boarded-up house amongst my animals, and stared out the window at the lights as they moved through the woodland. The faerie folk already had Adam. What more did they want? I held the changeling at my breast, but for nothing. He appeared gaunt, husked, as if the life were draining from him. But he had Gilbert's nose, the little cleft in his chin just like mine, the blonde hair of my dead mother. He looked every bit like my own baby.

When it came, the decision came easily. If I couldn't save Adam, I'd throw myself in the river. Gilbert would find himself another wife, one who could provide him with strong, healthy children.

I kissed Adam—no, the changeling—placed him on the mattress, and drew a long piece of timber from the fireplace. I went outside, holding the burning stick aloft like a torch. Walking towards the woodland, my pain turned to anger, and then flared into a kind of furious madness. I broke into a run across the meadow.

"Give me back my son," I screamed. "Give him back or I'll burn you all."

The trees loomed around me, their branches a crazy patchwork of witch fingers, black on black. The lights shimmered. As I ran further into the woodland, so the lights retreated. I tripped on an exposed root and fell full-length, winding myself. Panting, I heard the back and forth yipping of wolves. My fear lasted just a moment. Let the pack devour me, I thought. It'll save me a walk to the river.

"Beatrice!"

The shout was faint, but I recognised Cecily's voice. I lifted my head. The lights had gone. The moonbeams scarcely penetrated the canopy. My makeshift torch lay on the ground, smouldering.

"Beatrice, come quickly!"

The urgency in Cecily's voice galvanised me. Perhaps I had cowed the faeries into returning Adam. I stood up, grabbed my torch. The woodland looked exactly the same in every direction. I had run too far; now I would starve to death, or stumble into the bog and drown.

"Beatrice!"

I turned and hurried in a straight line. If the trees didn't thin out soon, it meant I was lost. The darkness went on and on. I kept going. Then I glimpsed orange-tinted windows, the houses of my village, shining with firelight. Relieved, I broke into the meadow and dashed to my home.

Climbing through the boards on my doorway, I found Cecily within. She had the baby wrapped in a blanket, clutched to her chest. I flung my torch into the fire.

"Is it Adam?" I said. "Did I save him?"

I grabbed him from her. Unexpectedly, his body was shaking. I placed him on the mattress and opened the blanket. To my horror, he was convulsing violently, as if shaken by invisible hands, his eyes rolled up into his head.

"What's going on?" I said. "What does it mean?"

"You've weakened the spell," Cecily said. "When you ran to the woodland, I feared the worst and came here straight away, but you've done it, Beatrice. Now there's only one thing left to do. Throw the changeling into the fire."

For a moment, the world stopped.

The fire?

"Don't hesitate," Cecily said. "Quickly, before it's too late. The changeling will revert into sticks, and vanish. After that, we'll hear a knock at the door. It will be a faerie, delivering Adam back to you, safe and sound."

"No, I can't do it. I can't put him in the fire. My other children…"

"Forget your other children. They are damned. Think of Adam."

I picked up the changeling. His shaking had passed. I hugged him against me, tight, sniffed the warmth of his skin, the scent of his sweet breath. Cecily pushed me through the crush of animals in the common room towards the fireplace.

"After this, I'll drown myself in the river," I said.

"Don't be afraid. There will indeed be a knock at the door."

I gazed down at my baby. For the first time, he gazed back, his blue eyes focused, as if seeing me. Perhaps it was Adam after all.

"Wait," I said. "What about Gilbert? I need to make this decision with him."

"Do it," Cecily said, "before the faerie folk recast their spell."

With a sob, I kissed Adam on the forehead, again and again, my beautiful child. My only living child. But no, it wasn't Adam. This tiny precious thing, staring up at me with its blue eyes, was made from dirt, twigs and magic.

"Put the changeling into the fire," Cecily said. "Do it, Beatrice. Do it now."

And so, God help me, I did.

Fair-Haired Boy

William tickled the downy clutch of fur under the tabby's chin. Charlie was so soft, maybe softer than Bunny, and if he could only locate Bunny, he would compare the two. He decided to look again in his room because surely his favourite toy must be packed somewhere inside one of those boxes. He rolled onto his back, drowsing in the autumn sunshine, and Charlie curled herself against him. Then she stiffened and screamed. William lurched to his knees, yelling, "Charlie! Charlie!" but she was already streaking to the cluster of birch trees at the end of the yard, and on her heels was the bull terrier from over the road.

Charlie hit low-lying branches and disappeared, scattering leaves. The terrier dived in after her. William bolted across the lawn and whipped through the branches towards the cacophony of yowling and snarling. The terrier had her against the fence. Charlie's face was contorted with agony and fear, and the piteous sight made William cry out.

Dad's distant voice growled, "What the hell's going on?"

Dad was most likely at the open door of the garage, too far away, and William could not wait. The boy wrenched the dog's tail, and the startled terrier dropped Charlie and shot from the trees. Charlie lay twisted on her side, her mouth open. Blood was on her. William reached out, but she shied and limped away. He crawled from under the branches and watched her stagger to the corner of the house and squeeze through a broken weatherboard.

Anxiety needled through William like static. He couldn't go after her. Not in there. *Not into the…*

"That's payback, you stupid cat, for every bird you've ever killed on my property." Dad was glaring at the broken board and smiling. "I ought to seal you under there and let you rot."

"No, Dad, please, she's hurt."

Dad stormed back to the garage. William put his face at the hole to call for Charlie but the dank air fanned across his lips and he fell back. He had to get help. He raced across the front lawn and into the house but slowed to a creep once he was through the kitchen. The doorway at the end of the hall showed a feeble light. As he got closer, he could hear the droning mutter of Gran, "Fear God and give glory to him for the hour of his judgement is come."

He entered the room. The dresser, instead of housing what it once had—a hand mirror, make-up and combs—now held a wash basin, a bedpan and pill bottles. The curtains were drawn. The lamplight from the bedside table showed Gran in a chair. She had one bony thigh crossed over the other and an open book on her lap. Mum fidgeted on the mattress, knotting her long hair against the pillow.

"Worship him that made heaven and earth and the sea and the fountains of waters," Gran said, as she ran a finger along the text.

"Charlie's hurt and she's under the house," William said.

Mum sat up and put her hands over her ears. "No! Haven't I suffered enough already?"

Gran paled. "Hush, stop your fretting about the baby, it's finished with."

"Yeah, Mum, he's safe in heaven with Jesus," William said, but in truth, he hated his dead brother and blamed him for Mum's illness and Dad's temper and Gran's permanent residence in the house.

Gran put the book on the bed. She manhandled Mum onto the pillow and said, "That's enough now, child. Why do you have to cause so much grief all the time?"

"I'm sorry," William said.

Mum pulled the sheet over her head.

Gran snatched up the book, slapped it against her knee and

wriggled her finger over the page. "And there followed another angel saying, Babylon is fallen, is fallen."

William retreated to his room. After a while, hiccupping and sniffling, he perused the stacked crates. He flattened his face against an opaque plastic chest and whispered, "Bunny, where are you?" Through the plastic he could just make out a box of some sort, a loop of string, something with stripes, but there was nothing that was blue and soft. He longed to press that toy rabbit to his face, to feel its fur, its fluffy ears. "Bunny," William sighed, mashing his nose against another crate, straining his eyes, "I really need to find you."

William caught his breath. He bent his head to the heating duct and listened. There it was again, a faint whimpering.

He ran down the backyard to the weatherboard's manhole. The door of the manhole was tiny and he stopped and stared at it, his heart fluttering into his throat. He felt a sudden need to pee. So it was dark under there, so what? Charlie was in trouble. Nothing else mattered. He would just open that dumb old door and go straight in and rescue Charlie and come straight out again, that's all. He took a step and eventually another. He dropped to his knees and fumbled with the latch while his mouth dried out. Clammy air closed over his face and tamped his throat. Then he heard the plaintive little peep and, shutting his eyes, he dived into the manhole.

It smelled rank and green like a stagnant pond. The floorboards were close to his head and he had to kick against the dirt to push deeper into the cold. Something as light as fairy floss settled across his face—a web—and he thrashed at the strands, fearing the spider.

"Charlie!" he hissed and forced himself to be still.

But she did not make a sound. Maybe she was gone. Maybe she had heard him open the door and had slipped out of the hole in the wall and fled to her real owners who would drive her to the nearest vet, so he was under here for no reason, stuck here alone and now he could not breathe. A rush of panic welled up from his guts. He had a frantic urge to scramble out of the manhole as fast as he could before whatever it was trapped there in the dark with him could make its move.

Wait.

That sorrowful sound: was it Charlie?

The black of the crawlspace was knifed every now and then by glints of light between the boards. About two metres away shone the hole that Charlie had climbed through, and next to it, half-lit, was Charlie herself.

"I'm coming, don't worry," William said, and struck out with his feet, scrabbling forward. But Charlie ducked William's hand and vaulted in a single smooth movement, like liquid pouring from a jug, through the hole in the boards. *Darn it.* Now he really *was* under here for nothing. Then William's empty fingers fell against something, a box of some sort, a chest with a rounded lid.

A pirate's chest! Of all things!

But how did the chest get all the way into the furthest corner? Someone must have pushed it with a broom handle. The safety of the manhole clamoured for his attention but the chest had lit a flame in his belly. Hoping for something wonderful, like doubloons or at the very least a treasure map, he grasped the wooden lid. Its roughness chafed his palms. The lid dropped back on twin leather straps, yawning like broken jaws.

William, disappointed, grabbed at photographs. He held one to the light. There was Mum before she got sick, looking happy with some kind of parcel in her arms. And here was one of Dad, smiling too and holding… William let go of the photographs. He snatched at something else, a doll-sized jumpsuit.

Baby clothes.

He scrambled backwards, broke from the manhole, ran across the yard. At the garage door, he hesitated. Gran was inside the garage with Dad. William could tell by the set of Dad's shoulders that Dad was angry. They hadn't noticed him. William stepped back.

Gran said, "She's getting worse."

"I know. I'll call the doctor tomorrow."

Dad prowled to one of the shadow-boards lined with carpentry tools and took up a hammer. He stood by the workbench with his back to Gran and stared at the birdhouse. It was almost finished except for the roof. A plastic container on the bench held the loose shingles no bigger than postage stamps that Dad had snipped from a sheet of cedar. He selected a shingle and placed it on a birdhouse rafter. Then he plucked a tack from the corner of his mouth, steadied it against the shingle, and brandished the hammer.

"She doesn't need any more pills," Gran said. "She needs a priest."

"What for? She's not dying."

"You know why."

Dad let the shingle and tack fall to the bench. He tightened his fist around the handle of the hammer. "All right, that's enough."

Gran stuck out her chin. "But it's true."

"Don't say it."

"She can *hear* him."

Dad turned to face Gran. For a moment, nothing happened. Then Dad shifted his weight onto one foot and Gran fled from the garage in jerky marionette steps, hands flailing.

William said in a rush, "Dad, I found some of the baby's stuff under the house, should we get it out? Dad?"

Dad swiped a forearm across his red and watering eyes, flipped the hammer so that the claw faced outwards and brought the hammer down, exploding the birdhouse to pieces. Then he threw the hammer and it bounced along the bench, upsetting the plastic container and strewing the shingles.

William ran and pitched himself through the manhole. *That damned kid*. He grappled with the chest and hurled the photographs, baby bottles, a pair of crocheted shoes, all the while crying and cursing the baby that had spoiled everything for everybody.

That is when he pulled out Bunny.

William's fury dropped away. Relief settled into him like warm milk. He closed his eyes and nestled his face between Bunny's soft blue ears. For a time, there was nothing but comfort until a snippet of memory tugged at him. A snippet from a bad memory.

A voice.

Shut up.

His stomach turned over. In a slice of light through the boards, he could see Charlie lying in the far corner. She lifted her head and looked at him, blood running.

Shut up, you little bastard.

In his mind, the voice came closer, loud and slurry. William jolted. He sat up fast and banged his head against the floorboards. He pressed Bunny against his cheek but the realisation came back anyway, crashing through in bright, jagged lines—*he didn't have a brother*—and he dropped Bunny to the dirt.

He rolled his eyes, white in their sockets, and saw IT in the crawlspace with him. IT was a patch of soil with a different texture from the surrounding soil and if he clawed through that patch he knew he would soon find what was left, wrapped in a rug and a black garbage bag, buried just beneath the surface. He lost control of his bladder. All at once the remainder of the memory rose up and here it was, strident and terrible, so real he could almost feel it…

—the pain in his arm, the wall rushing to meet him, the explosion in his skull and the voice's garbled bawling, "That'll teach you, you little bastard, now quit your sandbagging and get up. Get up, or I'm really going to hurt you…"

—and next, the horror of realising that he had recalled and forgotten this memory countless times before and would recall and forget it again and again in endless torment.

After a time, he could hear Charlie howling.

William sat up.

He didn't have a heart any more but it was hammering, which frightened and confused him. Nothing made sense. One thing became increasingly clear, though; he had to go inside straight away before the knowledge slipped away from him. And because he knew now what he was, he did not have to go the long way via the yard and back door. Instead, he rose through the floorboards.

Mum thrashed aside the blankets and gaped at him wild-eyed. "Haven't I suffered enough?" she yelled, and clutched the sheet to her chest as if naked and ashamed. "Go away, you little bastard, get away from me."

Gran's footfalls started down the hallway at a run but William did not need to bother about her. He did not register with Gran or Dad, it was just Mum, just this bitch right here. He pulled his mouth into something resembling a smile and floated towards the bed. Mum shrank back, gibbering. William put his hands around her throat and the fright opened her eyes until they were as big as peeled eggs. Gran, at the bedside, grappled with her daughter but her efforts were for nothing. William sat on Mum's chest and tightened his grip. He looked deep into her astonished eyes, seeking the oblivion at the bottom of those black pupils. He could hear Charlie from beneath the floor, screaming as she bled out, and he said, "This time you're coming with me," but he was not sure which one he meant.

Species Endangered

The empty beach looked so sumptuous, so tantalising, that it actually made her mouth water. The colour of the sand reminded Helen of canned pineapple, while the Coral Sea shone with the kind of bright and luminous blue she associated with travel brochures for infinity pools at five-star resorts. She slammed the car's passenger door.

"Last one in is a rotten egg!" she called, and broke into a run.

"Hoi, wait for me, you cheat!"

She had a good head start; Lou still had to get out and lock the car. Helen dodged through the palm trees and ferns that grew between the highway and the beach. The sand felt soft but hard-packed, easy to traverse. Hanging between the sea and sky sat a hump of land, presumably Dunk Island. Helen slowed, hopping on one leg to shuck a sandal. Lou flashed by, laughing, sprinting flat out. He kicked off his shoes and, bare-chested, ran into the sea.

"Rotten egg!" he shouted.

Cheeky bugger. Helen shucked her other sandal and waded in after him.

It was winter, July, but the dry season in tropical Queensland heated the seawater like a bath. The shelf went on and on at a gentle gradient. Helen caught up with Lou, who stood waist-height. They must be fifteen metres out or more. Fish darted. Sea grasses tickled her feet. She should have taken off her singlet and shorts. Now she would have to sit on a towel when they got back to the car.

"Come here, you," Lou said.

She moved in for his embrace. Instead, he gripped her waist, lifted her and dropped her. She came up, wet and giggling. He hugged her and kissed her crown.

"Babe," he said, "this has been the best holiday ever."

"Ditto."

Soon they would have to drive back to Sydney, to the cold wind and rain, to the noise, traffic, to their respective jobs; Lou at the building site, Helen at the start of third term with her rowdy grade five students.

Lou pulled away. "Did you hear that?" he said, facing the shore.

"Huh?"

"Listen."

There was the languorous whish and whoosh of the tide, the chatter of lorikeets, and something else: a low, almost subsonic growl from the lush vegetation.

"It sounds like a tiger," Lou said.

She laughed. "Or a truck's engine brake."

"Wait," Lou said, pointing. "What the fuck is that? You see it?"

Helen lifted a hand to shade her eyes.

Yes, now she could see it.

A shadow moved beneath the trees. She squinted. Whatever was slowly creeping nearer was tall, as tall as a man, yet impossibly slender and without shoulders. It resembled a head and spine with the arms torn off. Helen edged closer to Lou. They were alone on this stretch of coastline. The tyre iron Lou kept for protection while free camping was in the car boot, their phones in the centre console. The growl sounded again.

"Can you see what it is?" she said.

"Not yet."

The figure stepped out onto the sand and into the light. It looked prehistoric.

Lou said, "Babe, is that an emu, a giant turkey, or what?"

For a second, Helen didn't know either. Then she recognised the scaly legs, huge and black-feathered body, the long throat which her imagination had suggested was an armless man. *The most dangerous bird in the world*… During first term, Helen had taken her students on an excursion to the zoo. Afterwards, each child had made a poster on an Australian animal. Most had chosen cuddly favourites—koala, sugar glider, wombat—but not Brianna. That quiet, intense little girl had formed her poster's heading with letters clipped from a newspaper like some kind of ransom note: *The most dangerous bird in the world*.

Helen said, "It's a cassowary."

"Yeah? Cool, I've never seen one."

"It's only found in north-eastern Queensland," Helen said, "and Papua New Guinea. I think it's endangered."

"How come it sounds like a tiger?"

"No idea."

Lou put his hands on his hips. "The fucker's looking at us."

The bird had stopped its advance a metre or so onto the beach. Now it stood completely still and silent, observing them. The high crest on its head (the *casque?* she wondered) looked made of bone. The face and neck were featherless. A wattle, two red and flabby tags of flesh resembling an empty scrotum, hung obscenely from the blue neck. Helen grimaced. Jesus, the bird was ugly. No, not ugly—*scary*. The bird must have come from the national park, drawn by Helen and Lou calling to each other. It must have crossed the highway, seen them, and decided to confront them. But why? They did not have any food. And cassowaries were not meat-eaters. Were they? No, the poster had featured pictures of fruits and berries. Yet the bird kept staring. The sneering beak and orange irises gave its face a grotesque, demonic cast.

The bird cocked its head, fast, and Helen jumped. The bird froze again.

"What's the matter, babe?" Lou said, and grinned. "Crapping yourself?"

"For sure. Cassowaries have killed people."

"Bullshit."

"Honest, I swear." If only she could recall every detail on the poster. "A boy got killed a long time ago. He and his friend had clubs or something and were trying to bash one. It turned on him, and cut open his neck."

"With what? Its beak?"

"No, its foot. Each toe has a long nail, sharp as a knife."

"Shit, hey." Lou rubbed his chin. "Well, it'll piss off into the bush when it gets bored. Let's just have our swim, okay?"

He floated onto his back and made leisurely strokes through the water. Helen paddled in his wake. The bird watched them. Lou swam parallel to the beach. Helen noticed that he kept the motionless cassowary in sight. Soon, the bird was a long way distant. Lou stood up and flicked water. Helen splashed him in return and tried to laugh.

"Stop fretting about the damn bird," Lou said.

"Me? You're as spooked as I am."

He looked past her shoulder, and his face tightened. She turned. The cassowary was treading across the sand in their direction, its gait slow and cautious, body and neck tense and rigid, eyes fixed. Helen's cat, Toby, moved in such a stealthy fashion whenever he hunted a pigeon. The bird's rasping growl started up again.

Lou said, "No wonder it's endangered. It's obviously thick as shit. Doesn't the bastard have sense enough to stay away from humans?"

"They're territorial," she said. "It must have a nest close by."

"Well, I've had enough. Let's head to the car."

Freestyle, he swam back the way they had come, parallel to the beach. His shoes stood out against the sand like a pair of black beacons. Helen followed but kept glancing behind at the cassowary. It watched them swim away.

Lou stood, shook the wet hair from his eyes, and strode toward the shoreline.

In her hurry to keep pace, Helen lost her footing in the slippery sea grasses and fell. Water closed over her head. She stood, coughing, blowing her nose.

Christ, she had to calm down. In a controlled manner, she began to wade using high and careful steps. Already, Lou was clear of the water. He picked up his shoes and clapped the soles together, knocking out sand. The cassowary, some fifty metres away, lowered its head and sprinted. It moved faster than Helen thought possible.

She screamed.

In the time it took Lou to turn and brace, the cassowary had closed the distance. It jumped. Both legs flew out in front of it, toes pointed, talons slashing. Lou lunged out of the way. The bird kicked again. Its rasping snarls sounded reptilian, primordial, like a dinosaur. Lou was a tall man, but the bird dwarfed him.

Helen cried, "Get back in the water."

Lou kept his arms outstretched, a shoe in each hand, trying to swat the bird away. Despite its massive size, the bird moved fast, bounding and springing, charging, thrusting its talons. One strike and Lou would be disembowelled. Helen rushed ashore. Waving her arms, she yelled as loudly as she could, stripping her throat raw. The cassowary balked. Helen grabbed Lou's elbow. Together, they stumbled and floundered into the sea, scrambling backwards. The bird made a move to follow. Could the cassowary swim?

Yes. Oh, yes it could.

She remembered Brianna's penmanship, the cursive letters in hot pink pencil: *It swims like a champion in rivers and even the sea!* But the bird stayed onshore.

At waist-height in the water, Helen stopped and said, "Are you all right?"

"Nah," Lou said, panting. "The prick got me."

He had one palm held flat to his chest. Where were his shoes? He must have dropped them. God, was that blood oozing between his fingers? She dragged insistently on his wrist until he allowed her to look.

The gaping slash on his chest was about ten centimetres long. At its base, the flesh showed a glimpse of something white, something that must be, oh Jesus, must be bone…a rib bone. What if Lou had a punctured lung? Blood drizzled lazily from the wound. Surely, that was a good sign; if the talon had hit an artery, the blood would be spurting. *Don't freak out*. She tightened her grip on his wrist, felt his thready pulse beneath her fingertips.

"Can you breathe okay?" she said.

"Yeah, I'm all right."

The cassowary let out long, barking grunts, and stamped at the sand. Those legs belonged on a T. Rex. Helen wanted to cry but held on.

"So what do we do now?" Lou said.

Helen scanned the shoreline: deserted. Behind them, the Coral Sea was deserted too: no jet-skis, parasails or boats.

"We wait," she said. "Sooner or later, it'll leave for its nest."

He nodded. They held hands. The bird had again turned into a statue.

The black feathers were coarse and hair-like, falling on either side of its body as if from a central part. Where its wings should be were two stumps with blade-like quills. Perhaps these quills were secondary weapons. The bird kept hissing like a snake. Helen glanced at Lou. A flutter of panic started up in her stomach. He was pale beneath his olive skin, his green eyes glazed and sunken in their sockets.

"Pinch the edges of the wound together," she said. "That'll slow the bleeding."

He did as he was told. She squeezed his other hand.

Time passed.

The bird did not leave.

They began to speak quietly of many things: how much they had enjoyed their week in Cairns, snorkelling the Great Barrier Reef, trekking the Daintree Forest, river rafting at Barron Gorge; what they would do in Townsville, such as water-ski the Ross River Dam, hike Castle Hill; their work commitments; options to celebrate Lou's upcoming birthday, including a pub crawl, a party at the holiday house owned by Helen's parents on Phillip Island. Then the conversation petered out.

And still the bird had not left. And still it watched them.

The sun marched steadily toward the west. Its rays started to bite. Neither of them wore sunscreen lotion. This was supposed to have been a quick dip. During the drive south out of Cairns, the beach had kept peeking at Helen through the palm trees that grew alongside the highway. She had nagged Lou to stop.

"Are you in much pain?" she said.

"The salt water stings like fuck."

"At least you won't get an infection." She licked at her dry, cracking lips. "You realise the bird hasn't moved an inch."

"Yeah, I know."

"Maybe it's asleep," she said, and when Lou gave a snort, she added, "We don't know anything about this creature. It might sleep standing up, like a horse."

"With its eyes open?"

"Let's get low and walk sideways," she said. "We might sneak away."

They crabbed. The cassowary let out a shuddering bray and stalked the beach, following them. Helen felt the tears rise. At twenty-three years of age, she had not given death much thought, but she had never imagined dying from an animal attack.

"Oh, this is pointless," she said. "Let's stop."

The cassowary stopped too. It inflated its neck and made deep, booming sounds for a minute. Then it became silent and still. Its immobility chilled her.

She looked down at her bare shoulders. The skin glowed, a deep angry crimson. Lou's face and neck were reddening too. The blistering would soon start.

"How long do you reckon we've been out here?" she said.

"Couple of hours, maybe. We're gonna get heatstroke."

The reflection of sunshine on the water was giving her a headache. *Water, water, everywhere, nor any drop to drink*...what was that from, Coleridge? Something heavy bumped against her leg. A frisson of sudden terror made her shriek.

"What is it?" Lou said, clutching at her. "What's wrong?"

Shark.

Lou's blood must have attracted a predator, a fish with many teeth and an empty gullet. Her feet drew up involuntarily and her toes curled. But no, no, wait; it was a sea turtle. A bloody sea turtle… Relief made her sob.

"Hey," she said, and hiccupped. "Look."

The turtle swept its flippers and disappeared from sight.

Were there sharks off this coast? Saltwater crocodiles? Both? She had not seen any warning notices along the highway, but Australia's east coast was about a zillion kilometres. How could the authorities signpost it all? The expectation of teeth made her feel faint. She turned, scanned the vast expanse of the Coral Sea behind her, and saw the tip of a dorsal fin or the bump of eyes in every sparkling wave. The skin of her legs crawled in anticipation of the bite. *Don't freak out.*

"Find a stick or a rock," Lou said. "We'll have to smack the bird's head in."

"That's how the boy died, remember?"

"Yeah, but if we stay out here and do nothing, we'll die anyway."

Helen's heart pounded. "Don't say that."

"Babe, come on. Find a weapon."

Lou released her hand. Looking down, he searched the seabed. She did the same. There was sand and more sand, undulating grasses, fish, shells. The urge to scream began to build inside her chest. She clenched her jaw and swallowed hard.

"It's no use," she said at last, throat aching.

Movement from the cassowary drew her attention. Helen and Lou had drifted some distance apart. This must have confused the bird. It was pacing the beach, first one way and then the other.

"Check it out," she said. "It can't decide who to follow."

"There's our answer," Lou said. "We'll split up, put a hundred metres between us, and both make a run for it. The bird will have to choose which one to chase."

"What? Oh my God. Are you kidding me?"

"It's our best chance."

"No, that's a stupid idea." She swam over, grabbed him, and said, "We'll stay together and wait for help."

"There's no help coming, babe. Listen to me. The car's unlocked, keys in the centre console. Whoever gets to the car first drives over the beach and rescues the other one, okay?" He held her at arm's length. "Ready?"

"No. Shit, no. I mean, where's the car? All the palm trees look the same."

"Run in a straight line to the highway. You'll see the car once you're through the trees. Ready?"

"Please," she whispered. "I don't want to do this."

"Me neither." He kissed her crown and gave her a little shove. "Get going."

He loped through the water, heading north. The cassowary walked along the beach opposite him. Helen swam south. Her breathing sounded too loud. The pulse thudded in her ears. Every time the sea lapped at her mouth, she resisted the urge to drink. After a minute, she halted, stood, and looked around. The cassowary and Lou were a long way off. However, Lou must have been watching for her.

"Go," he yelled. "Hurry up."

Impatiently, he waved his arms. Helen stumbled towards shore. One step after another made the sea drop away, exposing her thighs, calves, ankles, until, oh God, her feet were on dry land. Had the cassowary noticed?

Yes. Even from this distance, she saw the bird turn to face her.

Lou—so brave, so gutsy—bounded from the surf. The bird sprinted at him.

Helen broke into a dash. The sand gave way beneath her heels, as if she were running in a dream, getting nowhere. The cool shadows of the trees and ferns seemed to mock her. Faster, she had to go *faster*. Her heart knocked chaotically.

Lou called, "Look out!"

She glanced. The cassowary was coming for her.

The bird powered over the beach, legs pumping. A fact from the poster: *It runs at fifty kilometres per hour!* Helen bolted into the vegetation. Branches whipped and lashed. Trampling sounded close behind. With a burst of speed, she emerged into the light. The car was some five metres to the north. She raced hard along the highway's shoulder. Gravel cut her feet. She focused on the driver's side door. Reaching out, she grabbed the handle, which stopped her momentum and spun her around.

The cassowary leapt.

Its huge, three-toed feet flew like a volley of arrows. Helen opened the door, creating an impromptu shield. The force of the kick pinned her against the car body. Pain flared in her collarbone. The bird dropped, preparing for the next kick. Helen slipped into the seat and slammed the door shut.

Relieved, panting, she pressed a hand to the stitch in her side.

The bird's head shot through the half-open window.

Its peck struck her scalp, ripping out a hank of hair. Dazed, Helen dropped across the front seats. Blade-like nails screeched against the door. Snarling, the bird lunged, its breath fruity and sour, beak snapping.

The window cracked.

Helen scrabbled through the centre console, found the keys, and started the engine. The bird squawked and withdrew. When she leaned on the horn, the bird shied, fled across the highway, and disappeared into the forest of the national park.

Gasping, Helen leaned her forehead against the steering wheel. Then she put the car into gear, swung the wheel and ploughed over the ferns, plants and grasses, crunching vegetation beneath the tyres. The car sank as it hit sand. Jesus, would the car bog? It was only a sedan, not a four-wheel drive. But no, it was okay, she was driving north and at a reasonable clip, but…

But where was Lou?

Fright gripped her by the throat. Had he fled to the water? She slowed the car. Nowhere, dear God, he was nowhere…and then she spotted him, about thirty metres away. Her relief quickly turned to panic. Why was he lying motionless on the beach?

Pulling up next to him, she left the engine running and got out.

His eyes were closed, his face grey beneath the sunburn.

"Lou?" she said, voice quavering. "Can you hear me?"

He opened his eyes. His gaze seemed blank, as if he could not recognise her. His shorts were covered in blood, and something else. What the hell was sitting on his hip? A steaming pile of greyish-purple, glistening loops…intestines…she was looking at Lou's intestines, extruded through a slash in his groin. Nausea washed over her.

"I think the bastard got me," Lou said. "Is it bad?"

Helen dropped to her knees and took his hand. "No," she lied. "Not too bad."

"So where's the bird?"

"Gone back into the bush."

Lou smiled. "Thank fuck for that. Help me up?"

"Hang on. Let me think."

If he tried to stand, the abdominal pressure would push more of his guts through the wound. First, she had to bandage him somehow. The car did not have a first aid kit. *Don't freak out*. Her mind raced. She took off her singlet and bra.

"What are you doing?" he said.

"Taking care of you. This might hurt a bit, okay?"

She wrapped her singlet around the top of his thigh, covering his guts, and secured the t-shirt with her bra. Lou did not react. Why not? He should be screaming in agony. She had to get him to hospital. They were midway between Cairns and Townsville, with nothing but sea, beach, and bush.

"Listen," he slurred, gazing blindly at the sky. "Can you hear that?"

A deep growl sounded nearby. Adrenaline shot through Helen's limbs.

"Sit up," she said. "Hurry. Roll towards me and lean on your elbow."

Complying, Lou grimaced. "Something doesn't feel right."

She draped his other arm over her shoulders and held his wrist. He smelled coppery, of blood and offal. Bile rose in her throat. Straining, she tried to lift him. He was too heavy. The growling came nearer. Helen did not have the breath to scream.

"Stand," she wheezed. "Put your feet underneath you and stand."

The car was only a metre away. Lou grunted. Short-winded, leaning his weight on her, he finally got up, swaying. A sharp pain twanged low in Helen's spine. She tottered beneath his arm, dragging him to the car. *Please don't let me drop him.* At last, she was close enough to open the back door.

"Get in and lie down," she ordered through her teeth.

As if unconscious, he collapsed across the back seat. The makeshift bandage at his groin bulged. The cassowary stepped from the vegetation. Helen grabbed Lou's ankles and hoisted his legs into the car. Pain lanced her lower back. Slamming the door, she limped to the front seat and fell behind the wheel. She locked eyes with the cassowary. A wild, crazy hatred flew through her body.

You're dead, fucker.

She aimed the car and floored the accelerator. The tyres spun in the sand. Hissing, the bird raised itself to its full height, glaring through the windscreen, its irises as orange as fire. Helen eased off the pedal. The tyres found purchase. Her fingers squeezed the steering wheel. The car lurched forward.

The cassowary turned and ran.

Helen bumped and smashed through vegetation in pursuit.

By the time she reached the highway, the bird was gone, lost in that vast, green forest across the bitumen. She braked. The bloodlust drained away. Now she could feel the pain in her back and collarbone, the cuts in her feet, the tight and hot scald of her sunburnt skin, the hammering of her heart. She grabbed a mobile. Perhaps an ambulance could meet them halfway. She thumbed the buttons. A bland, recorded voice said, "You have dialled emergency Triple Zero. Your call is being connected."

"Babe?" Lou murmured. "I don't feel so good."

"Don't worry. Everything will be all right."

Pressing the phone to her ear, Helen steered one-handed onto the highway and stamped the pedal. The bitumen felt smooth and flat. The speedometer needle climbed. Lou uttered a moan. Helen tried not to cry. The Coral Sea winked through the trees, and the beach shone bright, as yellow as pineapple straight from the can.

Nocturnal Fury

Dr Constance Bain picked up a pen and notepad from the side table. "Tell me about your nightmares."

Tuesday Rossi opened her mouth to speak to the psychiatrist, but faltered. Her gaze darted about the consulting room. Chiaroscuro oil paintings in baroque frames hung from every wall. A casement window overlooked a garden. Fog and misting rain swirled in a grey soup beyond the panes.

At last, Tuesday said, "A skittering noise wakes me, like claws moving over the hardwood floor. I open my eyes. An old woman is at the foot of the bed. She's hunched over, with long grey hair. I can't move or scream."

"What happens next?"

"She climbs onto my bed and sits on me." Tuesday shuddered. "She smells awful, like dust and rotten eggs, like shit."

Something moved out of the corner of Tuesday's eye. On the window ledge sat a black and white cat, motionless, watching.

"Don't be alarmed," Dr Bain said. "It's only Popobawa."

"What kind of name is that?"

"It's Swahili. What does the old woman do once she perches on your chest?"

"Nothing. She looks at me, squinting, like she can't make me out."

"And that's all?" Dr Bain tipped her small, bird-like head to one side. "She doesn't touch you?"

"I think I'd piss my pants if she did."

"What else do you notice?"

"That everything in my bedroom is in its rightful place, not like in regular dreams where scenes are weird. My doctor says I'm having sleep paralysis."

Dr Bain smiled. "And what does that mean to you?"

"He told me that it's a waking nightmare." Sitting still had brought the fatigue to Tuesday's attention. Her bones seemed filled with concrete. "But it feels real to me. After I clenched my jaw so hard I broke a tooth, I knew I had to get help."

"Very good. How often do these attacks occur?"

Tuesday gave a little start. "Attacks?"

"Dreams. Do they occur every night?"

"No. About two or three times a week."

Dr Bain nodded, touched idly at the tight bun sitting high on her crown. The grey hair reminded Tuesday of her nightmares. She looked away. The cat on the window sill was gone.

"Some medicines can cause hallucinations or sleep disturbances," Dr Bain said. "Are you taking any drugs: prescription, over the counter, recreational?"

Tuesday shook her head.

"Ah, yes." Dr Bain made another note and then laid the pen and paper aside. Gazing at the ceiling, she took a long breath, and sighing softly, whispered, "When doomed to death, I will attend you as a nocturnal fury, and as a ghost, I will attack your faces with my hooked talons, and brooding upon your restless breasts, I will deprive you of repose by terrible visions."

Goosebumps prickled along Tuesday's arms.

"That's a quote from the works of Horace," Dr Bain said, "a Roman poet in the time of Augustus, first century B.C. People of all cultures throughout the ages have documented encounters with the Old Hag, or versions thereof."

"The old hag?"

"In English legend, hags are spirits of dead witches. An old hag enters your house through a keyhole and roosts in dark places such as under the bed. She sleeps by day and feeds by night."

"Feeds?"

"On a person's life force," Dr Bain said. "On your life force."

Tuesday felt a hot mottle spread across her face. "I want professional advice, not fairy tales."

"Yes, of course. Ask whomever you live with to maintain a vigil in your bedroom overnight. An eyewitness report may point us in the right direction. Sleep disorders are a common cause of sleep paralysis."

"I live by myself."

"Is there no one you could ask?"

Tuesday shrugged.

"I see." Dr Bain steepled her fingers. "I can prescribe tri-cyclic anti-depressants to curb REM sleep, which is when attacks are most likely to occur. There are side effects, and the medication is not a cure. It will also take weeks for the ingredients to take effect."

"Weeks?" Tuesday said. "All right. I guess that'll have to do."

A soft rain fell. Constance Bain stoked a fire in the consulting room. She sat in an armchair and looked through Tuesday Rossi's file, taking a sip every now and then from a generous glass of sherry. A faint hum, an internal noise, a droning of wasps started up within Constance's muscles. She checked her watch. It was time.

She took the pillbox from a pocket and dissolved the combined tablet of levodopa and carbidopa on her tongue. The medicine tasted like chalk. As time passed, the droning within her muscles fell away until it was gone.

Constance glanced up. The folds of the curtain shifted, minutely at first as if by a trick of the eyes, but as she continued to watch, the curtains writhed and slithered more vigorously, like a nest of cobras. She observed the familiar serpentine movements without interest. When she had started taking the Parkinson's medication, these hallucinations had frightened her. Not any more. They were a necessary evil. From experience, she knew that any attempt to stop the hallucinations by reducing the dosage would cause the return of debilitating tremors.

Also from experience, she knew what was coming next.

Constance stared at the cupboard door and waited. Over the murmur of rain came the squeak of hinges. Out of habit, Constance glanced at Popobawa, asleep on the couch. As if he had heard the squeaking sound too, the cat raised himself, hissing, fixing Constance with yellow eyes. Behind him, the cupboard door opened a sliver. Talons clutched the door and swung it open. A dark and hunch-backed figure hunkered close to the floor.

"Hello, old friend," Constance said.

Arching, the cat poured himself in a single motion from the couch and fled the room. The dark shape bobbled its head, shifted on its haunches. Constance finished the glass of sherry in a single swallow.

"This one and no more," Constance said. "We have to stop."

She put the empty glass on the table and crossed her arms. The dark figure retreated into the cupboard and shut the door behind it, slipping back its talons before the latch clicked. Constance took off her glasses and rubbed at her eyes. She waited a long time with her eyes shut. When she looked again, the curtains hung lifelessly, once again two inert sheets of fabric.

"The pills don't work," Tuesday said.

God, she felt groggy, bone-tired. Last night's dream or attack or whatever it was had left her unable to go back to sleep. Today at the office, she had mislaid paperwork, forgotten to return calls. The world seemed to be lurching as if she were drunk in a hammock.

As Dr Bain made notes, Tuesday looked about the consulting room. There were many side tables. And so many lamps, a ridiculous amount, in fact: a dozen or so. Maybe Dr Bain was a collector. Or maybe she was afraid of the dark too.

"Why do you specialise in sleeping disorders?" Tuesday said.

"I'm interested in how the brain works once the unconscious takes over."

"Have you got other patients like me?"

Dr Bain took a sharp breath. "I've had three, in fact."

"Were they cured?"

"One of them is able to manage the condition, yes."

"And the other two?"

Dr Bain hesitated. Tuesday felt a quiver of anxiety. A movement caught the tail of her eye, startling her. The black and white cat padded across the room.

Dr Bain said, "I can remove Popobawa if you like."

"No, it's okay, as long as he doesn't jump on me."

The cat slipped beneath Tuesday's armchair. She had not expected that. Her ankles were bare, exposed between shoes and trouser hems. The flesh crept, anticipating the touch of claws, of teeth. She fought the urge to draw up her legs.

"Don't be concerned," Dr Bain said. "You're not a child and Popobawa is not a monster under your bed."

Tuesday flushed. "What about the other two patients like me? If they didn't get cured, what happened to them?"

Dr Bain removed her glasses. She looked old and pale. Finally, she said, "Have you heard of Sudden Unexplained Nocturnal Death Syndrome? Healthy adults with no history of disease pass away in their sleep. Medical science can't offer a reductive explanation. The Laotian Hmong population in the United States is especially prone."

"Let me guess. They blame the old hag?"

"A similar being they call Dab Tsog. A comparable phenomenon occurs across Asian countries. Some African communities protect themselves with Koran pages worn against the body. In Arabian countries, they call this entity Ya Thoom."

"These are folk tales," Tuesday said. "What does superstition have to do with your two patients?"

But she had already guessed, and her stomach churned. Momentarily, she fretted about the cat that she could not see. She shifted her feet, glanced across the rows of lamps, felt the nauseating slew of vertigo. God help me, she thought.

Dr Bain said, "Both patients died."

"Died how?"

"The autopsies were inconclusive. I have my own theory: obstructive sleep apnoea, undiagnosed at the time. Of course, there is no way to prove that after death."

The cat streaked across the room and out the door, giving Tuesday a fright. Uncharacteristically, she wanted to cry. She set her teeth instead.

"I have a suggestion," Dr Bain said. "A sleep trial. With your permission, I'll come to your house and watch you overnight for any signs of a sleep disorder."

Constance Bain placed her laptop on the blanket chest at the foot of Tuesday's bed, and aimed its camera at the pillows. Tuesday stood by, looking uncomfortable and embarrassed in flannel pyjamas.

"So that's it?" Tuesday said.

"Correct. I'll sit all night in your kitchen, monitoring you from my phone. Don't switch off the nightlight." Constance went to leave the room and paused. "I would wish you pleasant dreams, but unfortunately, that would defeat the purpose."

Constance shut the door. In the kitchen, she placed her phone in its stand on the table. The droning came from far away. She left it for as long as she could bear. A thousand angry wasps began to vibrate along the muscles of her arms and legs, fidget within her torso. She took her tablet. The wasps rose up, agitated. Finally, they started to weaken and withdraw.

She glanced at her phone. Its grainy image showed Tuesday in bed, mouth dropped open as if in deep sleep. Constance took the brush from her handbag and padded on stockinged feet to the bathroom. There, she unpinned the bun and finger-combed her hair so that it fell about her shoulders. The droning had gone.

As she brushed her hair from root to tip, firmly and methodically, the vertical blinds hanging behind the bath started to bunch and move. She did not look at them directly. Instead, she kept eye contact with herself in the mirror. The vertical blinds moved in her peripheral vision, each slat rising up like a cobra, swaying from side to side, as if to strike.

It was time to enter Tuesday Rossi's bedroom.

Tuesday's eyes flew open.

The silence ticked on. She held her breath and kept listening. The noise sounded again: the flitting of claws against wood, toes skimming without weight over the floorboards, scritching across the room towards her.

Dr Bain, she wanted to yell.

Sweat broke out.

The old hag approached. Awkwardly, with a great flapping of arms, the hag lifted up and alighted on the bed. The stink made Tuesday want to retch. Crabbing along the blankets, hands tucked beneath her sagging tits so that her bent arms resembled wings, the hag finally reached Tuesday's chest and rested there.

One of Tuesday's teeth cracked, then another.

The hag leaned in, grey hair falling forwards to whisk against Tuesday's face, their noses almost touching. The hag unfolded both arms with a dry rustle. The hands, unnaturally thin and long, dropped to the blankets and began to crawl.

"This is the last and no more," a voice whispered.

Was that Dr Bain? Was the psychiatrist in the room?

Cold fingers settled around Tuesday's throat and began to squeeze.

Gasping, Tuesday stared into unblinking irises, yellow as gold, and for a confused moment, recognised Dr Bain.

The crushing grip on Tuesday's throat pounded the blood inside her skull.

She could no longer breathe.

No, I'm just having a nightmare, she thought. To struggle would be pointless. Surely, Dr Bain would soon wake her. This dream was nothing but a deadfall in her unconscious mind. She had merely slipped into it, and would eventually climb out the other side, cured and at peace, ready to enjoy at last the untroubled sleep of the dead.

Closing her eyes, Tuesday surrendered.

A Haunting in Suburbia

A Barry Manilow song, tinny and faint, broke into his sleep. Leonard rolled over and switched off the clock-radio alarm. He squinted at the red numerals: 3.08 a.m. What the hell? Propping himself on an elbow, he checked the alarm, which was set as usual for 6.45 a.m. A loose wire, maybe? He scrubbed his hand over his face, groaned, and dropped back to the pillow. Just go to sleep, he told himself.

He snapped open his eyes and listened. Other electrical devices had come alive throughout the house.

The wall-mounted air con in the bedroom whirred and fell silent. From the kitchen, the pump for the fish tank clicked sporadically. The oven timer was making that weird buzzing noise it always made after a blackout, when only cycling manually through its modes from *cook time* to *clock* would stop it. A brownout must have occurred. In the morning when he backed the Volkswagen from the driveway, he would no doubt spot a frazzled possum lying beneath the power lines.

Sighing, Leonard got out of bed. He could just see his wife, Tanya, with her mouth dropped open, snoring gently. She must be more tired than usual to sleep through this racket, and for a moment, he felt resentful. He had a full schedule today. Then again, he reminded himself, so did Tanya with the children.

He padded down the hallway in his boxer shorts.

Thanks to the moon glowing through the bay window, he could see well enough to fix the oven timer. The aquarium pump had righted itself. He glanced around the kitchen. Everything else was fine. Lord, these tiles were freezing. He should have worn slippers. The house felt colder than usual. On his way back to bed, he would check the thermostat.

A loud hiss and a flare of light made him jump.

In the lounge, the TV had come on and selected an empty channel of static.

Goose bumps rose across Leonard's chest and arms.

Snatching up the remote, he pressed the off button. Now the house seemed too dark and very quiet. The word *stealthy* came to mind. He groped for a light switch. The halogen bulbs winked and wavered, emitting a strange yellow luminescence. He watched them, his breath held, and his heart beating hard. If they went out, he knew he would be scared, as mindlessly scared as a dog in a thunderstorm. But the lights recovered and shone their usual clear white. With some reluctance, he flipped the switch and stood motionless, waiting for his vision to adjust to the darkness, listening to the silence. Finally, he blew out his breath, embarrassed.

On the way back to bed, he checked on the kids. Both slept deeply, which was odd, considering he had tramped from one end of the house to the other, stepping on every goddamned floorboard that creaked. Usually, he and Tanya could not sneak a piss in the ensuite without one of them calling out. He got into bed.

Sleep would not come.

The ceiling bothered him.

As time passed, he became more and more convinced.

Something was on the other side of the plasterboard.

Telling himself to grow up, that he was forty-two years old for God's sake, did not help; the queasy, fluttering churn of his guts told him that some kind of *thing* lay quiet and watchful in the roof space. Meanwhile, his family slept on, undisturbed. At 6.45 a.m., an Aretha Franklin song began to play through the clock-radio. On cue, Oliver cried and wailed in his cot. Four-year old Chelsea ran down the hall and threw herself across Tanya.

"I dreamt about magical monsters," Chelsea said.

"Did you? That's nice." Tanya turned a bleary eye towards

Leonard. "How was your sleep?" she said.

"Fine."

"Here, go to Daddy." Tanya moved their daughter to the middle of the bed. "I need to get Oliver before he screams the house down."

Chelsea flung her arms around Leonard's neck and kissed his stubbled cheek.

"Yuck," she said, "your breath smells gross."

"So does yours."

"Does not."

He smiled despite his fatigue. "Does too."

For some reason, the ceiling appeared benign now that his family was awake.

It was the first Friday in June, the third day of winter, but due to Melbourne's unseasonably warm autumn, most of the leaves remained on the trees. Ten minutes after getting out of bed, Leonard, now wearing a tracksuit and trainers, exited the back door and whistled. Duke, their three-year old German shepherd, bounded from his kennel, his tongue lolling in a big, doggy grin.

"Come here, mate," Leonard said, and scruffled Duke's ears. "Ready? Huh?"

The dog leapt and panted.

Leonard jogged the path through the yard, lifting his knees high to warm up. Duke dashed to the gate and waited, tail wagging. The air pinched Leonard's nose. He opened the gate. Duke bolted. Their house, along with twelve others in the street, backed onto a sports oval that was lined with gum trees, had a modest pavilion on the far side, and goal posts. What it did not have, however, was patronage. There had not been a local footy or cricket club here for years. Leonard occasionally rang the council to complain about youths lingering at the pavilion, smoking and drinking, or else riding their bikes over what remained of the grass. No action was ever taken. A sign forbade dogs, but since the council did not give a shit about the youths, Leonard did not give a shit about the sign.

Duke broke into a dash. The oval lacked a running track but had a circumference of compacted dirt. Leonard set the timer on his watch for twety minutes and started off at a slow pace until his hamstrings felt elastic and a spring came to his Achilles tendons. Near the cricket pitch, a quartet of magpies warbled and pecked. Duke bolted at them. It seemed as if the birds would stand their ground but just before Duke was amongst them, they took flight and landed a few metres behind. This tactic confounded the dog. Leonard smiled. Duke was loyal, but dumb as a plank.

Leonard opened his stride, running now. Breath plumed from his mouth. He scrolled through his mental checklist for the day: advising three landlords via email that their tenants were in arrears; booking an NBN installation at a duplex where the builders had neglected to connect both units; attending a property with a Court Sheriff and a locksmith to secure the premises on behalf of a ripped-off landlord; arranging the landscaping of a vacated property for an open house next week. At least he did not have to attend court. God, his head felt woolly after such a bad night's sleep. His thoughts momentarily slipped into treacherous territory—stealthy house, watchful ceiling—but he pulled them back.

Duke stopped chasing the magpies and began sniffing at the grass. Was that a vent of steam rising from the ground? Leonard strayed from the track and ran over. What he saw perplexed him and made him kneel down for a closer look.

Some kind of gemstone; that was his initial thought.

Duke nuzzled at his side, whining. Leonard pushed the dog away, hesitated, and then poked a finger experimentally into the divot. The gemstone felt smooth and warm. Nothing terrible happened. Emboldened, he pulled out the object and rubbed it against his tracksuit pants, buffing away the dirt. Then he held it up.

The object, about the size of his palm, appeared to be metallic, or perhaps glass, and gleamed like an opal yet it was hotter than skin temperature. Leonard figured that soil must hold heat, just like it holds water. He lifted the object to the sky and looked through it. How beautiful: so many swirling and delicate patterns, so many whorls within whorls. The object had an uneven edge, obviously smashed, but the edge felt blunt and rounded, like melted glass. He noticed other pinpoints of steam all around; so there were more pieces. But pieces of what?

A meteorite?

Perhaps these shards had landed last night, broken up by the meteorite's fiery passage through the atmosphere. And meteorites contain metal, which would explain the electrical disturbances. He spent the rest of his run-time gathering the other pieces. Meanwhile, Duke ran laps but occasionally came back to circle him. The pockets of Leonard's pants and jacket soon bulged and dragged with stone. The pieces were much heavier than they appeared.

"All right, let's go home," he called, and the dog looked at him, its head on one side, an ear folded over.

In the kitchen, Chelsea, already dressed, nibbled toast inside the crusts, while Tanya in a stained wrap spooned oatmeal into Oliver's dribbling mouth. Strapped into the highchair, Oliver flung his arms about like a crazed conductor.

Tanya glanced up. "How did you go?"

"Great," Leonard said, dragging out a chair. "Guess what I found on the oval?"

"Dried-up dog poo," Chelsea said.

"No, you little dope; something much better."

"A million dollars," Tanya suggested with a wry smile.

Oliver piped up, "Juice," one of the few words in his repertoire.

Leonard reached into his pocket, took out a chunk of stone, and turned it around and around in his fingers while it caught the light. "Look. It's gorgeous, right?"

Even Tanya seemed interested. "What is it?"

"Unicorn poo," Chelsea said with authority.

"No, come on, it's got nothing to do with poo," Leonard said, and emptied his pockets, even putting a chunk onto the tray of Oliver's highchair. "It's a meteorite."

"A meatier what?" Chelsea asked.

"A rock from outer space," he said. "It broke up and landed in the oval."

"Gosh. Did it hit our house too, Daddy?"

Hmm, he had not thought of that. But rocks smashing through terracotta roof tiles would have made a god-almighty noise, right? He noticed that Oliver was chewing on his piece of meteorite, and took it away. The boy's lip crumpled.

"Nothing from outer space hit our house," Leonard said.

"Well, that's weird," Chelsea said. "It hits the oval but not us. Lucky, hey?"

Leonard could not answer. The rocks dragged in his pockets. Oliver bawled.

Looking exhausted, Tanya stood. "Hon, you ready for breakfast?"

He nodded. She made him an espresso at the coffee machine, and then went to the stove to prepare his regular fry-up of eggs, bacon and tomato.

In typical big sister fashion, Chelsea waved a clump of meteorite at Oliver, who cried when she would not let him grab it. Outside, Duke paced the patio. The time was 7.28 a.m. Leonard glanced at the ceiling. It looked ordinary. Everything was fine. He had let his imagination run away with him last night. That's all.

He would call a museum on Monday. Surely, finding a meteorite was a big deal.

Leonard yawned through his day at the office. At home after dinner, he took a beer into his study and locked the door. As usual, he was pretending to work but was actually watching porn with headphones on. The video had just reached a particularly interesting part when Leonard knew, with a sickening conviction that flooded him with adrenaline, that he was no longer alone inside this small, locked room. Some *thing* was behind him, millimetres away, staring at the back of his neck.

He flung the headphones and nearly fell in his panic to turn around.

Nothing, there was nothing there. Just the leather armchair, the filing cabinets piled with dusty issues of *Elite Agent* magazine.

Calm down. Yet his nervous system would not relax. His nervous system knew better. Carefully, he scanned the room. The air looked different somehow; viscous and hefty.

His mind grappled for an explanation and came up with *ghost*.

Fumbling, he stopped the video, deleted the browser history, and flung open the door. Now that he was standing in the hall, the oppressive atmosphere was gone. He waited for his booming heart to slow. From the lounge, he could hear Chelsea giggling at The Powerpuff Girls. Tanya was at the other end of the house, giving Oliver his bath, singing as Oliver crooned along in his baby babble, not a lullaby but Adele's latest hit. The dishwasher clunked and whooshed. It seemed to be a normal Friday night. See? Leonard wiped sweat from his brow.

Carefully, he gazed into the study. At first, it appeared normal, but no, no. The colours were hyper-saturated, the air pregnant as if carrying a clear gelatinous presence, largely invisible. Then the presence—the ghost—retracted back through the ceiling and was gone. The shock of it took his breath. Lord, there was a ghost living in the ceiling. He knew it. He knew it as surely as the faces of his wife and children, and his guts churned. Teeth clenched, he rushed down the hall.

"Where are you going, Daddy?" Chelsea cried. "What's the matter?"

Ignoring her, Leonard strode through the lounge, into the family room, and straight to the door that opened to the garage. The stepladder leant against the brick wall. Snatching it up, he hurried back through the house.

"Daddy?" Chelsea said, the TV forgotten. "What are you doing?"

"Be quiet and watch your show."

"Leonard?" Tanya called, who must have heard the exchange.

But there was no time to answer stupid questions. He shoved open the door to the laundry, and set up the ladder beneath the manhole. Next, he retrieved the torch from the kitchen cupboard. He gripped the ladder's handrail, and put his foot on the first step. His guts cramped into a tight knot. You can do this, he thought. *Do it.*

"Is something up there?"

He looked around. Chelsea was standing behind him in the hall, her face set.

Leonard tried to smile. "Course not, sweetie. It's nothing."

"Tell me," she said. "What's up there?"

"A possum."

Chelsea regarded him solemnly. He felt himself blush.

Tanya yelled, "Can someone please tell me what's going on out there?"

Without breaking eye contact, Chelsea called, "Daddy wants to check the roof for possums." Giving him a hurt look, she turned on a slippered heel and headed back towards the TV and The Powerpuff Girls.

He opened the manhole, scaled the ladder, and poked his head and shoulders into the roof space. It was dark and cold, draughty, with a strong smell of timber and dust. He turned on the torch. There were insulation batts, cobwebs, old rat baits, the desiccated remains of leaves that had blown in through the tiles over the years. Leonard began to feel foolish. What had he expected to see? A ghoul dragging a chain? He aimed the torch into the far corner of the roof space and the torch went out.

The fright of it gave him a stabbing chest pain. He swung the torch away and the beam returned. Shit, just a loose battery. He aimed once more at the far corner. Once more, the torch went out.

An icy dread settled around him. Slowly, he began to move the torch in a methodical arc from left to right and back again. Whenever the beam was about to alight on the far corner, it would flick off, then flick on a moment later. This was not his imagination. And there was nothing wrong with the torch. The ghost was stopping the beam in order to remain hidden in the dark.

Now what?

Leonard jumped from the ladder, hurried to the garage, and retrieved the fluorescent lamp and an extension cord. In the laundry, he plugged in and switched on the lamp, flinching at the dazzling 300-watt white light. Grimly, he scaled the stepladder.

As soon as he got the lamp into the roof space, the tube went out.

Sweat popped across his body, chilling him.

Suddenly he did not want to have his head sticking up into this dark space, where he could not see if some *thing* was crawling towards him, preparing to touch him. He ducked down, replaced the manhole cover, turned off the lamp, and paused, trying to think.

Tanya approached. Held on her hip was Oliver, wrapped in a towel with his blonde hair tousled and damp. She looked at Leonard and her face showed concern.

"Hon, what's up?" she said. "You look like you've seen a ghost."

He laughed. "I'm fine."

"Do we need to call somebody? A pest control company?"

He laughed harder as the 'Ghostbusters' song lyrics came to mind. Then he said, "No, everything's all right. I made a mistake. There aren't any possums."

Tanya studied him dubiously. "Well, okay, if you say so."

He sat in the study, biting his fingernails. Their house was indeed haunted, but how? He and Tanya had built it off the plan some eight years ago, so there were no skeletons in the closet, no murders committed by previous owners. And the estate used to be a brickworks factory, not a cemetery or ancient burial ground… It occurred to him that his knowledge of hauntings came solely from the movies. He Googled, 'How to tell if your house is haunted', and clicked the first link. Slamming doors, disembodied footsteps, cabinets opening and closing by themselves; no, no and no. But apparently, children and pets were particularly sensitive to ghosts.

Yet Oliver did not seem perturbed. When Leonard tucked his son into his cot, the child settled down happily, content and relaxed, clutching his stuffed toy rabbit. Perhaps Oliver was too young to sense the paranormal.

Later, when tucking in Chelsea, Leonard said casually, "You haven't noticed anything funny around here lately, have you?"

"Funny like what?"

"Oh, I don't know." He gazed at her bookshelves, her collection of dolls on the bedside table, unsure of how to proceed. "Strange noises or odd things happening."

She put a solicitous hand on his. "Daddy, are you okay?"

He blushed. "Of course I am, little petal."

"Then why did you lie? You weren't really looking for possums."

"Hush, forget all that. A daddy never lies. Sweet dreams. Now give me a kiss."

Before he retired to bed, he went out on the patio and coaxed Duke from the kennel. He led the dog to the far end of the house where the ensuite to the master bedroom was situated, to the corner where the torch kept snuffing out. He stopped and watched Duke. Meanwhile, Duke sat down, tail thumping softly against the lawn, gazing up at him quizzically. Leonard began to feel ridiculous.

"Can you smell anything, boy?" he whispered. "See anything?"

"Hon, what are you doing out there?" Tanya called from the back door.

"Nothing. Duke got out of his kennel, and I just wanted to see why."

Tanya retreated inside.

Sighing, Leonard regarded Duke, and whispered, "Fat lot of good you are."

Leonard slept badly that night. The electrical devices behaved as normal, but he could not shake the creepy sensation of being watched, studied, *observed* by that *thing* hiding in the roof. The sensation made him sweat. Occasionally, he batted the air above his face with both hands, expecting to feel a viscosity, an otherworldly resistance. The bedroom was too dark to reveal if anything gelatinous and transparent was hanging from the ceiling, but he knew it was there somewhere, and thanks to Google, he knew it was ectoplasm, a physical manifestation or exudation of a ghost.

Nothing like this had ever happened to him before. A rational man, a logical thinker, an agnostic, he had never seen an apparition or believed a ghost story; had never spotted a UFO, did not consider cryptids such as Bigfoot to be real, and thought anyone who believed in ESP, little green men or the paranormal to be simple or naive.

So what the hell was actually going on here?

And why was no one else in the family affected? Not even the dog?

The most reasonable answer: Leonard was going mad.

But how did that explain the behaviour of the torch and the fluorescent lamp? Had he imagined that too, perhaps?

No. Some *thing* was up there in the roof. And tomorrow, he would expose it. He knew exactly what to do. His plan comforted him enough so that he fell asleep.

Saturday morning began like most other days, with Oliver bawling from his cot, and Chelsea running down the hall and flinging herself across Tanya. Leonard, exhausted, felt as if he were dragging himself out of molasses.

"Guess what?" Chelsea said. "I dreamt of magical monsters again."

That braced him, quick smart. "What did they look like?" he said.

"Like monsters, silly."

"Go to Daddy," Tanya said, and got up. "Don't forget we're off to the mall straight after breakfast."

Damn. Leonard *had* forgotten. "Why are we going again?" he said.

"You already know why." Tanya counted the reasons on her fingers. "Shoes for the kids, pyjamas for Oliver, birthday presents for your mother—the nail-spa stuff, the moselle, ginger chocolates—remember? And coffee beans. Suits from the dry cleaners..."

"Sorry, I can't go," he said.

"Oh no, come on, you told me you'd give me a hand this time."

"Daddy, they're *your* coffee beans," Chelsea said reproachfully, "and *your* mother and *your* suits."

"But I have to do something important."

Tanya huffed and stamped down the hall, muttering, "For Christ's sake."

"Now you've upset Mummy," Chelsea said. "Good job."

"She'll be all right."

They could hear Tanya in Oliver's room, chatting with him softly, as his crying hitched and stopped.

"How come you don't want to come to the mall?" Chelsea said. "You promised me a cheeseburger and a milkshake."

"Mummy can buy those."

"Is it because of the possum?"

Leonard stared at her carefully. Perhaps his daughter had sensed something after all, but lacked the maturity to express it.

"Tell me about the monsters in your dream," he said.

"Um, I can't remember," she said, sliding from the bed. "Make me scrambled eggs? On a muffin, though, not toast. I absolutely hate toast."

"But you ask for toast every morning. You had it yesterday."

Instead of answering, she raced down the hall.

Leonard rubbed at his bleary eyes and stared up at the ceiling. The ceiling stared back. He took a deep, steadying breath. Not long now, he thought, and I'll expose you for what you are.

Duke loped around the patio, watching as Leonard carried the extension ladder through the garden to the far end of the house, to the corner that held the ensuite, and the ghost. Tanya had driven off with the children a few minutes ago, refusing to kiss him goodbye. Oh, well. She would get over it. She might pay him back by purchasing an expensive handbag, but she would get over it.

Leonard propped the ladder against the guttering.

A spasm of panic ran through him.

He paused and looked around the backyard. The reddened leaves on the Japanese maple were starting to shed, peeling off in every gust. Clouds dotted the blue sky. A wattle bird could not decide which side of the fence it wanted to face, and so kept hop,

hop, hopping as it clucked. A lawn mower droned nearby on the street. Duke, puzzled, watched him from the patio.

"It's all right," he told the dog. "No one in the history of the world ever got killed by a ghost. I just have to make sure I don't fall off the ladder."

Leonard climbed. The atmosphere felt more and more oppressive the higher he climbed until, by the time he reached the top, the skin on his arms and back had turned to gooseflesh. He took gloves from his pocket and put them on. Gently, so as not to break the terracotta, he removed the roof tiles one at a time, and stacked them. The ghost may have switched off the torch and the fluorescent tube, but let's see it turn off the goddamned sun. His smile felt mirthless and fake.

Finally, he cleared a hole in the roof about half a square metre. He took off his gloves. In his pocket he carried something idiotic: Chelsea's miniature bible, purchased a couple of years ago when Tanya decided to expose their toddler to 'spirituality'. Thankfully, the phase had not lasted; Tanya could not swallow the bullshit. And yet here Leonard stood, a grown man, hoping to protect himself with a kid's bible against, of all things, a ghost. Shame made him groan.

"I'm a stupid dickhead," he said to Duke. "I should have gone to the mall."

Then he heard it.

A scrabbling, scratching sound…

His blood chilled. The noises were coming from inside the roof. Leonard ducked his head into the hole. Duke whined. Whether the dog had finally sensed something amiss, Leonard could not tell. He was too busy staring at the monster.

The *monster*…

And yet, it was so small, the bluish-grey body about the size and shape of a hen's egg, with six legs and no visible eyes or mouth. The monster clenched into a little fist, like a startled huntsman spider.

Leonard tensed.

A swirl of thickened air appeared in front of the monster, wavering like a heat haze. A-ha, Leonard thought, there's the ectoplasm. But this *thing* was not a ghost. No, it was…

The realisation made him choke on a laugh of disbelief.

It was an *alien*.

A creature from outer space…

Oh, Christ, really? Leonard shook his head. Yes, really. The alien was sitting right *there,* within arm's length. Right there… He was staring at it, the miniature monster crunched up in a ball, as if frightened.

"Hey," he murmured, and tried to smile. "Hey, little mate. It's okay."

Could the alien understand him? Read his facial expressions? Leonard's mind raced. The shards buried in the oval were not from a meteorite, but a spaceship. The term 'spaceship' sounded ludicrous, but Jesus, its pilot was shivering not half a metre away from him, throwing out ectoplasm, or whatever the hell the substance was.

Leonard withdrew from the roof to seem less threatening.

The monster—alien—seemed to relax.

"Well, I'll be damned," Leonard said, and whistled. "You smell this, Duke?"

The dog, lying down on the patio, had his head in his paws, eyes closed.

"Greetings," Leonard said to the alien. "I come in peace."

He laughed and could not help it. The alien flinched at the sudden sound. Leonard held his breath and stayed very still. He should have brought a camera instead of a stupid bible. The alien clicked its spindly legs against the roof beam. Then the ectoplasm receded.

God almighty, an actual being from another world…

Leonard felt a crazed and wild joy. This might be the First Contact. He could well be the only human to have ever come face to face with an alien.

Upon reflection, this struck him as an anti-climax.

Surely, the First Contact would involve fleets of spacecraft crowding the skies, thousands of people crying and screaming in the streets. But that was movie lore again. This was something else. This was *reality*: a tiny, cowering alien that could fit in his hand.

Wait a minute.

If he had an alien, the world would pay to see it.

Forget a camera; Leonard should have brought a net up here. But why had his family sensed nothing wrong? A story from Chelsea's bible came to mind, something about a burning bush, which made Leonard think that while many are called, few are chosen. Was that a quote from the bible? In any case, the alien must have chosen *him*. Perhaps he could lure it with soft words and catch it. He leaned into the roof space and made kissing noises.

"Come on, come here," he murmured, offering his hand. "I won't hurt you."

The alien unclenched. It took a couple of hesitant steps closer on spiny legs.

Grinning, perspiring, feeling like the only Earthman alive, Leonard reached in to grab it. The alien lifted the front of its body like a snout to reveal a circular mouth lined with teeth. Leonard froze. *Holy shit*. The alien charged at great speed.

Dozens and dozens of identical aliens poured out of the shadows.

Leonard shrieked.

The frontrunners leapt. It felt like handfuls of gravel hitting his face. Slurping, the aliens latched on like snails. Leonard tried to dislodge them, raking with frantic and clawed fingers. They attacked his eyes; not with teeth but with a gritty, wet slurry that burned like acid. The pain was excruciating. He toppled from the ladder.

His initial thought was for Tanya, Chelsea and Oliver.

His next thought was the fervent hope that the fall would break his neck; that he would die before the aliens dissolved his eyeballs and sank into his brain.

It seemed to Leonard that he fell for a long, long time.

Griselda Gosh

Little Daughter was five years old and did not know about ventriloquist dolls so the thing sitting on the man's knee appeared to be a deformed child. Its limbs hung slack and its mouth, frozen into a toothy grin, clacked open and shut like a beak. Little Daughter groped blindly for Mother, but Mother was already holding hands with Big Daughter, and her free hand would not let go of her purse. Little Daughter hunched down in the seat.

Mother leaned over and whispered, "You watch every second. These tickets cost money. Now sit up straight."

Little Daughter sat up but instead of looking at the stage, she looked around. There were mothers and grandmothers and children of all ages laughing and clapping. Little Daughter peeked at the stage. The thing propped on the man's knee was swiveling its oversized head from side to side and singing in a thin, high squeal, "Cock-a-doodle-do, my dame has lost her shoe; my master's lost his fiddling stick and doesn't know what to do."

The man on the stage mugged at the audience and said, "Hang on just a minute, Griselda Gosh, exactly who is fiddling with what stick?" and the mothers and grandmothers and children started laughing again. The reflection of the stage lights gave their rapt faces a shining yellow cast.

Mother hissed, "I won't tell you again. Now watch the goddamned show."

The thing shrilled, "A-who and a-what stick? Oh don't ask me, Mr Patterson, I'm nothing *but a blockhead!*"

And on cue, the audience shouted in unison, "Uh-oh! Whoops-a-daisy!", so loud that Little Daughter jumped. The thing's jaw fell open as if a wire had been cut. A square patch of scalp on its woolly blonde head flew open like a hatch. Little Daughter sucked in a great draught of air and screamed and screamed and screamed.

The man on stage leapt to his feet. The thing dangled dead from his hand. Little Daughter screamed harder. The audience scrambled, turning to her, pointing, staring, gasping, and Mother slapped her and yelled, "Stop it, stop it," but the screams would not stop, even as Mother dragged her out of the theatre by her arm.

Outside in the red velvet foyer, nine-year old Big Daughter smirked and Little Daughter ran out of screams. Mother dug her fingers into Little Daughter's shoulder and shook her, rattling her teeth, and said, "How dare you embarrass me like that."

A startled face appeared behind the candy counter, a teenage boy's gaped mouth and popped eyes. Mother towed Little Daughter through the double doors and onto the street. The sunshine blazed sharp as a headache. Little Daughter began to howl. People in the car park looked over.

"Oh that's right; keep it going," Mother said. "Make everyone think I'm the worst mum that ever lived, why don't you?"

At dinner, Little Daughter had to sit at the table with an empty plate while Mother and Big Daughter ate lamb chops, mash and peas. Big Daughter kept looking over and sniggering. Little Daughter wanted to take hold of the knives and forks and poke out her sister's eyes.

"Get that angry look off your face," Mother said. "Right now or you can go stand in the broom cupboard for a while. How would that be?"

Little Daughter said, "I want Daddy."

"Well, too bad, he's working on the road."

Little Daughter thought of *Ontheroad* as a town: with many iron-latticed bridges spanning a river that teemed with fish and paddleboats. The last time she had seen Daddy, a long time ago, she had sat on his lap while he told her that his visit home was only brief, that he would be gone and working *Ontheroad* again before breakfast, before Little Daughter was awake. She pictured the two of them walking along the riverbank while a family of ducks cleaved a V-shape through the water. She put her arms around his neck and said, "Take me with you."

"Oh no, working *Ontheroad* is no place for a young girl."

"Please, Daddy."

"You wouldn't like it, it's no fun, believe me. It's better that you're here with your mother and sister." And Daddy had smiled and kissed her.

Now, Mother took the dinner plates to the kitchen sink. Little Daughter's stomach rumbled.

"You can do your homework," Mother said to Big Daughter, who pushed off from the table and sauntered into the living room. "And *you*," Mother said. "You can go straight to bed, and think about how horrible and mean you were today."

It was still light outside but the bedroom curtains were drawn. The dark held images of Griselda Gosh. Little Daughter hugged her teddy bear and pulled the sheet over her head.

Much later, when the light had faded from around the curtains, Big Daughter came into the room and climbed into the other single bed. Mother tucked her in and left. As soon as the door closed, Big Daughter scrunched the doona cover and whispered, "Hey, did you hear that? It's Griselda Gosh and she's coming for you."

When Little Daughter fell asleep, she dreamed of falling through an open hatch into blackness, into nothing.

The next day when the girls came home from school, there was a rectangular box sitting on the kitchen table. Little Daughter could not read the writing on the sides but she hung back. Stamped along the box were cartoon images of a goofy grinning face with yellow braids.

Flushed and happy, Mother put down her wineglass, flung

out her arms and said, "Surprise! I went shopping today. Go ahead and open it. It's for the both of you."

Big Daughter reached into the box and pulled out Griselda Gosh.

Little Daughter knew the sorts of things that would be coming next and wanted to run and run but she had nowhere to go and could not manage her buttons or shoelaces by herself.

Mother said, "Isn't she great? It's a replica, of course; not the real thing. But I just love her cowgirl outfit. Look at the fringe on her skirt."

"She's perfect." Big Daughter kissed the doll then held it out to Little Daughter. "Now it's your turn." She took a step closer.

Little Daughter took a step back.

Griselda Gosh had bulging and lidless eyes with whites that showed all the way around the painted irises. The baby-pink lips were pulled back over two rows of tiny white teeth.

"Go on," Mother said. "I spent a lot of money on that doll. Do as your sister tells you. Give Griselda a kiss."

Little Daughter shook her head. No one spoke or moved. The sound of Mother's breath moving in and out of her nose got louder and louder.

Then Mother snatched up Griselda Gosh and thrust it into Little Daughter's face, demanding that she kiss it, *kiss it*, go ahead and kiss the goddamned doll, while Little Daughter stumbled and flailed. She bumped her head somehow and ended up on the hallway floor. Mother hauled her back to the kitchen. Big Daughter watched with cool green eyes.

Mother said, "I do my best to make you happy, and I've had it. I tell you, I've had it up to *here* with you."

Mother opened the broom cupboard and shoved her inside and shut the door. Little Daughter fell in the darkness against the stack of toilet paper and hit her head on the wall. Broom bristles like spiders whiskered at her ankles.

"Is it lonely in there? Well, is it, you bad girl?"

The door opened a crack and Griselda Gosh flew in. Mother slammed the door as the oversized head smacked into Little Daughter's chest. The body rustled and tumbled down to her feet. Little Daughter jumped and kicked but Griselda Gosh would not stop touching her.

"Now stay in there until I tell you otherwise."

Later, Little Daughter heard canned laughter. The cupboard door opened when she pushed it, and she stepped out. Mother and Big Daughter would be sitting in the living room watching television. On the floor of the cupboard lay Griselda Gosh, her skinny limbs in an untidy sprawl and her head angled into a corner.

Little Daughter whispered, "I tell you, I've had it. I've had it up to *here* with you."

From the wardrobe in the master bedroom, she got one of Daddy's golf clubs. Back in the kitchen, she hooked the putter around Griselda Gosh and dragged her out onto the tiles. She made sure the doll was looking at her and then raised the club. It whistled through the air as she brought it down.

The head cracked on the first blow. Little Daughter lifted the putter again. She had seen a smashed bird's egg before and expected Griselda Gosh's innards to be the same, a yellow and red pulse of custard. The cheek broke away on the second blow but there was nothing behind the shattered plastic, nothing at all. Little Daughter stared into the void.

Mother and Big Daughter came running and stopped. Like twins, their faces fell open in identical shock.

Big Daughter recovered first. "Oh no, my beautiful doll," she whined, clutching and plucking at Mother.

Mother's mouth hardened into a line. She took slow and deliberate steps towards Little Daughter. Big Daughter sat up on the kitchen bench, eyes shining.

Mother said, "Drop that golf club. Drop it right now."

Little Daughter squared her shoulders and set her teeth and tightened her grip on the handle, which made Mother hesitate.

But only for a second.

The Brightest Place

"Hugh, wake up."

Menaka was next to me in bed, running her cool fingers across my brow, through my sweaty hair. Just the sight of her brought such relief that tears stung my eyes. I held out an arm. She cuddled alongside me, her head on my chest.

"You had that dream again," she said.

"Did I talk in my sleep?"

"I wouldn't describe it as talking." Menaka lifted her head and stared at me. "You were making those weird noises, like an animal stuck in a trap."

I tried to smile. My lips trembled. Fear still had me by the throat. To calm myself, I looked around our bedroom, seeking and finding comfort in its familiarity. The linen, carpet, walls, ceiling; all were lilac, Menaka's favourite colour. The curtains hung open. Sunshine drenched the room. Perhaps sunshine triggered my nightmares? Beyond the window, a breeze moved through the Japanese maple, swaying the branches and shivering a thousand green leaves. I watched the tree for a long time. At last, my heart began to slow down.

"When we buy a house," I said, "I want a maple tree just like that one."

"But I like our apartment."

"It's not big enough for children."

"Children?" Menaka giggled, kissed my cheek, and then moved to straddle me. "We have to make them first."

I gazed into her eyes, the colour of milk chocolate, and held out my arms. She lowered her body onto mine and kissed me on the mouth. Every morning when I wake, I thank my lucky stars for Menaka. Some people live their whole lives without finding someone to love them. Their whole lives, from start to finish. That's difficult to comprehend.

Disembodied, I float within an intense white light, as bright as a burning ribbon of magnesium. Somehow, I'm not blinded. My heart pounds, yet I have no substance. I am a weightless blip, existing nowhere in time or space, a random electron.

Dark shapes begin to sweep in and out of my field of vision: looming, shifting, circling. My terror is a kind of drawn-out suffocation. I can't move. The light no longer resembles burning magnesium. Instead, it is a supernova swallowing me whole. The dark shapes are planets, similarly panicked, as desperate for life as I am. We are all moving inexorably toward oblivion. Each one of us fights for as long as we can, but only for as long as Fate allows. Mathematically, free will isn't possible. Time is a circle. Events have been decided already.

I blink hard. The shapes momentarily come into focus.

They aren't planets but heads.

Giant elongated heads bobbling on stalk-like necks, the heads of aliens. I am on a spacecraft. The aliens are touching me, doing things to me. Can I feel probes, tubes, slender instruments moving into my body, puncturing my skin? Or am I conjuring these dozens of small pains? It feels so real that I scream and scream.

"Hugh, wake up."

I told Menaka about the nightmare. She was next to me, the sheet tucked around her.

"It's a good sign," she said. "If the shapes get clear enough, you'll finally see what you're dreaming about."

"Aliens." I hesitated. "Real ones."

"Real aliens? Are you serious?"

"Everything is possible, or at least, conceivable."

She laughed. "I didn't think right-minded physicists believed in aliens."

"Hey, I'm just telling you what the shapes looked like, all right? Jesus."

She regarded me, frowning. "Do you honestly suppose that aliens are abducting you every night?"

I shrugged.

"Hugh, trust me," she said, stifling a grin. "They're not."

"Stranger things have happened."

"So they're floating you out the window? Come on, now. Don't you think I'd notice? We sleep holding hands."

Instead of answering, I scrubbed my knuckles over my unshaven cheeks. I could feel the skull beneath the skin, as if I'd lost weight.

"You're working yourself to the bone," she added. "Too many hours at the lab, that's the problem. It's not aliens you're dreaming about, but humans from the future. You're scared of making time travel a reality."

I gave a derisive snort. "Now, why would that scare me?"

"Your guess is as good as mine." Pouting, she stared at the maple tree. "But we can't go on this way. You can't continue these dreams night after night, over and over. Something has to happen. Something has to break."

A chill went through me. Menaka seemed to know that Fate was coming for us. I knew it too. Not in my mind but in my body, the way you can feel the approaching change of seasons with your eyes closed, by some invisible charge in the air. Novikov's Theorem states that in order for time travel to exist, free will cannot. As a physicist, I believe in Novikov's Theorem. But it means that all things in the universe must succumb to Fate, including Menaka and me. I didn't want us to succumb to anything. Not now, not ever.

Sliding across the mattress, I put my arm around her.

"Do you love me?" I whispered.

"Yes. Promise you'll never leave."

"Leave?" I touched her face. "I'd rather die."

"Don't say that. Just promise me."

"Okay, I promise."

Squeezing her eyes shut, she turned her cheek into my hand.

"What's wrong?" I said. "Tell me."

But I understood already. Somehow, we both stood on the edge of an unseen precipice, afraid of what lay on the other side, afraid of never seeing each other again.

The interior of the spaceship is so dazzling that it hurts my eyes. Aliens grab me, handle me. Their backlit heads appear human-shaped instead of elongated and otherworldly. They aren't aliens, I realise, but demons.

Desperate, I flail my limbs.

The demons gibber to each other as they clutch at me, scrabbling for a firm hold. I must be dead. What about Menaka? I have fallen over the precipice and left her behind. The demons want to drag me down into Hades. I fight them off.

Menaka, I shout, Menaka.

She hears me. Thank God, she hears me.

"Hugh, wake up."

Her cool hands reach into the light.

"A near-death experience?" Menaka turned over in bed to face me. "No chance. You're as healthy as an ox. Besides, you're a good man. Why would you go to Hell instead of Heaven?"

I knew why: for an attempted murder I hadn't yet committed.

As soon as I managed to build a working time machine, I would try to kill one of my grandfathers in his childhood. The Grandfather Paradox states that any change to history via time travel is impossible: by killing my grandfather, I'd prevent my own birth; ergo, I wouldn't exist to go back in time to kill him. I wanted to prove the self-consistency theorem. Oh, to be the first person in humankind to categorically show that the probability of making changes to history is zero…my name would live forever and ever.

As if reading my mind, Menaka said, "Your grandpas can't die in childhood. Stop looking for things that aren't there. It's just bad dreams."

I fussed with the pillow. Finally, I said, "Maybe not."

"Meaning what? Alternate universes?"

Sighing, I gazed at the maple tree. Sunshine glistened off its leaves. If only a bird would alight upon one of those branches. I hadn't seen a bird in quite a while.

Menaka continued, "Einstein's general theory of relativity doesn't allow for alternate universes. Our single universe resembles a curved hallway with entries and exits, like doors. Remember?"

Yes, I remembered. I'd explained it to her myself. You can't travel to another era unless that era has a pre-existing 'door' or time machine: the ultimate definition of paradox. I grappled with this mess of equations every day at the lab. Constant theoretical thinking must have loosened my grip on reality. Of course, there are no alternate universes. If there were, my work on time travel would be futile. Einstein would be wrong. Novikov would be wrong. Everett with his fanciful theories of alternate universes would be correct, and no physicist in their right mind would believe in that kind of comic-book stuff.

"Don't forget," Menaka said. "The universe is a hallway with doors."

She turned over, as if preparing for sleep despite the sunlight pouring into our bedroom. I stared at her glossy, dark tresses splayed out across the pillow. How many more days would I wake up and see her lying next to me in bed? Everything in life must eventually happen for the last time. Was this my last sight of her? I had no way of knowing.

None of us has any way of knowing.

Floating, I move forward. Shapes whisk past me like ghosts. Every part of me hurts. It seems that I am standing, perhaps walking. My bones are frail, light as fairy floss. If I squint, I can make out where I am: inside an infinite tunnel.

No, it's a hallway. Those dark, rectangular maws at regular intervals are doors.

My heart lifts. I can leave this terrifying dimension by stepping through a door and ejecting myself into another moment along the space-time continuum.

I lurch sideways. Nothing happens. Deviation from the current timeline is impossible. But why? With horror, it dawns on me that demons are holding both my arms. They intend to march me right down the middle of this endless corridor and past every single chance of escape. This is torture. I can only scream for Menaka.

"Hugh, wake up."

I opened my eyes. I was lying in bed. Outside the window, a shrieking wind rattled the bare branches of the maple. This confused me. Where were its leaves? My surroundings were cream instead of lilac, my bedroom huge instead of small. Unfamiliar noises rose all around me: voices, electronic beeps, the trundling of trolley wheels, footsteps on linoleum.

"Hugh, wake up."

I turned my head. An old woman I'd never seen before sat by my bed, holding my hand. She had tears in her eyes. I tried to pull away but didn't have the strength. I felt like I'd been swimming underwater for a long, long while.

"Hugh, are you awake?" she said, and gave a choked laugh. "He's awake again," she shouted to someone behind her. "Come quickly."

Half a dozen faces loomed over me at once. I flinched at the demons.

"Don't be afraid," the old woman said. "The nurses have to do their checks. Everything is all right."

I whispered, "Where am I?"

"Still in hospital. They had to tie you down. You kept ripping out your IV lines. But you're getting better every day. This morning, I helped you walk the corridor. Do you recall? You were actually out of bed and on your feet." Overwhelmed, the old woman ran a wet hanky beneath her eyes. "Oh, blessed is our Lord. Blessed is our Lord Jesus Christ. Amen."

"I need to get out of here," I said.

"You don't recognise me yet, do you? It's me, Hugh. It's Mum."

She squeezed my hand. My heart began to pound. The demons hovered and fussed and touched at me. The branches of the Japanese maple shook hard. It was hailing out there in this place, the ice sheeting in sideways and hammering the window. Across the room, an elderly man in a nightgown slumped against the edge of a bed, coughing and hacking into a kidney dish.

"Menaka?" I said. "Please wake me up. Menaka?"

The old woman patted my hand. "She's just a character in your story."

"What story?"

The old woman smiled gently. "The one you were writing."

"But I'm a physicist, not a writer. I live with Menaka. Our bedroom is lilac."

"Hugh, listen, you're a science journalist working on some kind of novel about time travel. You were riding your bike and got hit by a car." She hiccupped on a sob. "You've been in and out of a coma for nearly two months."

None of this was true. None of this had happened. I tried to recall my lab and drew a blank. Never mind. This was only a dream.

"Where's Menaka?" I said.

The old woman smoothed the hair back from my forehead. God, I hated this manifestation of the nightmare, but it wouldn't last. I merely had to close my eyes and wait it out. The noises in the room started to fade.

Menaka.

My beautiful Menaka…

I could feel her cool fingers across my brow already. Any moment now, I'd be home and safe. Any moment now…

Any moment…

"Hugh, wake up."

Angel Hair

The river overflowed a few times every year, but this time it was different. Amy woke often during that final night. She would startle as if from a bad dream, and listen to the sop and sigh of the floodwaters lapping against the house until her heart slowed and she could drowse again. The digital clock remained blank, meaning the house was still without electricity, but at sixteen years of age, she was not scared of the dark any more. When she woke and noticed daylight around the curtains, she sat up. Something was wrong. It took her a moment to figure it out.

The silence.

The utterly profound silence.

All the outside noises had gone. No bubble and burble of floodwater, which was a good thing, since it meant the river had receded and her parents, stranded at their butcher's shop in town, could now come home. But no sounds of traffic either, no Saturday morning music from the neighbour's house, no barking dogs or crowing roosters, no bird calls, no wind sighing through the trees. Amy got out of bed. The silence pressed around her, thickly, as if she were underwater.

She opened the curtains.

What she saw did not make sense.

The five acres of their rural property should be covered in autumn leaves, not snow. And when had it ever snowed in this part of Victoria? Not in Amy's lifetime. Yet the snow must have been a metre thick on the ground.

"Grandpa?" she called behind her. "Are you awake?"

He did not answer.

An early riser, perhaps he was downstairs already, out of earshot.

Amy stared again out the window. At first glance, yes, it had appeared to be snow, but now she was not so sure. Could it be fog? Some bizarre weather anomaly triggered by the flood? Her bedroom overlooked the fruit trees. They should be bare yet they were lost beneath a giant sheet, buried, an orchard of smothered white humps, row upon interlocked row. The gauze that stretched between each tree reminded Amy of the netting her parents would throw over the canopies in summer to keep the birds from pecking holes in the apricots and peaches. But that unnatural, pale mesh was not snow, fog or netting.

What the hell was it?

Amy's heart thumped. The pane must be dirty, tricking her eyes. She turned the latch and lifted the sash window.

Oh, God. The air smelled unwashed and musky, a complex mix of sweet, sour and rancid notes. Recoiling, pressing a hand against her nose and mouth, she went to shut the window. But then, against the clear and sharp blue of the sky, she saw them: a mess of long, dangling threads, each one finer than a human hair, glistening in the early morning light, twisting in the breeze, showering down by the thousands, by the hundreds of thousands, a silent rainstorm.

Transfixed, Amy watched.

It was an eerie, yet beautiful sight.

A raft of streamers blew in through the window. They swept over her, sticky and wiry. Insects, she just knew it, *shit*, they were moving over her. With a shriek, Amy slammed the window closed. She slapped and swiped at her face and hands, and ripped off her pyjamas, throwing them to the floor. She leaned in for a closer look. Countless spiders swarmed her pyjamas, so tiny that dozens might fit on a button. Alarmed, disgusted, Amy stamped the fabric, over and over.

Jesus.

Gasping, she pulled on a t-shirt and jeans. She had to find

Grandpa. Then she saw the closed window. The glass was frosted with silk, and crawling with spiders.

"Grandpa!" she yelled. "Where are you?"

"Downstairs."

She raced to the mezzanine. The door to her parents' bedroom stood open, the bed still unslept in and neatly made. She took the stairs two at a time. The ground floor stank of mould and swamp. She reached the kitchen. Her bare feet landed in a centimetre or so of cold floodwater. A muddy line along the walls showed the waters had peaked at knee-height. The ground floor was in disarray: the entry-table on its side, wet sofa cushions piled up against the front door, twigs and leaves thick over the boards, random shoes scattered like beached fish.

Grandpa stood up from the kitchen table and smiled, patting the air with both hands as if to shush her. "Everything is all right," he said. "It's only angel hair."

"Angel hair?"

"It happens sometimes after a flood. Instead of drowning, baby spiders throw out a line of web and float away on the wind like this, see?" He waved his hand through the air, wiggling his fingers. "It's a kind of migration. Now take a seat. I'll make you breakfast." He went to the stove and clicked the burner. "At least the gas still works. Omelette?"

She nodded, sat at the table, and looked out the back door, which was a sheet of glass set alongside a floor-to-ceiling window. Normally, she would see a brick path lined with Mum's rosebushes. Instead, there were billions of white, cross-hatching silk threads, and the wriggling black dots of the spiders that made them.

She said, "It looks like the end of the world."

"Not everything's a zombie apocalypse. Notice how quiet it is? The webbing soaks up the sound waves."

"It's creepy. I don't like it."

"No one said you had to." He cracked eggs into a pan and began to whisk. "If you think this is bad, you should have seen Esperance back in, oh, sometime in the nineties. I happened to be there on business. The angel hair covered about a hundred square kilometres, believe it or not. Spiders floated so high, they even got stuck on aeroplanes. But the webs were gone by next morning. Angel hair leaves the way it comes, like magic. You want herbs?"

"Okay," she said. Another drift landed against the glass. The spiders seemed intent, determined, angry. "When do you think we'll hear from Mum and Dad?"

"As soon as the landline comes back on, I expect. They're probably staying at the motel and having a grand old time."

Amy did not reply. Her mobile was dead too. She and Grandpa were cut off. The pile of silks and spiders against the glass was growing higher. She became aware of a strange noise coming from all around; a flittering against the roof, walls and windows, a whisper that seemed to be getting louder.

Grandpa put the omelette in front of her, with a knife and fork.

"Are we going to be okay?" she said.

"Sure we are. Now tuck in."

She ate but mechanically, hardly noticing each mouthful. Angel hair piled up on the door and window like snowflakes driven by the wind, yet there was no wind. She watched Grandpa lean against the servery bench and stare at the phenomenon. He began to frown, gnaw at his lips. Amy's stomach tightened. Finally, he took his glasses from his shirt pocket and put them on.

"Look at that," he said, jolting, and pointed a finger. "You see that?"

He was pointing at the frame around the back door. Yes, she saw it. The house was old, had settled over the years, and the doors and windows did not fit squarely within their frames. Gaps that let in the draughts were now letting in the spiders. Webbing bulged and foamed. Scores of little arachnids broke away from the foam and eddied on their long, cotton-like strands across the kitchen. They were floating towards Amy and Grandpa.

Grandpa took the fly spray from the pantry. "Cover your omelette."

He fired a stream of fly spray around the door and window

frames. The chemical stink made Amy want to sneeze. Angel hair drooped wetly.

"There," Grandpa said. "That'll fix 'em."

Gossamer threads drifted into her field of vision. She turned in her chair. From the ventilation slots high in the wall swelled a great bubble of silk, with spiders breaking off and showering the air.

"There's more," she said. "Up there."

He shook the can and sprayed the ventilation slots.

"Let's check the rest of the house," he said. "You ought to be wearing shoes. Christ knows what the floodwaters have left behind."

She found a muddy pair of runners and pulled them on. Grandpa had already left for the lounge room. She hurried after him, the rubberised soles of her runners squeaking and squealing against the wet floorboards, the only sound apart from the feathery fall of angel hair against the house.

With a hand to her mouth, Amy stopped dead.

Grandpa stood in the middle of the lounge, stunned, the can of fly spray held by his side, forgotten. The half-dozen sash windows frothed with angel hair. Great clumps kept breaking off and releasing puffs of spiders. Each puff directed itself towards them. Amy experienced a moment of clarity: the creatures must be sharing a consciousness, acting in concert like the cells of a single animal.

"Let's go," she said, dragging Grandpa by the wrist.

The laundry had a single fixed window and no ventilation slots. Amy slammed the door behind them. For the next minute, she and Grandpa crushed all the spiders they could find on themselves and each other. When they finished, they were both covered in tiny spots of spider guts.

"What's going on?" Grandpa muttered. "Some kind of plague?"

"We need to fumigate every room."

From the cupboard, Amy brought out packet after packet of bug bombs, which Grandpa lined up on the lid of the washing machine. At certain times of the year, the house suffered from cockroach infestations. Dad preferred to deal with the problem himself rather than call in a pest control company. God, were her parents okay?

Grandpa said, "We've got enough chemicals here to sink a ship."

"If we hide in the bathroom and chock the door with wet towels, we'll be fine. We can hold out for hours with running water and a toilet."

Grandpa suddenly looked older, as if his skull had shrivelled inside his flesh. The sight unnerved her. She pulled towels from the hamper and gave one to him.

"Put this over your head," she said. "You do the ground floor. I'll do upstairs. We'll meet in the downstairs bathroom, all right?"

They both left the laundry. Amy took the stairs. As she hurried from room to room, setting each bug bomb, the fogs of swirling gossamer threads seemed to chase after her. Impossible. She must be disturbing the air with her passage, drawing the gossamer in her wake. Threads stuck to her. Whenever she wiped her hands along the backside of her jeans, she felt the crack of exoskeletons.

The stink from the hissing bug bombs started to choke her.

She had to hurry, go faster, faster.

The carpets crawled with spiders, popping softly in the hundreds with her every footfall. When she reached the stairs again, grabbing the banister and looking down to make sure of her step, she flinched.

Both feet were swathed in webs. Swarms of spiders charged up her legs.

She bounded down the stairs. Hysteria broke a long, wailing scream out of her. Once in the bathroom, she ripped the towel from her head and used it to beat at her jeans. Spiders flew in every direction. They scattered over the tiled walls, scampered across the floor, ran around inside the bath, the sink, drowned within the toilet bowl. The can of fly spray was in the laundry. Why hadn't she thought to bring it with her?

Amy's breath came and went in ragged, jagged gulps.

Stop it.

Get a grip.

But in the mirror, she saw wriggling black dots all over her.

She turned on the shower and stood under it, fully clothed, the water ice-cold. The spiders sluiced away in sheets and whirled in clots, thick as mud, down the plughole. *Get off me, get off me, get off me…* She kept scrubbing at her hair, t-shirt and jeans with clawed hands, until the water ran clear.

Now what? The bathroom was infested.

She got out of the shower, flushed the toilet over and over, and ran the taps in the sink and bath to swish the tiny monsters down the drains. Wetting the towel she had worn on her head, she wiped at the floor and walls, and then flung the towel into the still-running shower and shut the glass door. Only a few spiders remained, high on the walls, on the ceiling… Amy's breathing started to slow down.

Everything was okay, she was okay. She was dripping wet, shivering, but at least she wasn't covered in spiders, and everything was okay. Except…

Except, where was Grandpa?

Dread prickled at her nerves. She opened the bathroom door a crack, put her mouth to it and yelled, "Grandpa!"

No answer.

She closed the door. What should she do? Wait? Go out and look for him? He might have had a heart attack. Or he may have been overwhelmed by spiders. Right now, they might be cocooning him, stopping his nose and mouth with silk.

The towel in the shower recess was sopping. She wrung it out and put it over her head. If only she had that goddamned fly spray. Bracing herself, she tightened her grip on the doorknob. On the count of three…

One…two…

"Open up!" Grandpa yelled.

His weight thumped against the door. Amy let him in. He was covered in webs and scraping at his eyes. She manhandled him under the shower and helped him rinse off the spiders. When the water ran clear, he shut off the tap. She gave him a dry towel from the rack. They stared at each other for a few moments. Amy imagined that her own face must look as grey and frightened as

Grandpa's. Slowly, absent-mindedly, he began to dry his head and hands. Amy watched him, her heart pounding.

Movement caught her eye. Scuttling under the door were more hordes. She stamped on them, then dropped her wet towel and pushed it against the door.

Grandpa began to nod. He said, "The authorities will take care of this. Don't worry. Any minute now, we'll hear fire trucks, police sirens, alarms."

They sat down together on the edge of the bath. Amy reached for his hand. Grandpa interlaced their fingers. During the two hours they waited for the bug bombs to work, they heard nothing but the continuous, soft pelting over the house.

Grandpa looked at his watch. "Let me check," he said at last, and exited the bathroom. Within seconds, he was back, eyes wild. "We've got to leave."

"Huh? What about the bug bombs?"

"There's too many."

The sound on the roof and weatherboards was no longer muffled. No, it was loud, like pattering rain, a steady and relentless drizzle; the kind of drizzle that threatens to become a downpour. The frosted glass of the window looked white.

"I'll get my car," Grandpa said. "I'll drive it out front so you can hop in."

The garage was not attached to the house. It was a half-minute walk from the porch across open ground.

"But the spiders," she said. "How will you reach the garage?"

He frowned, tugged at an earlobe. "Well, I guess I'll put on a raincoat, gumboots, take an umbrella. Once you're in the car, we'll drive to town and find out what the hell's going on." He seemed to consider this for a moment, and added, "We might have to drive further, perhaps to the city. I'm not sure. God only knows how much angel hair is falling. Maybe it's not angel hair after all."

He nodded to himself, as if making up his mind, and draped a towel over his head. Panicked, Amy gripped his hand. It felt cold.

"Don't go," she said.

He shook his hand free. "When you hear the car horn, run to the front door."

"Let me come with you."

"I won't be long," he said, taking hold of the doorknob. "Keep an ear out. I'll lean on the horn."

He kissed her, a peck on the forehead, and then closed the door behind him, but not quickly enough to stop the flurry of incoming spiders. Amy beat them to the floor with a towel and trod on them. The acrid stink from the bug bombs had wafted in too. After a while, she sat on the edge of the bath and listened for the car horn. There was no clock in the bathroom. How much time had already passed?

She began counting.

One *cat-dog*, two *cat-dog*, three *cat-dog*…

When she reached five hundred *cat-dog* and Grandpa still hadn't sounded the horn, Amy draped a towel on her head, and left the bathroom.

Her home resembled a Halloween-styled haunted mansion. The webbing on the walls, from floor to ceiling, created round tunnels throughout every room. Dead spiders crunched underfoot like powdered snow. The live spiders were slow, drowsy, affected by the bug bombs.

Amy ducked into the laundry for the fly spray. From the cupboard by the front door, she took out her gumboots, raincoat and umbrella. She sprayed each item liberally, and put the can in the deep pocket of her raincoat. The car horn still had not sounded. Amy did not want to think about this too much. She put on the raincoat, slipped the gumboots over her runners, and unfurled the umbrella. Thrusting her hand into webbing, she flung open the front door and stumbled onto the porch.

Her breath hitched.

The outside world had disappeared. In its place lay a single, endless, smothering blanket. Trillions of spiders dropped from a giant cloud. In the distance, the familiar sights of sky, horizon and earth were gone, replaced by a grey and billowing mist. Aghast, lifting the umbrella, Amy hurried to where the garage ought to be. Was the spider-rain getting thicker, heavier? Had the spiders sensed her?

"Grandpa!" she yelled.

The webbing swirled about her legs with each step, as if she were wading through cotton candy. Spiders poured in the hundreds off the umbrella. She was close enough now to see the garage. The double doors stood open. Grandpa had made it that far. Staggering, panting, Amy ran inside the garage. Her eyes took a few moments to adjust to the dimness. Then she saw it, and dropped the umbrella.

On the floor, shrouded like an Egyptian mummy, lay a human shape.

Spiders scuttled across the cocoon. Amy emptied the fly spray over them. The arachnids shrivelled. Collapsing to her knees, weeping, she ripped at the cocoon with both hands. At last, she tore away the silk from Grandpa's face. His staring eyes crawled with spiders. Webs filled his open mouth.

She fell back to the concrete floor, retching, whimpering.

Angel hair crept up her limbs.

She clawed at Grandpa's cocoon and found the car keys in his hand. Amy had her learner permit, had taken a few driving lessons with Dad, but her fear was not in operating Grandpa's old Commodore. No, it was in keeping to the long, winding driveway when she could not see the bitumen. Near the front gate, the driveway ran over a creek. She would have to negotiate the bridge. If she put the car into the creek, she would never get it out again.

Once inside the car, Amy took off the raincoat and gumboots. She had brought spiders in with her. She crushed as many as she could with her fingers. She started the engine. Pulses drummed madly throughout her body. She put the car into 'drive' and coasted out of the garage and into the webs.

The car's passage made cracking, shearing, creaking, rending noises, which made her shiver in revulsion. Angel hair soon covered the windscreen. The wipers mashed and smeared it into grey paste. Amy leaned over the steering wheel, squinting, searching for landmarks. The angel hair that had gathered at the bumper began to creep up and across the bonnet. What if the radiator overheated?

Don't think about it.

The sound of spiders hitting and sliding over the roof scraped at her nerves. She put on the radio. It was an old-timey song, from a station that Grandpa liked. Tears pricked. She snapped off the radio. Grandpa was dead because of her. She should have gone with him. She should have insisted…

There!

The sight galvanised her. There, the railings of the bridge, she could see them. She would make it after all. She would drive to town and find her parents. Together, they would head for the city and away from this nightmare. The tyres smushed over angel hair, yet she could still hear the rhythmic *drub-dub drub-dub* of the bridge's wooden planks. She scrubbed away the tears on her cheeks.

She reached the highway. Or did she? It was difficult to tell. The neighbouring houses, the petrol station, the milk bar, the buildings that should be right in front of her, were reduced to gauzy lumps. And further back lay an impenetrable fog where the vineyard should be, and the hills beyond it, and the sky.

The car's engine coughed, wheezed. The red needle of the temperature gauge rose as she looked at it. Sweat trickled from her hairline. A few stray spiders tickled at the back of her neck. She turned the steering wheel, ploughed on.

Was she on the highway or not?

Something lay ahead, something large. As she got closer, she recognised its shape. It was a sedan, completely cocooned. Were people trapped inside? Yes, there would have to be at least a driver. Amy sounded the horn.

No response.

Maybe the driver had ditched and made a run for it.

Carefully, she steered around the sedan. Her armpits felt clammy, her mouth dry. She put the windscreen wipers on top speed and flicked the lever for the washers, trying to clear the angel hair. She feared crashing into a ditch. Every now and then, she spotted the mound of a roadside post, and adjusted her course.

Tiny arachnids gathered at the edges of the windows, as if trying to find a way inside. Cars were not airtight, she knew that. The spiders would get inside. They would find a way. Her legs felt itchy. From real or imagined spiders? She could not afford to check. She had to keep both hands on the wheel. The webbing pulled and dragged at the tyres. Her foot was flat to the boards, yet she was travelling at only twelve kilometres per hour, now eleven, now ten, as if she were driving into a bog.

Up ahead were more cocooned vehicles.

Amy leaned on the horn. No answering honk came back.

There was just silence, an utterly profound silence out there, and the whisper of angel hair as it landed and collected itself on the car.

Stagecoach From Castlemaine

A dozen stagecoaches were lined up alongside the kerb of the station. Chafing, the yoked horses whinnied and shook their heads. The air smelt of dust, animal sweat, and leather. Passengers, both arriving and departing, crowded the footpath. Minnie Sutton left her son with their luggage and walked the kerb until she found the correct stagecoach. Painted russet, it proclaimed *ROYAL MAIL—COBB & CO* on its body in gold letters and *MELBOURNE—BENDIGO* under the roofline. Minnie went back for her son, and flagged a porter. The constant clamour of voices sounded from all around. She showed their tickets to the driver, an elderly man wearing a cap and a sour expression. He nodded and waved them impatiently towards the open door.

While she settled herself inside the coach, taking off her bonnet and gloves, placing them next to her on the bench, nine-year old Edward swung his legs and gazed without interest at the people thronging Castlemaine station.

"How are you feeling?" Minnie said gently.

"I'm fine."

"Looking forward to seeing Father?"

He turned to her and smiled. "Oh yes, more than anything."

The shadows under the boy's eyes stood out against the pallor of his cheeks. Minnie ran a hand through Edward's blonde hair, a habitual gesture of affection that allowed her, these days, to surreptitiously check for signs of fever. His skin felt cool today. It was the first week of spring. The mild weather had brought a cloudless sky.

"When are we leaving?" Edward said.

"In no time at all, I'm sure. We shall reach Bendigo by dinner."

The porter offered his palm through the open window. Minnie gave him a coin. The porter tipped his hat and turned back into the press of people. Meanwhile, the driver cursed as he secured their luggage to the roof rack, his efforts rocking the coach back and forth on its thorough-brace suspension. Edward flinched.

"It's all right," Minnie said. "Your father swears the journey is smooth."

"Promise? I don't wish to feel sick again."

Minnie put an arm about his shoulders, and gave what she hoped was a jolly smile. "Nor do I," she said, and kissed his forehead.

Yet she was all out of promises. She and her son had already travelled for three days, from their farmhouse in the southeast to the city of Melbourne, and thence to Castlemaine. The overnight stops had provided deficient accommodation. Minnie's back ached from the last mattress. Edward had hardly slept or eaten.

The coach dipped hard towards the kerb-side.

A portly middle-aged man, suited and holding a cane, struggled to alight. He exuded an unpleasant smell of tobacco and unwashed undershirt. With a grunt, he dropped onto the opposite bench and sprawled there with his legs apart.

"Good morning," Minnie said.

The man took off his hat, and leaned from the waist as if bowing. He had greasy hair and a meagre, greying beard. Perspiration dotted his forehead.

"And a good morning to you, madam," he said, thrusting out a hand for her to accept. "The name is Pollard."

His skin felt clammy. When he let go, she wanted to wipe her fingers along the folds of her dress, but resisted out of politeness.

"Mrs Minnie Sutton. And this is my son, Edward."

"Charmed. I've spent the past fortnight with my brother, a shameless laggard, but I shan't bore you with any vulgar stories." His twitching smile kept hiding and revealing his stained teeth. "So, you're off to Bendigo? To visit or stay?"

"Stay. I hear it's quite pleasant."

"Pleasant? Well, it's a boomtown, still thriving on gold. You'll find it grander than the likes of Castlemaine. You have business there?"

"Yes."

Pollard raised his eyebrows. "I'm a hotel proprietor, vying with too many other establishments already. You're not planning to compete with me, I hope?"

Of course, the man was a drinker, and of whiskey too, she supposed. "No, my husband and I intend to open a clothing store," she said. "He has gone ahead to secure the premises. By trade, he is a tailor, and I am a seamstress."

"From the old country too, by the sound of it," Pollard said. "London?"

"We immigrated some time ago."

On doctor's orders. Edward, their only child, was born with a weak constitution. The cold, damp air of England might be the death of him. They had arrived in Melbourne near to Christmas of the previous year, 1879. The oven-hot wind and baking sun were almost unbearable. Yet Minnie and her husband, Richard, were determined to adapt to their new country. In fact, Richard had been so taken with the swathes of open, cheap land that he had bought, of all things, a poultry farm. The foxes and wild dogs had killed their stock despite the fences, despite the armed vigils. They had sold the farm and lost money on it.

The stagecoach jolted as the driver dropped to the footpath. He stood at the doorway with his fists on his hips.

"Ready to go?" he said.

Pollard blinked about as if surprised. "No other passengers?"

"There's nowt else but mail. Call me Blyth. If you've a concern, knock on the ceiling. I'll hear you, more likely than not. Otherwise, give us a shout."

Blyth secured the door and lifted the windowpanes to a couple of inches from each sill, to keep out the dust yet allow a little air. The carriage rocked as he stepped up to the driver's seat. The horses neighed. A whip cracked. With a groan and creak of leather and wood, the stagecoach pulled away from Castlemaine station.

"We're off," Edward said, and clapped.

"Oh, what a delightful boy," Pollard said. "If only I'd brought a bag of sweets."

Minnie offered a tight half-smile, and fixed her gaze out the window.

The town buildings thinned out. Soon, there were farms on either side of the trail, with tin-roofed shacks and sheds, and paddocks holding cattle or sheep. The coach jiggled and shook on its wooden wheels. The endless rows of eucalyptus trees scented the air with mint and honey. Cockatoos cried and swooped through the sky. Magpies warbled. Edward yawned and leaned against her.

"Do you wish to sleep?" she said.

Pollard began to struggle with his jacket. "Allow me to furnish a pillow."

"That's quite all right," Minnie said. "Edward, put your cheek in my lap."

The boy complied. She stroked his hair. He fell asleep within minutes.

"If you'll excuse me," Pollard said, "I think I'll have a kip myself." Propping his head in his hand and leaning his elbow on the windowsill, he dozed.

Minnie had never travelled so far north. Castlemaine and its surrounds, cupped within a valley, were almost as verdant as Victoria's southeast where the Suttons had had their poultry farm. As the hours passed, however, the landscape became rockier, dry and craggy, with scrubby bush and ironbark trees.

The coach rocked like a baby's crib. Minnie drowsed.

A loud, sharp toot of a bugle, sounding three times, woke them all with a start. Minnie sat up and wiped her eyes. They must be approaching a changing station. The coach veered from the trail and bumped along a dirt track. Over the rise appeared a homestead of logs and wooden shingles, with smoke curling from its chimney. The driver's bugle had brought a flurry of activity to the homestead, with figures hurrying out the door. A woman in an apron ushered a handful of running, squealing children back inside the house. Dogs leapt about, barking with excitement.

The coach pulled up outside the stable and jerked to a stop.

"Here we are, lady and gents," Blyth called, as he climbed down. "Lunch."

A middle-aged man was already attending to the sweating horses, preparing to swap them for a fresh team. The woman, presumably his wife, stood at the window.

"Stew and damper?" she said.

They were accommodated in the kitchen, a large and airy room. The stew was tasty—lamb in gravy with onions and carrots—and the damper surprisingly light. But the wife kept hissing, trying to attract Blyth's attention. When he grudgingly stood up and joined her at the back door, Minnie watched and listened.

"Keep your horses at the gallop," the wife said. "Have you a firearm?"

"I store a rifle under my seat. Why, what's the news?"

"There's a Hairy Man about."

Blyth snorted. "Gad, you and your blasted yen for native superstitions. There are beasts aplenty out here without need for make-believe ones."

Gripping his arm, the wife said, "It sounded like a Yahoo-Devil-Devil."

"My only concern is bushrangers." Blyth pulled away. "Next you'll be warning me about Spring-heeled Jack."

Minnie had heard of the latter; a demon with burning coals for eyes that could vault across London rooftops. But what on earth was a Yahoo-Devil-Devil?

Blyth approached and rapped the kitchen table with his knuckles. "We'll be off," he said. "To make Bendigo by six, there's no more delaying to be had."

The party returned to the coach. The whip cracked. The coach squeaked and whined and gained purchase. The homestead was left behind. The wife stood on the edge of the dirt track, clasping her hands to her mouth as if praying, getting smaller and smaller in the rear window. Minnie felt a stir of unease. The coach turned onto the trail and the homestead was lost from sight.

"I'm tired," Edward said.

Minnie smoothed the skirts over her lap. "Rest your head."

He did, and seemed to fall asleep.

"Mr Pollard," she whispered. "Did you hear that gossip at the farmhouse?"

"The Yahoo-Devil-Devil?" Pollard nodded. "Some blacks call it the yowie."

"Yowie? What is that? A type of dingo?"

"Oh, no," Pollard said, "something like the orang-utan of Malay, but larger and more ferocious, with a body the size of a water-barrel, arms that reach to the ground, and hands the size of dinner-plates. They say if a yowie catches you, its first instinct is to dash the brains out of your head."

Edward stirred. Minnie ran her hand through his hair until he settled.

Finally, she glared at Pollard and said, "Blyth has never seen it, and he must travel between Melbourne and Bendigo many times a week."

"He's new to this route; less than a month, I'm told."

That gave her pause. "Even so, if Blyth doesn't believe in the yowie, then I shan't either." And with a dismissive lift of her chin, she stared out the window.

In time, the rhythmic clopping of hooves soothed her. While in Melbourne, she had ordered bolts of fabric in a range of modern colours. She would introduce to the womenfolk of Bendigo the very latest in city fashion: the Princess line silhouette. The clothes shop would flourish. She and Richard would hire a milliner, perhaps a jeweller for cufflinks and hatpins. An emporium is what they would need, a giant department store, *Suttons Fine Suits, Dresses and Accessories…*

The coach slammed to a halt. The collective neighing of the horses was loud, high-pitched and tremulous, like the screaming of terrified women. Minnie gasped. Edward sat up and clung to her.

"What the devil is going on?" Pollard said, turning this way and that.

They could hear Blyth urging the horses, shouting, "Giddyup," over and over.

Pollard wrenched down the windowpane and stuck out his head. "What in blazes is wrong with your blasted nags?"

If he heard, Blyth didn't reply. "Giddyup," he kept insisting. "Go on, gee up."

"Hurry," Pollard yelled. "It might be a pack of bloody bushrangers."

Bushrangers? Minnie's stomach dropped. She pulled Edward closer.

The boy whispered, "They have guns, don't they? Are we going to die?"

"Of course not," she said. "Pay no heed."

Pollard flopped back into his seat, his face pale and sweating. "If it's a bushranger and this fool driver won't ride us out of danger," he said, wagging a finger, "I'll sue Cobb & Co. for all they're worth, you mark my words."

"I'll thank you not to scare my child any more than you already have," Minnie said. "Please calm yourself."

Instead, Pollard rapped on the ceiling with his cane. "Hurry," he bellowed.

Blyth cracked the whip. The coach remained stationary. The horses screamed. There was a great shaking and shimmying of the coach itself, as if the horses were pressing against each other, jostling the yokes. Minnie bit at her lips. Dear God, if only the animals would stop that unearthly screaming.

"Mother," Edward whispered, "I'm scared."

"Everything is all right," she said. "It's probably just a snake lying on the trail. Horses are frightened of snakes."

Aren't they? She wasn't sure. To show her son that she wasn't afraid, Minnie opened the door and leaned out.

The horses were, indeed, huddled in a bunch, their tails clamped down, ears flattened. They were responding to something on Minnie's side of the coach. As they looked at the bushland, she could see the whites of their staring, bulging eyes.

"Is it a snake?" Edward said.

"Yes, perhaps."

The horses stamped and shrieked. What could they see? She gazed into the bush. The countryside in Australia was nothing like that of England. No cheery, bright green grass; no inviting canopies of beech, yew and oak that beckoned for you and your picnic basket. Here, the colours were dirty shades of brown, rust and grey; the trees and shrubs gangly, stringy, misshapen and ugly; dangerous, covered in spiders. You would no more spread a blanket out here than on a grimy platform in London's underground Metropolitan line.

"Get back in the coach," Blyth told her, "and shut the door."

"Mother, please."

For her son's sake, Minnie obeyed.

Pollard, wan and haggard, murmured, "Something terrible is about to happen."

Edward squeezed his arms about her waist. Incensed, Minnie was planning to give Pollard a right dressing-down when the stink hit them. A combination of sulphur, decay and wet dog reached down Minnie's throat. They all coughed and held their noses.

"Oh Jesus, Mary and Joseph," Blyth wailed in terror.

The horses screamed with renewed vigour. The coach jumped and rattled.

She looked out the window and saw the monster.

It had emerged from the trees on Minnie's side of the coach, a few feet ahead of the trail. The sight chocked her lungs. Taller than a man, the monster's head seemed to jut straight from its chest as if it had no neck. Like the chimpanzee, short hair as black as tar covered its body except for the face. Its shoulders were impossibly wide. Beneath the slabs of chest muscle sat a round, bloated abdomen. She'd never seen anything like it. Not at the London Zoo, nor in encyclopaedias or newspapers.

"What's out there?" Pollard said, his cheeks draining of blood. "I can't move."

"Is it a yowie?" Edward said. "Will it dash the brains out of our heads?"

Minnie hauled their valise and a mailbag from under the bench.

"Hide," she said, and urged Edward with pressing fingers to clamber beneath the seat. She packed the valise and mailbag in after him. "Stay there until I tell you to come out. Be quiet. Don't make a sound."

Pollard remained frozen.

Minnie looked out the window. The yowie had taken a number of steps from the bush and onto the trail. Its face was matt black, with flaring nostrils that opened like tunnels into its head, and a bulging upper lip. What would it do next? Retreat or attack? She could not read its expression or body language. Whether the monster was angry, frightened or merely curious, she had no way of telling.

The coach jerked and rocked as the horses tried to back away.

"Giddyup," Blyth cried.

Minnie dragged down the windowpane. "Mr Blyth," she called. "Shoot."

The yowie ran fast, and launched itself. The coach rocked. Blyth's voice keened over the screams of the horses. The yowie dropped to the ground with Blyth in its arms, like a child with a doll. The yowie closed its gaping jaws around Blyth's crown and bit down with long, yellowed teeth.

The cracking sound caused Minnie to momentarily swoon.

Mewling, Pollard fell against her in his rush to look out the window.

Blyth's skull broke like an egg. Blood spurted. The yowie swept aside the shattered bone and tattered flesh, and slurped at the brain. The bulk of the pulsating organ disappeared into the yowie's mouth with the speed of a shucked oyster. Then, with great solemnity and concentration, the yowie poked a finger into the skull cavity, again and again, to suck at the blood and gore.

Minnie gagged.

"Mr Pollard, we need the rifle," she said, panting. "Retrieve it from the locker under the driver's seat and bring cartridges. I know how to shoot."

Pollard stumbled across the carriage and flung open the opposite door. Minnie felt a rush of gratitude. However, instead of heading to the front of the carriage, Pollard, whimpering and sobbing, cane flailing in one fist, sprinted towards the bush as if its limitless expanse held salvation.

Come back, Minnie wanted to cry, but feared drawing the yowie's attention.

"Edward," she whispered. "I have to fetch the rifle myself."

"Let me come too. I'll give you the bullets."

Edward had done that at the farm, on occasion, when the eerie howling of dingoes had prevented sleep. Their firearm had been a Martini-Henry single shot rifle. What kind of firearm might she find in Blyth's locker? Surely, she could figure it out, even if it were unfamiliar. A breech, a trigger, a sight: was there anything else?

"No, stay here and keep hidden," she said.

She glanced out the side window. Her heart jumped into her throat.

The yowie had gone.

A flash of movement caught her eye. She looked out the opposite side of the coach. With a pistoning of its great arms, back and forth, back and forth, the yowie was running through the bush at tremendous speed after Pollard, whose blue suit stood out against the scrub and black ironbarks. Minnie could shout a warning, but to what end? The monster would be upon him in seconds.

Scrambling from the coach, Minnie's shaking legs almost buckled. She groped to the driver's seat and, wrenching aside the folds of her skirt, hauled herself up. Her first instinct was to grab the reins and get the hell away.

"Hah!" she cried, flicking the reins. "Giddyup!"

But the horses stamped and whinnied and pressed against each other. Nearby lay the mutilated corpse of Blyth, the top of his head missing, his face twisted into a bloodied mask of horror. Minnie retched.

No, she had to find her courage, locate the rifle.

She dropped the reins and unlatched the driver's boot beneath the seat. To her relief, the rifle was a Martini-Henry. She took it and a box of cartridges. She opened the lever to expose the breech, slid a cartridge into place, and closed the lever. The rifle gave a satisfying click. She sighted along the barrel. Her arms shook violently. Shifting in the driver's seat, she crouched and steadied the rifle on the backrest. Now…where was the yowie?

She couldn't see it.

Oh God, she couldn't see it.

Lifting her head, Minnie scanned the bush, left to right. Her breath came and went in gasps. She looked about the stagecoach.

Had the monster circled back around?

Could it be behind her?

And then, far off through the trees, she saw the bright blue of Pollard's suit. The suit appeared to be moving towards her. Somehow, Pollard had survived. Had the yowie given up the chase? Pollard must have defended himself with his cane.

"Mr Pollard?" she called. "Are you all right?"

He didn't answer. A prickling of gooseflesh crawled over her body.

Minnie lowered her eye to the rifle.

Pollard appeared from the trees. The top of his skull was gone, his face a gory slop. The yowie held him by the neck in the crook of its elbow, and gnawed on the stump of the dead man's wrist. Dear Lord, it had eaten Pollard's hand, bones and all. Even as she watched, the yowie let go of Pollard's ruined arm and picked up the other. It bit off a finger and chewed. With a muffled shriek, Minnie pulled the trigger.

The shot rang out.

The yowie stopped walking.

Had she hit it? Or had it stopped because of the loud noise?

"Here, Mother."

Edward was standing alongside her, his face white and tear-stained, his jaw clenched, holding up a cartridge in one small hand, clutching the box of ammunition in the other. There was no time to chastise him for abandoning his hiding place.

Minnie reloaded, aimed and shot. Blood flowered on Pollard's lapel. Damn.

"Mother, quickly," Edward said, proffering a fresh cartridge.

She reloaded. The yowie bellowed. The deep, resonant roar sounded like that of a lion. The horses shrieked and jostled.

The carriage shook the barrel of the rifle. The yowie flung aside Pollard's corpse and began to run at her.

Panicked, Minnie pulled the trigger. The monster did not break its stride. She must have missed again. The yowie kept running. Oh God, was she hitting it at all? She reloaded, shot. Blood exploded from its temple. Doubling over, stumbling, the yowie put both palms to its face.

"Another bullet," she said, glancing at Edward.

He had wet himself, yet offered the ammunition. Oh, her poor, brave boy. His courage put iron into her spine. With a determined sense of calm, she reloaded the Martini-Henry, took careful aim, and shot the yowie square in the face.

Choking, the yowie clawed at the wound.

Eat that, she thought, with a giddy sense of elation.

With a terrible gargling sound, it shuffled towards the trail and headed for the horses, which bucked and reared. The stink of the monster was overwhelming. The lead horse took a few jerky steps forward as if readying to bolt. Yoked, the others had to follow.

"Hold this," Minnie said, and gave Edward the rifle, "and sit down." Grabbing the reins, she flicked them and yelled, "Giddyup."

The horses broke into a messy gallop. The coach rocked, threatening to tip. The yowie leapt into the path of the horses, arms outstretched. Screaming, the horses threw their heads, reared, and ran the monster down, trampling it beneath their hooves. The wheels bounced as the coach passed over the monster's legs.

Surely, their nightmare was done?

Standing in her seat, Minnie looked behind. On the trail, the yowie was gathering itself together, clambering to its knees. Minnie swore.

"Edward, take the reins," she said.

The rifle was loaded. Minnie rested the barrel on the carriage and squinted down the sight. Limping, the yowie was gaining on every stride. She aimed at its massive chest and pulled the trigger. The monster dropped.

After a moment, Minnie wiped sweat from her brow, sat, and took the reins.

"Did you get it?" the boy said at last.

"Yes, I got it."

"Are we safe?"

"As safe as houses."

One-handed, she reloaded the rifle. She would keep it at the ready.

Edward sagged against her. He was trembling. Minnie kissed his forehead. She was trembling too. The horses settled into a canter as they followed the trail from Castlemaine to Bendigo. On either side, the dark and dingy ironbarks leaned their branches at them, as if watching their passage.

Delirium of Negation

"A coffin?" Dave said. "You want me to build you a coffin?"
Jemima, the old woman sitting in the armchair opposite, nodded.

Dave had a sudden urge to leave. Instead, he leaned back into the sofa and drummed his fingers on his knee. The lounge room smelled of dust and mothballs. Yellowed doilies draped the furniture. A grandfather clock ticked in the entrance hall. Dave, a carpenter, had experienced plenty of mysterious calls from potential clients over the years. Usually, the request was for something the customer felt too embarrassed to mention over the phone. *Can you make me a sex swing? Yeah, no worries; tell me the features you've got in mind*. But a coffin? Dave was neither religious nor superstitious, but a coffin?

"That's not my field," he said. "You need a funeral director."

"Oh no, no, no." Jemima's tiny, arthritic hands fluttered and clenched, reminding him of bird claws. "That would be out of the question. A funeral director just simply wouldn't understand."

"Wouldn't understand what?"

Jemima clamped her lips, and regarded him with washed-out, watery eyes. "You look young," she said. "Are you?"

"I'm thirty-one."

"Would you consider yourself a spiritual kind of chap?"

"Not really. Well, as spiritual as the next bloke, I guess. Why?"

She tried to smile but it flickered and died at the corners of her mouth. Dave glanced at the front door. Pinned beneath the transom was a large wooden crucifix with a suffering Christ. A painting of Jesus hung next to the clock. When Dave looked back at Jemima, he noticed a small cross on a chain around her neck.

"The coffin must be the size and shape of a single bed," she said, "and quite deep. A mattress has to fit inside, you see. And we'll need a lid that blocks out light but not air. The coffin can't be airtight. That's imperative."

Dave's fingers stopped tapping.

When he did not reply, she added, "Can you make a coffin like that?"

"Yeah," he said, "but what for? I mean, isn't the person dead?"

Jemima tipped her head, as if considering. "Not really."

What kind of answer was that? He shifted in his seat. A spring in the sofa poked at his thigh like a bony finger. "Look, they're either dead or they're not."

"I'd like you to meet my husband," she said. "You'll stay, won't you? You'll sit here and wait while I get him, won't you? Promise you won't sneak away?"

Dave felt his cheeks redden. "Sure, okay."

Jemima put both hands on the armrests and gingerly pushed herself to her feet. Her posture was stooped. She had the appearance of someone in constant pain.

"I'll be back directly," she said, and turned towards the kitchen doorway.

Somebody was already standing there.

Dave and Jemima both startled.

Recovering, Jemima let go of the cross about her neck, her laugh brittle. "Oh Sylvester," she said, "I assumed you were resting. This is our carpenter, Dave."

Dave stood up, wiped his palm along his overalls, and prepared to extend his hand. Sylvester, the old man in the doorway, didn't move. He wore a shirt and tie, a double-breasted suit, and a fedora. The shoulder seams of the jacket sagged down his arms, and the trouser hems puddled around his shoes, as if the suit belonged to a much larger man. Dave got the idea that both Jemima and Sylvester were shrivelled versions of their younger selves; two fallen apples left in the hot sun to dry.

"I'll allow you gentlemen to talk business in private," Jemima said, and departed, walking gingerly.

The old man stepped across the room. He moved slowly, putting his weight onto one foot before lifting the other in a high step. The stiff, ceremonial gait was typical of pallbearers. Dave did not want to shake with this man any more. Instead, he slipped his hands into his pockets, gave a hearty smile, and said, "G'day."

Sylvester halted, looking surprised. "My word. You can see me?" His chortle sounded tired and weak. "Well, well. That's interesting."

Dave was not sure how to respond. Did the old man believe himself to be a vampire or something? These pensioners were nuts. He ought to leave. Perhaps he could pretend to receive a text message, offer his apologies.

"You can smell me too, I presume?" Sylvester said.

"I'm sorry, what?"

The old man took off his fedora and arranged himself in the armchair vacated by his wife. The front door was perhaps five or six easy strides away. The door had panels, sidelights, stained glass panes; a beautiful piece of work apart from the wooden Jesus hanging by his wrists, mouth agape, thorns gouged into his scalp.

"Please," Sylvester said, and indicated the sofa.

After a moment, Dave sat down again.

"I smell like rotten meat," Sylvester said.

Involuntarily, Dave flared his nostrils and sniffed. He could smell only the house: unwashed net curtains, naphthalene, and some kind of potpourri.

"I'm not sure why," Sylvester continued, "since my internal organs are long gone, and my skin, so far, remains intact. Perhaps the odour floats out of my ears. I've been dead for many weeks. By now, my brain must resemble a lump of burnt, leathery offal covered in mould, wouldn't you agree?"

Dave mulled this over, chewing his lip.

A couple of cars whooshed by on the street beyond the windows and the small, neat garden. Then a creaking floorboard attracted Dave's attention. In the kitchen, peeking out, was

Jemima. As soon as he spotted her, she ducked from sight.

That's it, he thought, I've had a gutful. He pushed on the armrest and stood up.

"Get in touch with a funeral director," he said. "And have a good day."

Sylvester raised his eyebrows. "Aren't you curious as to how I died?"

"Listen, mate, you're not dead, all right? Dead people can't walk and talk."

"Very true, but then again…" Sylvester trailed off, and gestured towards himself with a cold, amused smile. "Here I am."

"Yeah, well, take it easy. I'll let myself out."

"Wait a minute, you'll find this fascinating, I guarantee." Angling his face to the kitchen doorway, Sylvester called, "Dear, bring in Marmalade, would you?"

"Forget it," Dave said, "I've got to go."

Sylvester made an impatient, fussy gesture. The beds of his fingernails were an odd bluish-grey. Before Dave had time to contemplate this, Jemima crept into the room carrying a dog, a red corgi with a lacklustre coat. She must have had the dog already in her arms, waiting in the kitchen, waiting for her cue. Vigorously, Sylvester flapped his hands, indicating that she should bring the dog closer, closer.

"There, that'll do," he said. "Set him down."

With difficulty, Jemima stooped to put the corgi on the rug. Snuffling, the corgi pawed on the spot as if straining at the end of a leash, trapped.

Dave said, "What, he rolls over and plays dead?"

"Shush," Sylvester demanded. "Now listen."

At first, all Dave could hear was the clock. But then the dog growled. The dog growled quietly, threateningly, a repetitive one-note snarl. It seemed to be staring at Sylvester. No, not *at* him, exactly, but in his general direction…staring unfocused as if Sylvester were invisible. The flesh crawled across the nape of Dave's neck.

"So your dog doesn't like you," Dave said. "Big deal."

"Ah yes, but it's only since my passing that I frighten him."

"Marmalade has cataracts," Jemima said. "He gets confused because he can't see very well."

"Yet he can smell me. He can smell that I'm a rotting corpse."

"Oh, for Christ's sake." Dave put his hands on his hips. "Which one of you is going to tell me what's going on here?"

Jemima nodded. "Forgive me. My husband had a stroke. The doctors think it triggered a delusion known as Cotard's syndrome: the belief that one is dead."

"Dead? You mean undead, like a vampire?"

"Quite possibly. It's difficult to know what he's thinking these days." She sighed. "The doctors are confident he might recover, but he refuses to take his anti-psychotic medicine. He can't see the point, since he considers himself a corpse, and corpses don't need medicine." She shrugged wearily. "We keep going round in circles."

Sylvester laughed. "Oh, Jemima, shush with your nonsense. Let me tell the story. Please, sit down, both of you. Once you sit, I shall begin." He waved encouragingly at the sofa.

Dave sat because, okay, the old bastard had piqued his interest. And Dave was a tall, heavy and thickset man, with nothing to fear from these pensioners. Jemima sat next to him. The dog kept growling.

Sylvester interlaced his thin fingers and placed his hands in his lap. "Three months ago," he said, "I was hoeing the yard when lightning hit me."

"Not actual lightning," Jemima murmured. "That's when he had the stroke."

"Senseless, I fell to the ground. I woke up in a hospital bed. I was there for weeks. Many doctors visited me, many nurses tended me, and I had to take large quantities of medicines, both orally and intravenously." He leaned forward, his eyes shining. "I was on death's door."

"That's true, it was touch and go for a time," Jemima whispered.

"And yet I was still myself. I still knew myself to be alive. And one day…"

With a shrill bark, the corgi hurried from the room. Its nails clicked over the kitchen tiles in a frantic staccato. Dave began to tap at his knee. Jesus's agonised expression seemed to ask: *Why the hell are you still here? You ought to be running too.*

"Trainees always came to my bedside," Sylvester went on, and his hands wrung and rubbed at each other. "In particular, this one young doctor, a boy, took a liking to me. However, there was something wrong with this boy."

"Wrong like what?" Dave said.

"The staff sensed it too. They stayed away from him. The trainees always moved in a pack, you see, from bed to bed while the registrar pontificated on the ins and outs of each patient, but there was a force field around this boy. No one stood close. No one touched him. He always had about this much space around him." The old man extended one wavering arm to demonstrate. His nail beds were not so much bluish-grey, but black.

"So why didn't anybody touch this bloke?"

Jemima made a tiny exclamation and stood. As she tottered from the room, she gripped the cross around her neck. Dave watched her go and experienced a flush of unease. His mouth dried out.

"One day," Sylvester said, "this boy came to see me. He was alone. No one else was in the room. The other patient had been discharged that very morning. As soon as the boy drew near, I felt a great dread. The spit left my mouth. I perspired like a horse."

Dave stopped tapping his knee. Sweat had popped on his forehead, stubble, back. If he got up, fast, he might reach the door in three strides, open it, and have the weak autumn sunshine on his face, the car keys solid and sharp against his fingers.

"The boy told me he was leaving to continue his training at another hospital. He wished me well, and put out his hand." The old man's voice had dropped. And were those tears in his eyes? "Not wanting to be impolite, I shook with him."

Dave glanced at the front door. The suffering Jesus glanced back.

"I gripped his hand. It was like plunging my hand into snow.

The coldness travelled up my arm and spread throughout my body like poison. The boy laughed and laughed. I knew immediately that I was as good as dead."

The old man stared sightlessly at the rug. Dave kept very still. The clock ticked. Another car whooshed along the street.

Finally, Dave said, "Then what happened?"

Sylvester looked up. His eyes seemed cloudy and mottled. "What happened? Well, the doctors, in their infinite wisdom, discharged me. I came home. I continued to die, organ by organ, blood vessel by blood vessel, cell by cell. I died in totality some three weeks ago. Once I died, there was no need to eat. I'm not sure how it will end. Perhaps I will walk the Earth for eternity. Perhaps I will decay until I'm reduced to dust." He sat back in his chair and smiled. "I see that you believe me now."

Dave shifted, felt the prod of the sofa spring. "What does your wife think?"

"That I'm insane."

"Aren't you?"

"No. These days, I spend my time in cemeteries. I feel at peace amongst the dead, amongst my own kind. I'd sleep there too, but Jemima would fret. It's not right to purposefully upset one's wife. At least, not over trivial matters."

Dave wiped sweat from his brow. "So that's why you want a coffin-bed."

"Yes."

"To stay home and pretend you're sleeping at a cemetery."

"It would bring me comfort. Being dead is lonely. Despite my efforts, I've not been able to find the boy, the dead intern, who transformed me into this state."

Dave swallowed. A dry *click* sounded in his throat. "The intern was dead too?"

"Well, but of course."

A floorboard creaked. Dave looked toward the kitchen. Jemima ducked away. Had she seemed afraid?

"Ignore my wife," Sylvester said. "She worries about too many things."

Dave sucked in a breath and let it out. "Mate, I can't help you."

"No?"

"Coffins aren't my thing. Look, I'm not religious"—and he shot a quick look at Jesus—"but what you want is beyond my area of expertise. Decking, outdoor furniture, pergolas, that sort of thing, wardrobe makeovers, I'd be more than happy."

"What a shame."

Dave stood up. Sylvester stood up too.

Mate, I can't help you either, said the tortured face of Jesus. *You've left your run too late. Pater noster, qui es in caelis, sanctificetur nomen tuum…*

"No hard feelings?" Dave said.

"Ah, piffle. I'll simply ask Jemima to call another carpenter. Thanks for coming. I hope you enjoyed my story, at least."

Sylvester put out his hand. Automatically, Dave took it, and cried out.

Jemima wailed from the kitchen, "Sylvester, leave him be."

Somewhere, the dog barked hysterically.

The bitter chill cut through Dave's palm as if he had dipped his hand into liquid nitrogen. The pain was off the chart, on another scale altogether, more hot than cold, a glowing poker from a fireplace, burning through to his bones. Darkness crowded his vision. Oh God, he was going to pass out. He tried to pull away.

Sylvester's grip tightened.

"No, no," Jemima mewled nearby, disembodied. "You swore you wouldn't."

For a moment, Dave thought he saw an apology in the old man's face, a sop of compassion. Then Sylvester laughed. His yellowed, mottled eyes turned black as if flowering with mildew. The searing cold juddered up Dave's arm, spreading and cracking and freezing. His heart felt faint enough to stop.

Then, much to his surprise, it did.

Post hoc ergo propter hoc

The man on the gurney is my grandfather. I haven't seen him in years. Irritable, as if we'd argued only yesterday, Grandpa lifts his bony head and shouts, "Why the fockin' bejesus are you at work? You ought to be home raising bairns."

I've been an ER doctor for a long time. Now I'm a frightened child again. The nurses look at me, waiting for my commands. Meanwhile, the ambulance officer lists an array of symptoms: fever, rigors, myalgia, vomiting, headache, variable consciousness. Apparently, the housekeeper found him. She's in the waiting room.

Grandpa hasn't changed much in 28 years. It's Sunday afternoon with my parents, and I'm a little girl sitting on Grandpa's plastic-covered sofa. Daytime, the curtains shut. He's pontificating, lecturing, hectoring. To see a funeral procession before a wedding is bad luck. Never cross two knives on a table.

I'm frozen. My senior ER nurse takes charge, scissoring away Grandpa's clothes to check for wounds, yet there's nothing, nothing… *A good-for-nothing doctor? By Christ, any banogha of mine should be a wife and mother…*

"Jessica," the senior ER nurse says. "There's a suppurating ulcer on his heel."

My training comes back fast. "Test blood and urine for infection: sepsis, Lyme disease, brucellosis. Get his medical history." One of the nurses bolts. I shout after her, "Check for drug reactions, new prescriptions."

We work on Grandpa. He comes awake and stares at me, grabs

at my wrist. He whispers, "That fockin' housekeeper stopped me putting out the cream and cake. She turned my broonie into a fockin' bogle."

Nauseated, I leave for the waiting room. The housekeeper is short and round with a square haircut. I introduce myself as Grandpa's doctor, not his relation, and ask what happened.

She grimaces. "He's a hoarder. I clean the bathroom, bedroom and kitchen; that's it. Every night, he insists on putting out saucers of food. I think a rat bit him."

Something has bitten him, yes. My heart flutters, panicked, a trapped bird. I say, "Did he ever mention a broonie?"

"Oh, constantly. And I'd reply, stop the superstitious rot, you're in modern-day Australia."

To keep them happy, you must feed your broonie…

Yet correlation does not imply causation. I tell my staff to check for rat-bite fever. The test is positive. It is, indeed, *streptobacillus monilformis*. The diagnosis doesn't help. Despite life support, Grandpa dies.

As it turns out, he bequeathed me his house.

I hire cleaners used to dealing with hoarders. Next, I hire a decorator. Lastly, removalists transfer my belongings into Grandpa's house. No, into my house; it is my house now. And everything in it belongs to me.

Everything.

The scratching wakes me at night. Pitter-patter, pitter-patter. I stare at the ceiling, dimly lit by the digital clock. Something lives in the crawlspace. Exterminators can't find evidence of infestation. "The spoor is old and desiccated," one of the many exterminators says. "Whatever's creeping around up there doesn't take a dump."

Yet a creature is getting in and out, somehow.

I close off unused rooms; chock doorways with newspapers, shoes, empty wine bottles. It occurs to me that this behaviour resembles hoarding. I still hear the rat at night. Broonies don't exist. I believe in science, double-blind studies, pharmaceuticals. Actually, I am stealing pharmaceuticals from work, self-medicating. Perhaps I'm going crazy like Grandpa, crazy like his daughter—my mother—who killed herself, convinced of supernatural possession.

The scratching noises get worse over time. God, I'm tired despite the pills but I can't move out. To leave is to admit defeat. And a broonie, if it existed, would follow me anyway.

One night, I wake up. By my pillow is a tiny, corpse-white hominid without a nose. Its fingers are fused, so its hands look like mittens. The continuous row of nails on each hand resembles a blade. When those mitten-blade-hands reach for me, I scream and turn on the light. The broonie is gone. I mean the bogle is gone. Grandpa always told me that if you mistreat a broonie, it becomes a malicious bogle.

No, I decide it must be the pills giving me nightmares. I flush the pills down the toilet. The next day, I can't go to work because of the shaking, sweating, puking.

That evening—what the hell, what do I have to lose—I put a saucer of cream and cake on the kitchen floor. I scatter talcum powder around it. The morning shows footprints. Not those of a rat, but of a tiny hominid. Terrified, I look again, and laugh. See? There are no footprints. But how is the saucer licked clean?

It seems I'm losing my mind.

Yesterday's dishes and cups that I left on the draining board are in the sink, shattered into pieces. I didn't hear them smash. Did I smash them myself? The only thing I heard in bed last night was the scratching. Not within the ceiling as usual, but behind my head in the wall space, an insistent and frantic digging sound, as if something were desperate to break through the plaster so that it could flay its blade-like nails through my skull.

My pager goes off. I'm needed at work.

Exhausted, I stir my hands wrist-deep in the sink of broken crockery, drawing blood. Gradually I become aware of pain in my foot. I look down at four puncture marks. Something with needle-like incisors must have nipped me while I slept. Is that a temperature spike I can feel? I contemplate my shredded hands, tattered skin; the blood pulsing out of me in waves. Oh Grandpa, why did you bring me here? You knew what would happen.

Skittering footsteps approach from behind.

I'm ready to yield. I should be afraid but in fact, it's a strange kind of relief. I think I understand my mother now.

The Again-Walkers

1.

As she now must do every weekday morning, Svana left the house carrying the lunch-pail of bread, cheese and beer. The trek to the village centre was several miles. She walked faster than usual, a little breathless. The spring air was cool. A layer of snow still covered the peaks of the faraway ranges. She should have worn a shawl. Then again, she had planned all along to bare her shoulders and neck, regardless of the weather. Before leaving the house, she had laced her belt tightly to show off her narrow waist, had taken great care with her braiding so that an intricate criss-crossing of plaits encircled a cascade of yellow hair from her crown. Her mother-in-law, Dagny, had noticed. Looking up from the loom, the old woman had skewed an eye and said, "Don't be thinking about making mischief. Hallkell won't stand for it."

Humming, Svana patted at her hair with one hand, and swung the lunch-pail in the other. The lane began to widen and fill with foot traffic and people drawing carts behind horses or riding on horseback. No one waved or spoke to her. As a peace-pledge wife given by her father to appease Hallkell's family, Svana had resided here for about a month. Whether the villagers didn't talk to her because she was a foreigner, or because they were fearful of Hallkell's wrath, Svana didn't know. She had fled that first night, barefoot and crying, in the direction of her own village, but Hallkell had caught her and beat her. Neighbours had seen. They saw everything. No doubt, everyone in the village knew about Svana and Hallkell's wedding night.

Over the rise, the wooden buildings with their steeply pitched roofs came into view. Svana headed to the marketplace. A bustle of women, men, and children thronged the stalls. Dogs roamed. Hawkers called out to attract customers. Someone played a pan-pipe, the notes rising and falling. Svana headed to the foundry.

A great heat came from the furnace. She stood at Hallkell's side until he noticed her. He dismissed his apprentice, who left the foundry to purchase something to eat from the market. Putting down his tools, Hallkell strode away from the anvil and bellows, and took off his leather apron and gloves.

As was his custom, he didn't speak to her.

She handed him the lunch-pail. He sat on a bench and started eating. Hallkell was a giant of a man, fat and heavily muscled. He wore his dark blonde hair shaved apart from a single braid that followed the midline of his scalp to his neck and then dangled down his back in a long plait. He had a moustache and kept his beard in a half-dozen plaits. As he ate and drank, Svana regarded his grimy, sweat-stained body, his pot belly, and the whorls of hair matting his meaty shoulders. She curled her lip at the memory of his lovemaking. Just last night, he had lain on top of her, at arm's length, pumping mindlessly, staring at the wall. When she had tried to touch herself, he had slapped away her hands, saying, "Be still. You're a wife, not a whore." From the other bedroom behind a curtain, his mother, Dagny, had laughed.

Now, Hallkell belched and dropped the empty beer bottle into the lunch-pail.

"I need money," Svana said.

"For what?"

"Dagny has asked for skeins of wool."

Hallkell stood and searched through the leather money-pouch on his belt. He brought out some coins, and then a few more.

"Here," he said. "Buy yourself a piece of jewellery."

"I have enough jewellery already. Thank you, Husband."

"Then buy yourself a new dress." He gazed down at her and briefly touched her cheek. "You look pretty," he said.

"I try my best to please you."

"And you please me greatly. Now, be on your way."

He turned from her and picked up his leather apron. Svana pocketed the coins and moved through the marketplace. Hallkell had taken longer than usual over his lunch. It was past midday. Already, the meat, fruit and vegetable vendors were packing up and preparing to return to their farms. Was Svana too late? She hurried, slipping through the crowd, the pulse beating in her throat.

Relieved, she stopped.

Behind a trestle table arrayed with cuts of lamb and mutton was the shepherd, Agmundr, attending to a customer. Unlike the other villagers who had red, brown or blonde hair, Agmundr's hair was jet-black. He wore it parted on the side and long to his collar. Unusually, he was clean-shaven. Svana had never before touched the face of a clean-shaven man, and wondered how such a jaw-line might feel. Agmundr wasn't wearing his cloak today. Bare-armed in his tunic, the lean muscle and sinew moved beneath his pale skin as he wrapped the mutton for his customer. There was an exchange of goods and money. The customer spoke a few words and left. Agmundr looked across and saw her.

Caught, Svana held her breath.

The intensity of his gaze made her blush, clutch the lunch-pail in both hands.

She had first seen him three weeks ago at the Grand Hall assembly. The Earl and Wife had been recounting business affairs, conducting criminal trials and providing news of the outside world. As they did so, Svana had kept her chin in her hand, stifling yawns, when across the longhouse, she noticed a man watching her. His dark, heavily lashed eyes didn't look away. Jolted, Svana sat up. He smiled with one side of his mouth, his lips full and red. That night, she nudged at Hallkell for his sexual favour and imagined that she was making love with the mysterious, dark-haired stranger. By the next assembly in the Grand Hall, she knew the stranger's name and occupation: Agmundr Rask, shepherd. There was a dance to celebrate the start of spring, a line dance, men on one side and women on the other, so that everyone ultimately shared a turn. By the time she landed in Agmundr's arms, she was wet with anticipation. He held her close against his tensile body and seemed to stare into her very soul as he swung her around and around. She lost her breath, her gasp hidden in the tumult of music. Then the next man took hold of her and Agmundr was gone. They kept catching each other's eye as the music played on and on, his mouth lifting at one corner, his eyes never blinking as if he couldn't afford to miss a second of her.

Over the past weeks, she'd lived for these glimpses, these stolen moments.

Now, she reddened as she walked past his stall.

Agmundr called out, "Is there something you want? Anything you need?"

Halting, she looked at him. With a wry smile, he spread both arms to encompass the meat on the trestle table. Then he raised his brows and gestured towards himself. Svana giggled. He laughed too. A lock of black hair fell across his brow. She wanted to smooth it back, wind her arms about his neck, and taste his mouth. A woman stopped and studied her, frowning. Chastened, Svana scurried past, almost breaking into a run. Hallkell's beating had been so terrible. It had taken her days to recover. Could she risk it again?

Agmundr, Agmundr…

Is there something you want? Anything you need?

Yes, she went ahead and bought Dagny's stupid skeins of wool, fussed over a variety of dresses and finally chose an expensive linen tunic, one that would befit the wife of a blacksmith, yet her mind lay elsewhere. By now, the market lane was almost empty of farmers. Svana could go straight home…or not. Tradesmen like Hallkell would not finish work until dusk. She fidgeted at her complicated braids, ran a hand along the silky and golden hair that fell from her crown; touched the belt cinching her waist.

Then she walked north instead of east.

Agmundr's farm was a small, grassy plot with a thatched cottage at one end. Svana hesitated at the gate. Hurriedly, before she could change her mind, she entered the property and headed to the house. Sheep lifted their long, dull faces from the grass and watched her progress. Lambs broke away, kicking their heels and bleating.

The door was open. She stood within its frame.

Agmundr, sitting at the table with bread and cheese, stood up and swept the plates aside. He was wearing only trousers. His chest was wide and deeply split down the middle, his belly a cross-hatching of muscle. Svana's mouth went dry. She swapped the lunch-pail with its skeins of wool and its folded dress from one hand to the other. She'd prepared a speech before leaving home, had known all along what to say at this very moment, but the vision of a half-stripped Agmundr and those blue veins running along his forearms blasted her mind clean and empty.

"What are you doing here?" Agmundr said.

Svana fumbled with the money in her pocket. "I want lamb."

He smiled knowingly. Of course, she would have bought lamb at the market if needed. He gestured for her to come inside. Timidly, she stepped over the threshold. He took a wrapped piece of meat from a nearby bench and held it out. She took it and placed it in the lunch-pail. Numbly, she dropped uncounted coins onto the table.

"You are Hallkell's new bride," Agmundr said.

"Yes. My name is Svana Norup."

"You're a peace-pledge from another village?"

"My brother killed Hallkell's father. I'm the apology to stop the blood feud."

Agmundr moved out from behind the table. Svana's heart thrummed. Taking a step back, she remembered her suspicious mother-in-law, Dagny; the woman scrutinising her at the market; the various people who may have seen her walking to Agmundr's farm. She lost her nerve.

"I have to go," she said, and turned away.

"Wait."

He was behind her already, his hands gripping her arms. The air left Svana in a rush. Agmundr gathered her fall of hair and swept it aside to expose the nape of her neck. His touch brushed over her bare upper back, leaving trails that tingled and burned.

Then he slipped his fingertips beneath the cowl of her dress and slid the fabric off one shoulder. His lips moved along her skin. The lick of his tongue on its way to the base of her neck made her shudder as surely as if his mouth had been nestled between her thighs. She leaned back into him. He clutched her waist and spun her around. His kiss was long and deep. As he drew up the folds of her dress, Svana quailed, and pushed him away.

"What's wrong?" Agmundr said.

"I can't. He'll kill me."

She kissed Agmundr passionately, desperately, for it would be the last time. Breaking away, she raced from the house.

"Come back," Agmundr called.

She kept running. The long road kicked up dust with every footfall.

Close to Hallkell's house, panting, feverishly wild and intoxicated, Svana ducked behind a stand of trees and hoisted up her dress. Rubbing at herself, she imagined Agmundr doing the same and fantasised the look on his face at the moment of release. She came, hard, and wiped her fingers on the grass.

Knees shaking, she took to the lane again. The sight of the thatched house brought tears to her eyes. Dagny would be waiting.

Dagny's loom clicked and clattered. Ignoring the headache that clenched her temples, Svana stirred the pot. Dusk had fallen. Birds called goodnight in the fading light. Hallkell pushed open the door and strode in, stinking of sweat and ash.

"What's for dinner?" he said. "It better not be rabbit."

Svana didn't look up from the pot. "Lamb stew."

"Lamb from whose farm?"

She said nothing.

Hallkell approached. "Agmundr's? I told you to stay away."

"I was with him only a few minutes."

Dagny stood up from her loom and clucked. "That's all it takes."

Svana smiled rigidly at her husband as he glared at her. "You must be tired," she said. "I'll fetch you a beer."

Hallkell grabbed her wrist.

"You're hurting me," she said.

"I don't like how that shepherd looks at you."

"He looks at me with both eyes, like everybody else. Let me go. Do you want the stew to burn?"

"I'm no fool. Agmundr eats you with his eyes. I've seen him at it."

Dagny shouted, "And Svana laps it up. I'll bet she's as wet as porridge."

Hallkell went to grope between Svana's legs, but she kept them clamped.

He cried, "Woman, what shame are you hiding?"

"None," she said, trying to twist free. "I'm your wife, I do you no harm."

"I provide and this is how you repay me? By running after a shepherd?"

The force of Hallkell's slap knocked Svana off her feet and headlong into the hearth. Before the flames could touch her, however, Hallkell dragged her clear by her hair. He gripped the golden hank that Agmundr had smoothed aside in order to press his lips against the nape of her neck. Dagny laughed and clapped at the drama.

"Are you all right?" Hallkell said, grasping Svana's shoulders and shaking her with all the strength in his prodigious arms, so that the teeth rattled in her head. "Did the fire touch you? By the love of Odin, are you all right? Tell me."

"Yes," she stammered. "I'm all right."

He shoved her and she fell against the table, panting. Only one thing in the world appeared to frighten Hallkell: fire. As a blacksmith, his body was covered in shiny red welts, and scars from countless burns. At that moment, if she could, Svana would have tied him to a stake and lit a huge pyre beneath him.

"Next time, answer me when I speak to you."

"Yes, Husband."

"Do not provoke me."

"Yes, Husband."

"Look at her hair," Dagny said, sidling over to stand by her son. "Do you see how much time and care she put into it today?"

Hallkell's face darkened. He looked at Svana from top to bottom, scrutinising her. She blushed. Hallkell must have seen the guilt in her face, for his chest started to rise and fall rapidly, and his hands clenched. It was as if Agmundr's kisses and fingerprints shone on her skin.

"Dagny," she said, and fell to the old woman's feet, clutching at her dress. "It wasn't I who killed your husband. Help me. Take pity on me."

Dagny sniffed, and pulled her skirts free. She resumed her seat at the loom.

Feeling cold and faint, Svana stood up. Hallkell advanced. On impulse, she plucked the carving knife from the table and held it out. He seemed surprised, even amused. When he began to shake his head at her, as if she had made a grave mistake, Svana felt the tears come. He stepped closer, a giant, an ogre, built so large he could enclose her neck in one hand. Trembling, she put down the knife.

"Please," she whispered. "Please don't."

"Woman, you give me no choice."

The beating took only a minute. He paused midway to chastise her.

"Quit mewling," he said. "It gets on my nerves. I spank you as lightly as I would a child. Why, if I hit you square just once, I'd dash your brains out. You ought to thank Odin for my mercy."

When he finished the beating, he told her to serve dinner. She obeyed. The thought of eating turned her stomach, but Hallkell wouldn't excuse her from the table. He and Dagny chatted about the events of the day. After the meal, Svana cleaned up. Then she went outside and sat by the water barrel, washcloth in hand. She kept dipping it in the water, wringing it out and holding it against her eye as a compress.

The distant mountains looked black against the sky. The first stars had started to shine. Far away, a pack of wolves yipped and called. Svana looked down at her wedding ring, forged by Hallkell and inscribed with tiny runes. He wore a matching ring. During the ceremony, they had offered these rings to each other on the hilt of Hallkell's new sword, made especially for the ceremony, as was the Viking custom. The Earl, who officiated, had spoken of the sword as a symbol: that the sanctity of their marriage vows could be broken only by death. The ceremonial sword hung on the kitchen wall. Svana had often dreamed of taking the weapon and using it to cleave Hallkell's neck in his sleep. But what fresh vengeance would his family then wreak against her own? Svana thought of her little sisters, her mother and grandparents, and wept.

The door opened.

Panicked, Svana straightened up and stopped crying. But it was only Dagny.

"Where is Hallkell?" Svana said, watching the doorway behind.

"Washing himself." Dagny seemed to consider for a moment. Then she closed the door, sat next to Svana on the bench, and patted her shoulder. This small gesture brought fresh tears.

"Don't blubber," Dagny said. "You know Hallkell can't bear the sound of it."

Svana dabbed at her eyes with the wet washcloth. "It's not fair. My brother murdered your husband, yet walks free. Why must I take my brother's punishment?"

"Because, as a woman, you're no better than a horse or an ox, a possession fit to barter. Your father should have taught you that lesson from birth."

Svana's throat ached with the need to cry. She dipped the washcloth, squeezed it, and held it to her eye. "I should be free to choose my own destiny."

"Hah. Do you have a cock? No, a defenceless slit. The world belongs to men." Dagny offered a weary smile. "Never mind all that. You must learn how to be Hallkell's wife, and learn quickly. Otherwise, one day you will enrage him enough to kill you." She sniffed and looked away. "I don't want my son to suffer punishment because of you."

"He treats me like a dog." The tightness in Svana's chest made her choke on her words. "I hate him."

Dagny knocked the washcloth from Svana's hand and rose. "Return to your chores," she said. "And if you have any sense, mind your husband. Stop giving him reasons to beat you."

While Dagny sat at the loom, Svana spent the rest of the evening kneading and baking loaves of bread, hanging milk curds in muslin cloth over a bucket, salting wheels of cheese, sorting the clothes for tomorrow's wash. The whole time, Hallkell drank beer. Svana kept count of the number of bottles. Four, five, six... His broad face became ruddy. He began to watch her carefully.

Then he stood, took his last drink, and said, "Woman, come to bed."

"I must unbraid my hair."

"Do it later."

He strode from the table and shoved through the curtain to their bedroom. Svana hesitated. Dagny made a clucking sound to catch her attention, and then gave an impatient gesture, urging Svana to follow him. Svana braced herself. It felt like walking to the gallows. She went through the curtains. Hallkell was lying in bed, already naked and erect.

"Take off your clothes," he said.

She fumbled with the brooches that pinned the straps of her woollen overdress. The overdress dropped to the floor. Then she pulled the cowled, ankle-length shift over her head and cast it aside. Hallkell smiled tenderly.

"You're very beautiful," he said. "I'm proud to have you as my wife."

She lowered her face and gazed at the dirt floor.

"Come," he said. "Lie on your back."

She did as she was told. He opened her thighs and knelt there. He spat between her legs and, cock in hand, began to work it inside her. She winced.

He made an exasperated sound. "Relax. You're too tight."

"I'm trying." Svana put an arm across her face. "You've blackened my eye. I'll not go to the General Assembly tomorrow."

"You'll go. Everyone in the village needs to see how Hallkell Jenson disciplines his wife." Grunting, he gave a final push. "There. Now be quiet while I attend to my business."

2.

The following morning, they travelled to the village centre in the horse-drawn cart. Dagny sat up front, with Hallkell on the reins. Svana had to sit in the back. Despite her efforts with the cold washcloth, her eye was swollen and purple. Hallkell didn't appear to notice. He insisted that she wear her new linen dress to the General Assembly, her best necklace, and twist all of her hair into an intricate mesh of braids that sat like a crown on top of her head.

During the journey, Hallkell and Dagny kept waving and chatting to their neighbours who travelled the lane beside them on foot or horseback. Svana hardly dared look up. Any time she did meet someone's gaze, she saw pity or disgust.

What might Agmundr think of her now?

Outside the Grand Hall, the villagers gathered in groups to talk and laugh. Svana stood by Hallkell's side and stared at her boots. When the attendants opened the doors, Hallkell took her hand. Everyone filed inside. The Earl and Wife, richly dressed, sat high on a dais, their enormous chairs lined with furs. As usual, musicians played while everyone took their seats. Once the murmuring, shuffling of feet and coughing had stopped, the music stopped too. A horn sounded. The Earl began to talk of business, about a planned raid in another land far to the west. Svana didn't care. All she cared about was the humiliation of her swollen, purple eye. Next to her, she could hear Hallkell's nose whistling on each breath. Heat emanated from him like a fire, and he smelled sour and musky. Svana dug her fingernails into the wooden bench.

The Earl was a great orator. Villagers sat forward in their seats. Hallkell and Dagny were similarly transfixed. Keeping her head still, so as to not attract her husband's notice, Svana cut her gaze across the Great Hall. The sight of Agmundr clenched her insides. But Agmundr wasn't looking at her. No, he was glaring at Hallkell with a dark and murderous rage.

Svana could have wept in elation. There was a way out.

Agmundr loved her.

Now, by the gods, she had a way out.

The bruising subsided very slowly. Obsessed, impatient, checking her eye constantly in the mirror, Svana waited five days to see Agmundr. She hurried to the marketplace, gave Hallkell his lunch-pail as usual, watched him eat and drink. Then she stalked back and forth along the stalls. Kerchiefs, shoes, cloak-pins, caps, she cared for nothing of it. She watched the movement of the sun and waited. Whenever she passed Agmundr's stall, he stared at her and she looked back at him, brazenly. On each pass, the lust in his eyes made her loins shiver.

At last, the fresh food vendors packed up.

Svana waited a little longer, fussing over knitted socks. Finally, she bought two pairs: one for Hallkell and one for Dagny. She walked past Agmundr's empty trestle table. Steeling her resolve, she headed to his farm.

But he wasn't in his cottage.

Frozen at the doorway, Svana didn't know what to do. Perhaps he was consulting with a shearer or a wool-spinner. Disappointment hit her stomach. She ought to return to Hallkell's house, tend to the chickens, sweep the dirt floor; stop this fanciful nonsense.

"Svana Norup."

She turned. Agmundr stood with his bloody hands held out. She recoiled.

"Have no fear," he said. "One of my ewes gave birth. Give me a minute."

He shucked his stained shirt, scooped water from the barrel by the doorway and sluiced it over his head and body, washing himself. The water ran off him. Wet and shining, his brawn flexed and bunched. Svana, captivated, let go of the lunch-pail. It clattered at her feet. Agmundr shook his head. The droplets flew from his black hair. Smiling, he slicked back his fringe with one hand. His laugh brought out the muscles on his belly in sharp relief. Was he tormenting her, taunting her?

"What's so funny?" she said.

"I'm just glad to see you." He sobered. "I thought you'd never come back."

"If that were so, you could have visited me."

He raised his eyebrows. "And take on Hallkell Jenson?"

Svana picked up the lunch-pail in both hands. "So you're afraid of him."

"Any man with a grain of sense is afraid of Hallkell Jenson."

She turned away to leave. Walking through the grass, she focused on the gate and its wooden slats. Sheep moved aside. Her feet felt heavy.

"What if I killed him?" Agmundr said from behind. He had followed her, soundlessly. "What then?"

Svana looked back. "You're too timid for such a deed. I can't afford the risk."

Agmundr gripped her arm and dragged her against him.

"Leave me be," she said. "This fate is my own."

"No. It's our fate together. The gods have decided. I have decided."

She gazed into his dark, sombre eyes.

"What if you did find the courage to murder Hallkell?" she said. "What if he rises after death, seeking vengeance? What then?"

Agmundr ran his hand through her hair. "Then I'll strike him down a second time and cut off his head."

"You're not frightened of an Again-Walker?"

"If it meant that I could take you as mine, I'd slay Hallkell a dozen times over, whether he were alive or dead."

"You would do that for me?" she whispered.

He brushed his lips over hers. "I would do anything for you."

His voice and touch dissolved her common sense. Svana allowed him to lead her behind the cottage, permitted him to pull her onto the green, soft grass. Agmundr lifted her dress and removed it. His mouth found her nipples. She arched her back against his lips. He kissed down, down, down along her stomach. Spreading her with his fingers, he lapped between her thighs. She worked her hands through his hair as the sensations arced sweet and sharp, higher and higher, tipping her over the edge. She cried out to the sky.

Recovering, gasping, she murmured, "You're all I've ever wanted."

Agmundr moved up her body and kissed her. She tasted her own juices. He unbuttoned and removed his trousers. Svana reached down and gripped him. He was large and thick; to her surprise, much bigger than Hallkell. Agmundr slid into her. Svana clasped at his hips and buttocks. Instead of pumping, he stayed deep inside and rocked against her, rhythmically, over and over; flooding her with pleasure, the sensations rising up and up and up as she strained against him.

"Oh, Agmundr," she sighed, and gritted her teeth.

The climax rolled through her, the intensity tricking her mind. The ground beneath her disappeared. She wrapped her arms and legs about him, frightened and exhilarated, clutching desperately as if the act of letting go would drop her through empty air, as if Agmundr suspended her above a precipice.

He moved to a kneeling position and lifted her up so that she sat astride. They pressed against each other, skin on skin, kissing. He began to move faster. His breath hitched. Svana gripped his ears with both hands and, rapt, watched his face. He returned her gaze for as long as he could. At last, grimacing, his eyes squeezed shut and he let out a guttural moan.

Spent, the lovers collapsed to the ground, panting.

A couple of sheep wandered over, curious. Agmundr struck out with a leg to chase them away. Svana giggled. With a smile, Agmundr caressed an errant curl of hair away from her cheek. Love shone in his adoring gaze.

She didn't want the moment to end, but it was now or never.

"What about Hallkell?" she said.

Agmundr's smile drained away. "Divorce him. He beats you, doesn't he?"

"Not enough to break bones. And I'm a pledge-wife. I don't have any rights. The Earl would never allow it. The blood feud between our families would only continue." She grabbed his arm. "You told me you would kill Hallkell. Was that a lie?"

Frowning, Agmundr gazed at the sky. "I don't wish to hang."

"So make it look like an accident. Don't you want me for yourself?"

"I would be mad if I didn't."

Then he lay on his back with his arms behind his head and bit at his lips, deep in thought. Svana waited.

Finally, Agmundr turned his face to her. "Tomorrow is Sunday. Get Hallkell to visit me here at my farm. Now this is important: make sure he arrives on horseback. If he arrives on foot, my plan won't work."

"Do you really mean it?"

His eyes were steely. "I swear to you, Svana Norup, that Hallkell Jenson will be dead by this time tomorrow."

Unshed tears blurred her vision. She clasped her hands together at her mouth and laughed with relief, excitement, and gratitude. Then she took Agmundr's wrist and placed his palm directly on her breast, moving it so as to raise her nipple. When he stiffened against her thigh, she mounted him. Within seconds of entering her, Agmundr hardened into a full erection. He began to thrust.

She kissed him and sat up, riding.

"Oh, Svana," he chuckled. "If you keep on like this, you'll be the death of me."

After dinner, once the sun had set, Svana gave Hallkell and Dagny their presents: a pair of socks each. Dagny nodded her approval. Hallkell put his giant arm about Svana's waist and puckered his lips against her forehead.

"You are a good wife," he said, and then held out the socks to admire them.

"And you are a good husband."

"See, my little one?" he said. "I told you on our wedding night that we'd forge a life together."

Dagny stood from the table. "I shall gather the eggs."

She patted Svana's hair on her way past. When Dagny closed the front door behind her, Svana took a bottle of beer from the shelf, opened it and placed it front of Hallkell. Despite her resolve, her heart beat hard and fast with terror.

"Husband, there is something we need to discuss."

"I'm listening."

"You were correct about the shepherd, Agmundr Rask."

Hallkell slitted his eyes, swallowed his mouthful of beer, and carefully placed the bottle onto the table. "Explain."

"When I was at the market today…" Her throat closed up.

"Tell me."

Panic fluttered inside her stomach. "While I was buying your socks, I walked past Agmundr's stall and he told me that…he told me…"

Hallkell slammed his fist to the table. Svana cringed and gave a tiny shriek.

Mouth twisting, Hallkell said, "He told you what?"

"He told me that he wanted to bed me."

Hallkell's face filled with a slow, quivering rage. Blood suffused his cheeks. His arms trembled. Then he leapt from the table, grabbed his coat, and shouted, "I'll wring his head from his shoulders."

Svana panicked. "Now? But wait, it's too dark to travel."

"My fury will light the way."

"But the horse might stumble."

"I'll run every mile."

Svana flung herself on him and put her arms about his neck. Hallkell turned to the doorway. She swung helplessly, her feet off the ground. Agmundr had instructed that the visit be tomorrow. Agmundr wouldn't be ready yet, the plan wouldn't work.

"No, stay and give me comfort," she cried.

Hallkell paused. "Meaning what?"

"I'm frightened and need your warmth."

"Warmth?"

"I need my husband's love."

She began to kiss frantically at his cheeks, his beard, his mouth. Hallkell's beefy hands gripped her buttocks. Svana did her best not to flinch. His face still dark with anger, he walked her through the curtain and threw her to the bed.

"Lift up your dress," he said.

"But you'll stay the whole night with me? And visit Agmundr tomorrow?"

Hallkell stripped his trousers. "First thing after breakfast."

She opened her legs. "And take the horse. Don't waste energy on walking. You must be strong when you reach his farm. You must be strong and beat him."

Hallkell knelt onto the bed, his cock in hand. "Oh yes, Wife, but I'll do more than beat him. I shall kill that scrawny, boy-faced bastard."

She looked away.

He spat between her thighs. She pressed an arm across her face.

Sunday morning brought low clouds and a cool, misting rain. The horse's hooves beat a steady rhythm against the hard-packed dirt of the lane. Svana pulled the hood tighter around her face. Sitting behind her on the horse, Hallkell put his mouth to her ear, and said, "Are you cold? You're shivering."

"I shiver with worry. Please, halt the horse, let me get down. I'll walk home."

"No. I want to see Agmundr Rask eat you with his eyes one last time."

"But if you kill him, you'll hang."

Hallkell gave a dismissive grunt. "The Earl will forgive a crime of passion."

"I don't wish to see you fight. The very thought of it knots my stomach."

"Ease your mind, Wife. I'll not suffer a single scratch. If it's the violence that bothers you, look away and plug your ears while I deal the fatal blows."

She couldn't stop shaking. The journey to the village and beyond, to the farmlands, seemed to take an age. When she saw the thatched roof of Agmundr's cottage in the distance, dread ran through her. Hallkell must have felt it, for he took one hand off the reins to wrap a reassuring arm about her.

"Hush, little one, all will be well," he said. "You'll see."

"Perhaps you could just warn him."

He laughed. "Warn him? No. I'll not be cuckolded. Agmundr's death will be a lesson for any man stupid enough to covet my wife."

They reached the gate. Hallkell drew up the horse and dismounted. Svana raked her gaze over the property. There was no sign of Agmundr. Had he heard their approach? Was he prepared? Hallkell took hold of Svana's waist and lifted her down. He gave her the reins. Opening the gate, he smiled at her, and entered.

Palms sweating, knees quaking, she followed with the horse. Once she and the animal had passed through the gate, she found she could go no further. Hallkell strode across the grass towards the cottage. Both of his fists were clenched. Oh Frey, Svana prayed, son of Njord and brother of Freya, bestow your protection upon Agmundr, the man I love, the man who is to set me free from bondage. Please, Frey, I beg you…

Hallkell kicked open the cottage door and stepped inside. Svana put a hand to her mouth. But within a moment, Hallkell exited again, and shrugged.

The cottage must be empty.

Facing the grassy field with its dozens of sheep, he yelled, "Shepherd! You wish to bed my wife, do you? Come out from hiding and accept your punishment." He gazed around the field, as if expecting Agmundr to appear out of the faraway trees.

A movement caught Svana's eye.

Peeking from behind the cottage, holding a long-bearded axe, stood Agmundr.

Svana blanched.

He lifted a forefinger to his mouth—*shh*—and raced out, light-footed, silent and swift as a cat, the handle of the axe lifted over his shoulder.

With a great swing, he hit the blunt side of the axe against the back of Hallkell's head. Svana recoiled at the sharp cracking sound. Hallkell staggered, and dropped to his knees. Svana tried to look away but terror held her fast. Agmundr drew back the axe and swung again. This time, the blunt side of the blade made a wet and splintering sound. Hallkell fell onto his face. A small, burbling fountain of blood and dark curds erupted from the hole in his skull.

Working quickly, Agmundr wiped the axe on the grass and returned it to his cottage. He came outside again and flipped over Hallkell so that the dead man faced the sky. To do so took all of Agmundr's strength. Then he hurried to Svana and snatched the horse's reins from her. He turned the animal and struck its hindquarters. Whinnying, the horse took off through the gate at a trot, heading down the lane towards Hallkell and Dagny's house. Dizzy, Svana watched it go.

Agmundr grabbed her arms.

"Listen to me," he said. "This is what happened: the horse shied at something in the grass. Hallkell got bucked off and smacked his head. Cradle him in your arms and cry like a good wife. I will run to the village for a doctor. As far as we are both concerned, Hallkell is simply injured, not dead. When the doctor says that he is dead, you and I will be shocked and saddened at the news. Do you understand?" When she didn't answer, he shook her a little. "Svana, did you hear me?"

She nodded. Agmundr kissed her hard on her mouth, and ran out of the gate.

Long after he had disappeared from view, she kept staring down the empty path. The misting rain flurried and eddied in the breeze. Sheep bleated. Her heart boomed. She waited for Hallkell's giant hand to drop to her neck, for him to spin her around and slap her senseless. When nothing happened, she turned.

Hallkell lay exactly where Agmundr had left him.

She approached. His chest didn't rise or fall. His half-open eyes didn't blink. His frowning brows didn't relax.

"Husband?" she whispered.

She wiped rain from her face. Her hand trembled. She knelt down. The cold, wet dirt soaked through her overdress and shift. The ground near the cottage was indeed stony. It would seem plausible to the doctor that Hallkell had broken his skull on a rock. Hesitantly, she touched Hallkell on the arm.

He didn't respond.

A puddle of blood surrounded his head like a halo.

As Agmundr had instructed, Svana tried to cradle him. Gore smeared her palms. In revulsion, she wiped her hands on the grass. She decided to lie on his chest and stroke at his beard. To the doctor, racing to the scene of the accident, her posture would seem terribly sad and poignant, wouldn't it? She decided that it would.

She put her cheek to Hallkell's chest and stroked at his beard plaits.

Instead of relief, however, fear began to crowd her mind. It was important to placate Hallkell, for his spirit was close by and listening. Thankfully, he hadn't seen Agmundr's attack, and couldn't possibly know what had happened.

"Husband," she said. "When in your grave, please, sleep quietly. Your death was an accident. You fell and hit your head. Blame no one. Don't seek vengeance. What is there to avenge? You smashed your own brains. As your wife, I swear it."

But she could feel the coiled tension pent up within his corpse. Hallkell Jenson was not the kind of man who would surrender willingly to death. Anger would fuel his reanimation; transform him into a living corpse, an Again-Walker. She knew this to be true as surely as she knew that the sun rises and sets each day.

She began to cry.

By the time Agmundr returned with the doctor, and various other villagers who wanted to bear witness, Svana was hysterical. Two men hauled her by both arms from Hallkell's body as she wailed in horror of what was to come. Assuming her to be grief-stricken, the women tried their best to hold and comfort her. The men stood back, awkward and embarrassed. When the doctor pronounced Hallkell dead, Svana finally looked at Agmundr. He was staring back at her, white-faced, his black hair slicked down with rain and sweat.

3.

Hallkell's three uncles were as big, meaty, bearded and blonde as Hallkell himself. With their own hands, they built Hallkell's barrow, a pit lined with stone and fitted with a timber roof, which they dug high on the cemetery's hillside so that Hallkell's spirit could watch over the village for eternity.

Then the uncles had come to the house to help Svana and Dagny prepare the body. Upon arrival, however, they had first taken their revenge and slaughtered the horse, which had bucked off Hallkell and killed him with a hoof to the head, according to the doctor. The horse's last scream sounded like that of a woman.

Now, rattled, Svana gazed down at Hallkell. She, Dagny and the uncles had washed him, dressed him in his best clothes, put him face-up on a stretcher along the marital bed. In his arms, they had placed his blacksmithing hammer, tongs and poker, a pair of tweezers, comb, and a frying pan. He seemed larger in death than in life.

"We should cremate him," Svana whispered.

Dagny recoiled. "Put him in fire? With him so afraid of it?"

"Don't blame the child," one of the uncles said. "She fears he'll become an Again-Walker. We fear the same. Hallkell's spirit won't rest easy in the ground."

Another uncle added, "The only sure way is to burn his corpse to ashes. What difference would it make? He'll still have his barrow, after all, and his belongings to see him through the afterlife whether he's burned or not."

The third uncle said, "No. There are more respectful methods we can use."

"None of them as good as cremation," Svana said.

"It's up to Dagny," the first uncle said. "She birthed him. What is your word?"

Dagny glared at them, each in turn, with her rheumy and wounded eyes. "All right," she said at last. "We'll take precautions. But we'll not cremate him, you hear?"

The uncles agreed. Svana, uneasy, said nothing.

They placed an open pair of scissors on his chest, and twisted lengths of straw into crosses, which they put beneath his shroud.

They tied his big toes together and stuck the soles of his feet with many needles. When the uncles carried his stretcher from the house, they raised and lowered it a couple of times at the threshold to form the shape of a cross. While they placed him in the cart, and secured the cart to two of their horses, Svana and Dagny went around the kitchen and put all of the pots and pans upside-down, and turned over the chairs.

"Do you think that will be enough?" Svana said.

Dagny's eyes glittered with hatred. "I know it was you."

The blood left Svana's face.

"I don't know how, but it was you and that shepherd," Dagny hissed, and waggled a finger. "Sleep with one ear open. My son will come back for you."

Svana fled from the house. One of the uncles kindly helped her into the cart. For once, she sat in the front seat and felt great satisfaction. Dagny had to sit in the back with the two remaining uncles and Hallkell's corpse.

They travelled to the cemetery in silence.

The entire village turned out for Hallkell's burial.

The parson prayed for Hallkell with magical words meant to bind the giant to his barrow, yet Svana perspired. She allowed herself two glimpses of Agmundr. Both times, he was watching her. What if anyone else saw him staring like that? So blatantly, so hungrily? Svana put her face in her hands. One of Hallkell's uncles mistook her gesture for grief, and put his great arm about her shoulders. It felt like Hallkell's arm. It felt like an omen.

There was a funereal feast in the Great Hall. Speeches were given. Hallkell's apprentice, a young man with long red hair, was named as the new blacksmith. The whole time, Svana could feel two sets of eyes scalding her skin: those of Agmundr and of Dagny. She kept her gaze on the floor. She accepted the condolences of the villagers, one by one, without looking up. A few of the women, apparently moved by her stoicism, wept for her. "Look, Svana's broken heart is numb," she heard one cry.

Afterwards, drunk, one of the uncles took Svana and Dagny home in the cart. With a wave, he turned the horses around in the courtyard and headed back to the village at a trot. Now it was just Svana and her ex mother-in-law.

Once they lit the lamps, Svana said, "I'll wait one more week. Then I'll ask the Earl if my peace-pledge can be voided. If the Earl says yes, I'll return to my village. If he says no, I'll serve you until another man claims me as his wife."

"Either way," Dagny sneered, "you'll have Agmundr between your legs."

Svana offered a sly, smug grin.

Nostrils flaring, Dagny said, "Revolting child! Go and gather the eggs."

"Gather them yourself," Svana said, and went to bed. She couldn't sleep for frayed nerves, but nonetheless, it was gratifying to hear Dagny outside the windows, fussing and swearing around the chicken coop as the hens clucked and flapped.

Finally, when Dagny extinguished the lamps and retired, Svana turned over and closed her eyes. The smell of Hallkell rose from the linen. Her pulse skittered.

Husband, she thought, stay in your barrow. There's nothing for you here now.

It took a long time to calm herself. At last, exhausted, Svana fell asleep.

A continuous pounding at the door woke her. Svana rubbed her eyes and rolled off the bed. A faint light lay about the house. The pounding continued. Svana stumbled across the kitchen. Dagny flipped aside her bedroom curtain and, perplexed, scrubbed at her wrinkled face and wandered out, flat-footed.

Svana called, "Who is it?"

"One of the Earl's messengers," said a male voice. "All occupants within, come out directly. There's a cart outside for you."

"What's going on?"

"An emergency assembly at the Grand Hall."

Svana unlatched and opened the door. Dawn streamed inside the house. The messenger startled, appeared to recognise her, and looked her carefully up and down. Svana clutched the nightclothes about her throat. A premonitory chill ran through her.

"I'll not go anywhere until after breakfast," Dagny said.

"Get dressed, both of you," the messenger ordered. "We leave now."

The villagers in the Grand Hall clustered together in frightened groups. According to Dagny, the last time the Earl had called an emergency assembly was more than ten years ago, when a mysterious form of sleeping sickness had struck the cattle on a particular farm. Svana watched the front of the longhouse. While the Wife sat in her fur-lined chair, waiting, the Earl was off to one side of the dais, consulting with his messengers. When the messengers left the dais to stand guard at the doors, the Earl gestured to his musicians. One of them stood up, and blew a long note on the horn. The villagers scrambled to sit. A hush descended straight away. Nonetheless, the musician blew a short note on the horn to introduce the Earl, who took his seat next to his Wife and patted her arm. Together, the Earl and Wife gazed about at the congregation, tension etched in their faces.

Svana twisted on the thorns of a terrible anticipation. She knew what this emergency assembly was about. She already knew in the pit of her stomach.

The Earl announced, "We have an Again-Walker."

A loud murmur ran through the assembly. Svana felt faint.

"And we believe it to be Hallkell Jenson," he added.

People exclaimed. A couple of women shrieked. Svana's heart jangled. The villagers turned this way and that, looking for her and spotting her, some pointing her out to others. She wiped clammy hands along her overdress, over and over.

A short note sounded on the horn. The place fell silent.

"This is what we know," the Earl said, and crooked a finger.

A small, bent old man stood up and, blushing, faced the assembly.

The Earl said, "For those of you who don't know him, this is

Claus the goat-farmer. His property backs onto the cemetery. A few hours after sunset, he awoke to the sounds of his animals screaming. He went outside with a lantern and axe, fearing a wolf. The goats were running at full speed around and around the perimeter of the fence, frothing at the mouth in terror. Chasing them was not a wolf, but a huge, black bull, its skin half-flayed to show the red meat beneath. Only a man such as Hallkell Jenson would be large enough to transform into a bull."

Shocked muttering broke out in the longhouse. Svana peeked at Dagny beside her. The old woman was rigid and shaking, grinding her teeth, staring at the Earl.

Raising his arms to quieten the crowd, the Earl continued, "Knowing this huge flayed bull to be an Again-Walker, Claus went inside and barricaded the door. The bull ran his flock ragged for hours. The Again-Walker shifted its shape, for then Claus heard the beast climb onto his roof and start drumming at it with two heels. Sometime after midnight, the Again-Walker left. Claus went outside to check on his stock. Eight of his goats had been ridden to their deaths."

Discreetly, the Earl gave a small, dismissive gesture and Claus returned to his seat. The Earl crooked his finger at someone else.

Agmundr stood.

Svana's heart seemed to cramp. Mouth open, she gaped at him. Agmundr's eyes searched the crowd, found her. They stared at each other in shared agony for a moment. He lowered his gaze.

The Earl said, "For those of you who don't know him, this is Agmundr the sheep-farmer. His property backs onto Claus's property. In a similar fashion, Agmundr woke to the sounds of his animals in distress. When he went outside, he found a dozen of his sheep crushed to death. Of the Again-Walker, there was no sign."

The faint noise of crying took up in the longhouse. Young, frightened children were clutching at their mothers. Everyone looked ashen and pinched.

The Earl's Wife spoke up. "Until we can hire a warrior to hunt and kill the Again-Walker," she said, "we must take great care.

Do not go to the cemetery at any time. Do not be outside after dark. If you can, keep your animals inside with you at night. If there comes a knocking at your door at night, especially if it is a single knock, do not open it. Keep an iron sword on hand. If the Again-Walker rides your house, hide in case it breaks the roof beams and gains access. Do not try to flee, or the Again-Walker will catch you and destroy you."

Moans and murmuring started up.

The Earl raised his hands for attention, but was ignored. Lifting his voice, he said over the tumult, "We must pray to the gods for guidance. We don't yet know what torment has led the departed Hallkell Jenson to become an Again-Walker."

Dagny stood and shouted. "I know exactly what torment!"

Everyone fell quiet.

The Earl and Wife looked too shocked to be offended at the interruption.

Dagny pointed at Agmundr, who still stood at the foot of the dais, and said, "All along, he had unclean notions about Hallkell's wife, Svana. Like a whore, she invited Agmundr's attentions. Together, they drove Hallkell mad with jealousy."

The Earl and Wife gazed speculatively at Agmundr. A hot, prickling dread broke out across Svana's body. Sweat popped on her upper lip.

"Is this true?" the Earl said.

"The poor old woman is torn up with grief," Agmundr said. "She's keen to blame someone, anyone, for her son's untimely death."

Dagny said, "On the day he was killed, Hallkell visited Agmundr's farm to punish him. At the market, Agmundr had told Svana of his intent to bed her."

The congregation gasped.

The Earl said, "Svana, where are you?"

When she didn't move, Dagny slapped at her. Reluctantly, Svana stood.

"Come up here to the front," the Earl said, "where we can see you better."

Dagny shoved her. Svana sidestepped along the benches

to reach the aisle. Villagers pulled their knees out of her way, quickly, as if she might burn them with the merest brush of her dress. She approached the dais and stood there, hands clasped in front of her, skin flushed and hot.

The Wife said, "What have you to say about this?"

"Nothing, my Lady," Svana whispered.

"Nothing? Not a word in defence of your honour?"

"Ask anybody," Dagny shouted. "Agmundr is forever making cow-eyes at her."

"All right," the Earl said. "Any witnesses?"

Mortified, Svana looked about at the dozens of raised hands.

"So a man admires a beautiful girl," the Wife said, and shrugged. "A cat may look at a Queen, after all, with no harm done. Plenty of men would ogle Svana. How could they not? She is young with soft yellow hair, big blue eyes, and skin like milk. Hallkell should have known better than to lose his senses over one of his wife's many secret admirers. Svana, Agmundr, you may both return to your seats."

The relief surging through Svana made her legs shake. She glanced at Agmundr. He smiled at her, faintly, with one side of his mouth. His dark eyes shone.

"Wait, my Lord and Lady," said a male voice.

Svana turned to see who had spoken. The blood ran to her feet. Standing up was Esbern, the chicken farmer, and his wife, Kirsten. They were next door to Agmundr's property. In fact, she had twice passed by their fence on her way to Agmundr's gate. The Earl raised one palm to Svana and Agmundr, as if to say, *stay there*, and crooked the forefinger of his other hand at Esbern and Kirsten.

The couple approached the dais.

Svana felt ill.

"Speak your piece," the Earl said.

The couple regarded each other. Finally, after clearing his throat, Esbern said, "We are Agmundr's neighbours. On Saturday, the day before Hallkell died, my wife and I were tending to our chores when we heard noises of love-making. We went to the fence we share with Agmundr. There, we saw him lying in the grass with Svana."

Pandemonium erupted. The Earl's messengers had to race through the longhouse and strike out with staffs to force people to take their seats. The musician kept tooting his horn. Svana regarded Agmundr. His face was grey and frightened. She wanted to drop to the flagstones.

Order was restored after a long minute.

The Earl frowned. "Neighbours, are you absolutely sure?"

"Yes," Kirsten said. "They were naked and kissing each other. We saw them make love in various positions. He even put his mouth on her womanhood."

Uproar ensued. It took the messengers and the horn-player a good couple of minutes to calm the assembly.

"They murdered my son," Dagny shouted. "Svana lured him to Agmundr's farm where they both killed him. Our horse would never shy. Our horse would never have kicked Hallkell."

"Doctor," the Earl said. "Could Hallkell's cause of death have been something other than a horse's hoof?"

The doctor stood and scratched his beard. "Well…yes, I suppose."

The Earl sat forward in his chair. "Agmundr Rask, Svana Norup, it is time to confess. As lovers, did you conspire together to murder Hallkell Jenson?"

Lightheaded, Svana looked at Agmundr. Neither of them spoke.

The Wife clapped at one of the messengers and said, "Fetch a poker."

The room began to whirl. Svana felt a tight grip on her arms. Two of the Earl's messengers were holding her upright. A third was advancing with a poker. Glowing red and smoking, the poker smelt like sulphur, like Hallkell after a day at the foundry.

"Interrogate the girl first," the Earl said.

"Stop!" Agmundr bellowed.

Everyone froze. The longhouse went quiet. Dazed, Svana

looked at Agmundr. He was sweating freely, but kept his shoulders squared.

"Leave her be," he said. "And I'll confess."

The Earl nodded. The messenger wielding the poker stepped back.

"Project your voice so that all can hear," the Wife said.

"So be it." Agmundr faced the crowd and lifted his chin. "I fell for Svana Norup the first moment I saw her. She holds my heart even as I speak."

Svana went limp. The messengers held her firmly.

"I wanted her for myself," Agmundr continued. "I didn't care that she was married. On Saturday, the day my neighbours thought they saw us making love, I had lured Svana on false pretences. When she insisted on being faithful to her husband, I forced myself upon her. My neighbours heard her cries of pain, not passion."

The villagers reacted with hisses and angry clamour.

Svana's eyes stung with tears.

The Earl lifted a silencing hand. "So you admit to rape," he said. "Go on."

"The next day, she brought Hallkell to punish me. I slew him with an axe."

Waiting until the excited chatter around the longhouse abated, the Earl's Wife said, "Svana, why didn't you come to us and report these crimes?"

Agmundr said, "Because I swore I would kill her if she did."

The crowd turned ugly. The men were half-standing, shaking their fists, while the woman snarled through their teeth and whistled. Svana caught Agmundr's eye. He nodded at her, solemnly, and tried to smile with one side of his quavering mouth.

The Earl announced, "We have the full confession of Agmundr Rask, rapist and murderer. The sentence is death, to be carried out immediately."

Two messengers grabbed Agmundr.

A tidal wave of people carried Svana out of the double-doors.

Still held by her arms, she was marched to the courtyard behind the longhouse amongst a sea of furious villagers. They cheered and yelled. The sunlight dazzled her. She kept tripping over her own feet. The strong hands of the messengers kept hauling her up.

"Agmundr," she wailed, but her voice was lost in the hubbub.

She was tossed to and fro. The voices around her rose, fell, and screamed to a feverish pitch. She opened her eyes. High above her, standing on the wooden trapdoor of the gallows, stood Agmundr, his arms behind his back, the hangman already placing the noose about his neck. She and Agmundr gazed into each other's souls in terror and frantic longing.

"Have you any final words?" the hangman said.

"Yes," Agmundr said, his voice trembling with emotion. "Svana, I love you."

She couldn't bear to watch. She screwed her eyes shut. The trapdoor clanked and clunked as it dropped. She heard the whisk of his body through space, the snap of the rope, the kick of his legs, and then nothing but the baying crowd.

The world spun too fast on its axis. Svana lost consciousness.

4.

The rest of the day was spent at the Grand Hall, with animal sacrifices, feasting, music and dance to curry favour from the gods. Every villager tried to seem happy and confident, since tears and begging only peeve the gods and make them contrary. Svana, however, sat on a bench and stared at the floor. From time to time, people came by to press goblets of beer or plates of food into her indifferent hands. Well-meaning women came over to tell her that, while it was no consolation, at least her husband's murderer had been dispatched from this world. Svana never answered.

Eventually, the Earl's Wife approached.

"You're making everyone uneasy," she said. "Come with me." She led Svana to an antechamber at the rear of the dais, a dressing room richly decorated in furs, silver and gold. "Rest here," she added, gesturing at a divan.

Dutifully, Svana sat. The Wife took hold of Svana's feet and swung her legs so that Svana found herself lying down.

"There, is it not comfortable? I recline here to listen while the Earl rehearses his speeches." The Wife sat alongside and stroked at Svana's hair. "Poor girl, your short time in our village has been so very traumatic. I will appeal to the Earl to void your peace-pledge. You can return home to your family as soon as you feel able."

Svana nodded.

"Try to sleep," the Wife said, and left the antechamber, closing the door.

The merry, jaunty music sounded through the wooden walls. Svana stared at the rafters. Agmundr, Agmundr… *Is there something you want? Anything you need?* Yes, she thought, I need you, the warmth of your arms and the love in your eyes. On the other side of the wall, villagers gave out forced laughs and desperate cheers.

When the afternoon waned into early evening, the celebrations broke up so that everyone could hurry home before dusk.

Svana trudged along the lane. Dagny insisted upon walking next to her. Svana didn't wish to speak, but Dagny fidgeted as if she were full of words, opening her mouth and shutting it again, tutting to herself, stamping with a heavy tread.

Finally, she said, "Witch, Hallkell will come for you."

"Yes," Svana sighed. "I expect he will try."

"Despite your lies, I know you conspired with Agmundr. I know you're as guilty as he is. You should have been hanged too, and thrown away."

"Shut up, old woman."

Tears blurred Svana's vision. After Agmundr was flung onto the rubbish tip, all the villagers had filed past to spit on him, as was the custom for criminals. His blood had not yet settled, so he appeared alive and only sleeping. Svana had wanted to gather him against her breast. The messengers had shaken her, insisting that she spit. She had cried that her mouth was dry, but the messengers only relented once the fury and disgust of the villagers had shamed them into walking her past the body.

Now, Dagny gave a laugh. "Hallkell will pop your head like a bilberry."

Svana said nothing.

"You hope I'll put in a good word?" Dagny went on. "Not a chance. I shall stand aside and let him have at you. I'll applaud Hallkell as he rends your limbs."

The air held a chill. Svana gathered the cloak tighter around her shoulders. Her silence, however, seemed only to provoke Dagny's suspicion.

"Why aren't you afraid?" the old woman said.

Because I no longer care if I live or die, Svana thought. But she did not answer.

"Oh, I get it," Dagny said. "You imagine that love will transform Agmundr into an Again-Walker. You believe he'll protect you from Hallkell's wrath."

"I believe no such thing."

"Yes, you do. So young and stupid, hah, you know nothing of men."

Svana kept walking. In the distance, a pack of wolves yipped and bayed. The sky began to look bleached about its edges.

"A woman's love is selfless," Dagny continued. "She would die for her child, but a man can't fathom such a gesture. A man's love is fickle and self-centred. If you don't please him, and keep pleasing him, he will turn on you."

Not Agmundr, Svana thought grimly.

As if reading her mind, Dagny cackled. "That is the way of all men, your precious Agmundr included. He won't rise from death to help you. But he might rise to take vengeance upon you. After all, you're to blame for his hanging."

They reached the house. Svana chased the chickens into the coop and collected the eggs in the apron of her overdress. Momentarily, she considered bringing the animals inside the house, as the Earl's Wife had instructed, but upon reflection, she did not care a jot if Hallkell, in his supernatural form, slew his own livestock. She decided to leave open the door of the coop. If

Hallkell did not kill the chickens, let the wolves have them. She cast her gaze across the land. The stars had started to glow in the deepening sky. No one in the village would sleep easy tonight. In fact, no one would sleep easy again until the Again-Walker was killed.

Svana came inside. Dagny, wielding a large knife, was slicing root vegetables into a pot of simmering water over the fire.

Svana put the eggs into the basket, and said, "Do you want help?"

"So you can poison me?"

"You're a spiteful bitch. I hate you almost as much as I hated your son."

Svana stormed to the marital bedroom and glared about. She despised every piece of furnishing. Tomorrow, she would leave and never return. She began folding her clothes—tunics, overdresses, aprons, cloaks, hats, shoes—and placing them inside her two large leather bags. Hallkell had given her many items of jewellery over the weeks of their marriage. These items she placed inside a linen drawstring pouch. Once she was home in her own village, she would be safe. Again-Walkers could not trespass onto foreign soil. Hallkell's reanimated corpse would be stuck in this village until a warrior killed it and sent the restless spirit shrieking into the afterlife.

A corner of the bedroom curtain twitched aside.

"What do you think you're doing?" Dagny said.

"Packing."

Dagny opened the curtain. "To leave? On whose authority?"

"The Earl's Wife. She voided my peace-pledge. I'm going home tomorrow."

Dagny upended one of the bags and said, pointing, "Not with that or that or that. Hallkell bought those."

"And presented them to me as gifts."

Dagny tightened her lips. "Oh no, you won't take his gifts with you."

"And who is going to stop me?"

A single knock sounded at the door, impossibly loud, as if hammered not with a fist but with a tree trunk. The women froze.

With the same wide-eyed expression, they waited for the visitor to knock again. The second knock did not come. Svana's stomach clenched. The tendons along Dagny's stringy neck stood out in sharp relief. For a moment, the old woman appeared as scared as Svana, but a cruel smile lit up her face and made her eyes gleam.

"He has returned for you," she said. "Witch, it's time for your comeuppance."

She darted from the bedroom. Svana ran after her. Dagny was at the door.

"No," Svana yelled. "Don't open it."

Dagny threw the bolt. Lifting the latch and flinging aside the wooden door, she cried, "My son, my beloved son. Step inside and warm yourself. I shall bring you a beer. Slake your thirst, and then kill your stone-hearted viper of a wife."

Nothing happened for long moments.

The only sounds were the crackle of the fire, the bubbling of the stew, Dagny's excited puffing and panting. Svana stared at the doorway. It held total and utter blackness, as if a moonless night had somehow descended from the sky and wrapped its arms around itself, like a bat, and barricaded the single exit. The night moved. Svana saw that it was a humanoid figure, a titan. Dark as coal, it stooped to fit its head and shoulders beneath the lintel, and shuffled crabwise to squeeze its bulk through the opening. Standing to its full height, its head grazed the rafters.

Svana stopped breathing.

Dagny staggered back, clutching at her chest.

This thing was Hallkell, yes, but just barely. Svana recognised the single braid along the scalp, the pattern of beard plaits. Swollen to twice Hallkell's size, the bloated and blackened Again-Walker regarded them both with care, one at a time and curiously, as if it could not place them in its memory. The eyes were not human; they reflected the lamplight as would a pair of mirrors. The Again-Walker growled. Its breath stank, rotten and fetid, like the gas that rises from a swamp.

The four windows were small, designed to keep out the cold. The only one that might be large enough to allow egress was next to the fireplace.

"Step away," Svana said. "We can try to escape through the back window."

"Escape? Why should I, when I have nothing to fear?" Recovered from her initial fright, Dagny closed the door and drew the bolt, locking them all inside. Sneering, she hissed, "Look what you did to my boy. I shall laugh as he stamps you to death. Did you hear me? Laugh! And when he's done, I'll stamp on you too."

"That monster is no longer your son. It'll kill us both."

"Hah, watch this." Dagny spread her palms to the Again-Walker, and whispered, "Don't you know me, Hallkell? Your own dear mother, the one who brought you into this world and nursed you?"

The Again-Walker held out its enormous arms and cradled Dagny's head between its hands, tenderly, as if to draw her closer for a kiss. At first, Dagny smiled. Then, grunting, she began to struggle. She screamed. Blood ran from her ears. Her skull cracked as loudly as a nut. The Again-Walker released its grip. Dagny dropped to the floor, blood spraying in jets from her broken head.

Svana withdrew across the kitchen. The Again-Walker stared with a blank face. Its footsteps shook the walls. Svana backed against the fireplace.

Trapped…

No, perhaps she had a chance.

From the hearth, she drew a flaming log and held it out. In life, Hallkell had been afraid of fire. Surely, his Again-Walker would share the same dread?

"Retreat," she yelled, waving the log. "Retreat or I shall burn you."

The Again-Walker did not seem to notice. Its metallic mirror-eyes reflected the fire. Svana lunged with the flaming log, close enough to singe the beard plaits. The hair shrivelled and released an acrid smoke. Keening, the Again-Walker balked.

Svana, gasping, tried to make sense of this.

Had the heat of the fire stirred what was left of Hallkell's memory?

Yes, that must be the explanation. What else could it be?

Svana kept swinging the log. The monster kept backing up. She had to steer it away from the door. But no, too soon, the flames smouldered and went out. The Again-Walker regarded her with annoyance. And the fireplace lay too far away to grab another burning log.

She stared up into the monster's eyes. Reflected was her terrified face. The hands reached out to enclose her head. Ducking, Svana dropped the log. She ran to put the table between them. The table was too small to lead the Again-Walker on a merry chase, not big enough to allow her sufficient time to reach the door or climb through the window without being caught. Perhaps she could do laps of the table and grab one burning log after another, and scare the Again-Walker until sunrise when it must return to its barrow. But how long until the monster realised that all it need do was toss the table aside? Svana grabbed a carving knife from the table. Doubling over, she screamed from her diaphragm, ready to fight, ready to die.

"Damn you," she yelled. "You were never man enough to be my husband."

The monster paused, drew up a lip. The yellowed teeth were long and fanged.

"I despised being your wife," she said. "You were less than a pig."

The Again-Walker flinched as if stung. Svana lifted the knife. With its face twisting into a furious grimace, the Again-Walker began to suck air in and out of its mouth, as loudly as a pair of bellows, while it stood tall and taller still, ballooning higher and wider, its blistered skin splitting all over to reveal meat and a crawl of insects. Svana cowered. Soon, the Again-Walker was so big that it had to crouch beneath the ceiling. Now it would kill her.

A thundering noise began overhead.

Both Svana and the Again-Walker startled and looked up. Outside, on the roof, a noise like heels drummed, rattling the rafters. The drumming stopped. A section of thatching tore back. Svana stared into the patch of dingy sky. The knife shook in her fist. Could it be…?

Out of the darkness appeared a pale face framed by black hair.

Elated, Svana cried out, "Agmundr!"

He dropped from the roof and landed on the kitchen table.

She recoiled at his pungent stink of mould. His cadaverous face was mottled and white; his eyes, no longer dark, shone like polished steel. He gazed at her and Hallkell, angry but puzzled, as if unsure what to do next. Svana felt faint; Agmundr did not recognise her. But then he lifted one side of his mouth. At the sight of his gentle, familiar smile, Svana wept and laughed as tears spilled on her cheeks.

"Agmundr," she said, letting go of the knife. "My love, you've come back."

With a roar, Hallkell punched Agmundr clear across the room. Agmundr crashed into the wall like a cannonball, the force bowing and splintering the wood panels. His head and spine must surely be broken. Svana hugged herself tightly.

The fight was over.

But no, unfazed, Agmundr pushed himself clear and landed on his feet.

Svana put her hands to her mouth. This was not Agmundr anymore, she reminded herself, giddy with shock and revulsion, but a supernatural being.

The Again-Walkers circled each other. They stood between her and the door. Svana held the apron of her overdress to her nose. The stench of rotting flesh made her gag. She tore the blind from the largest window. Could she fit? Yes, she would be able to wriggle her shoulders through well enough, but what about her hips? The risk of getting stuck was too great. Reaching the door was her only chance.

Head down, Hallkell rushed and caught Agmundr. The momentum of the charge rammed Agmundr into the kitchen shelves. Shards of wood and broken ceramics exploded across the kitchen. Svana bolted for the door, her shoes crunching over debris. Something sharp opened her foot. She cried out and fell.

Hallkell slammed his massive shoulder into Agmundr once more. The wall behind them caved. Surely, neighbours must hear the commotion. But who would dare investigate? And with her foot split from toe to heel, running away would now be impossible. What should she do? Try to hide while the battle raged around her, praying to the gods that she wouldn't be crushed?

Agmundr grabbed the iron pot from the fire and struck Hallkell across the face. There was an audible crack. Boiling water and vegetables sprayed in an arc. Hallkell lost his grip and sprawled onto his back. When he gathered his limbs beneath him to stand up, Svana saw that the blow had sheared the skin from his cheekbone as neatly as if dissected by a filleting knife. Agmundr struck again with the pot. A dozen of Hallkell's yellow teeth spilled across the floor.

Of course, the supernatural power of iron…

To kill an Again-Walker, you must cut off its head with an iron sword.

Svana remembered the marital sword hanging on the wall, the iron sword that had held their wedding rings, and crawled towards it. Her injured foot left a long, wide trail of blood. She must have severed an artery. One way or another, she would die this night. Damn her brother. If he had held his temper, none of these terrible events would have happened.

The feud between the Jenson and Norup families had started because of cabbage seeds. At great expense, her brother had purchased 10,000 seeds from Hallkell's father and had sown an entire field. The seeds had rotted in the dirt. They had been too old to germinate. Hallkell's father had refused to repay the purchase price, let alone give compensation for the loss of income a failed acre would cause. The farm had only been three acres in total, with one acre already lying fallow to rest the soil. Enraged, her brother had killed him with a rock to the temple.

Hatred for her brother burned in Svana's belly and gave her strength. Crawling faster, she stayed along the walls, giving the Again-Walkers a wide berth.

Hallkell punched Agmundr across the room and fell upon him, pummelling with both fists, again and again, until Svana was sure that Agmundr must be in pieces.

Groping his hand along the floor, Agmundr found the knife she had dropped. With a shout, he thrust the iron blade into Hallkell's eye. Hallkell howled, staggered away, pulled out the knife and threw it aside. Agmundr leapt up, grabbed a chair and broke it over him; grabbed the table and broke that over him too. Hallkell swept an arm and slammed Agmundr to the ground. In a trice, Agmundr leapt up and attacked again. Neither of them seemed fatigued or bothered by injury, as if they could keep assailing each other until the end of the world, until Ragnarok.

Svana got to her feet, lunged for the sword, and pulled it from its bracket.

Nearly a metre long, the sword was heavy.

She staggered beneath its weight, her muscles straining and pulling. The hilt was wrapped in leather thong, the blade decorated with a herringbone pattern-weld. How fitting: Hallkell had made the very sword that would send him to the afterlife. With difficulty, she slung the sword over one shoulder.

"Agmundr," she cried. "Look out."

Clenching her teeth with effort, she swung the sword double-handed into Hallkell's neck. Sparking and smoking with an unknown alchemy, the iron blade sliced through the thick and sinewy throat as if through a bowl of soft curds. The head fell away. Svana dropped the sword. A blustery, sighing exhalation issued from the severed neck. Hallkell's remaining eye glittered once and went out.

"Is it over?" Svana said. "Is he finally dead?"

Agmundr did not reply. Together, they stared at Hallkell.

A ghostly blue mist rose from the body, curling like steam. The mist began to glisten with thousands of lights, each one as tiny as a dust mote. Hallkell's corpse rippled and wrinkled as if countless mice were running beneath his skin. Horrified, Svana could not look away. The blue mist flared and crackled. With a stink of ozone, the mist erupted into an intense bright light that shone through her eyelids. She flung an arm over her face and screamed. The light went out as suddenly as it had appeared.

Hesitantly, Svana dared to look.

The mist had cleared.

The colossal and blackened Again-Walker was gone. In its place lay Hallkell, human and dead for three days, waxy, streaming with putrefaction juices.

Praise Odin.

Exhausted, Svana collapsed. A puddle of blood surrounded her injured foot. She would have to staunch the bleeding, and quick. Already, she felt her strength waning and her vision fading.

Agmundr sat on the floor nearby. The awful marbling of his chalk-white face made her whimper. He smiled at her with one side of his mouth and reached out his hand, as if to say, *come to me, don't be afraid*. And what did she have to fear? His love for her was so great that he had defied death in order to save her from Hallkell.

Relief gave her the shivers. Beginning to sob, she crawled over.

Dagny's remains lay at the door. Stupid old woman, Svana thought. Not all men are as selfish as you would have had me believe.

Drained, Svana reached out to her lover.

Agmundr took her in his arms and held her tightly.

Her terror ebbed away. His body felt as cold and dense as clay, but it did not matter. She would get used to his physical changes; would come to adore his eerie, mirrored eyes, learn to put up with his dank smell. He had not spoken a single word this whole time. Had he lost the power of speech? Well, that did not matter either.

Safe, she relaxed against Agmundr's chest.

"Ours is a true love," she said at last. "Not even death can separate us."

He took her by the shoulders and held her at arm's length.

Svana opened her eyes, already smiling with gratitude and devotion. His smile, in return, was pitiless. Svana's heart began to thud. She tried to pull away but the grip on her was impossibly strong. Fingers dug into her flesh. Yes, she would die this very night, but not from the severed artery in her foot.

"Please," she whispered. "Please don't."

The Again-Walker's mouldering lips drew back to show long fangs.

And then it set upon her.

Story Publishing History

 All stories are original to this collection, unless listed below (first publishing instance).

"Across the White Desert" *Aurealis* 2016
"Fair-Haired Boy" *Page Seventeen* 2008
"Flight Path" *Pendulum* 2009
"Griselda Gosh" *Eclecticism Ezine* 2010
"In the Company of Women" *Pulp Modern* 2015
"Perfect Little Stitches" *Midnight Echo* 2015
"Post hoc ergo propter hoc" Allegory Magazine 2016
"The Brightest Place" *Polestar Writers' Journal* 2016
"What the Sea Wants" *SQ Mag* 2016
"When This You See, Think of Me" *Hell's Bells* anthology 2016
"Will o' the Wisp" *Lighthouses: an anthology of dark tales* 2015